Turner's Vignettes

JAN PIGGOTT

Turner's Vignettes

TATE GALLERY

Sponsored by Volkswagen

cover
'A Tempest – Voyage of Columbus' *c.*1831–2 (cat.27)

ISBN 1 85437 132 0

Published by order of the Trustees 1993
on the occasion of the exhibition at the Tate Gallery
29 September 1993 – 13 February 1994
Designed by Caroline Johnston
Published by Tate Gallery Publications, Millbank, London SW1P 4RG
© Tate Gallery and the author 1993
All rights reserved
Typeset in Monophoto Baskerville by Icon Colour, London
and Tate Gallery Publications
Printed and bound in Great Britain by Westerham Press, Edenbridge

Contents

Foreword

Very little work has previously been done on Turner's vignettes, the tiny intricate and brilliant watercolours which Turner produced to be engraved as book illustrations in the 1830s and for which he was widely known during his lifetime. Now, as a result of the researches of Dr Jan Piggott, a far greater knowledge and understanding is possible of the extent of Turner's involvement in the production of these jewel-like miniatures.

Jan Piggott was appointed a Turner Scholar in 1991 and is the fourth scholar to receive this award, which is supported by Volkswagen. A master at Dulwich College, where for ten years he was Head of the English Department, he comes to the subject through literature and his own particular interest in the authors and their works for which Turner provided the illustrations. He has studied the development of the images from the earliest sketches to the finished watercolours, through to the engravers' proofs 'touched' by Turner and the final engravings.

This catalogue discusses the place of the vignettes in the context of Turner's ideas and achievements and reveals Turner's skill in their execution and his constant involvement at every stage of their engraving. It also explores the history of the printing commissions.

Although most of the works in the exhibition come from the Turner Bequest, we have also benefited from the generosity of a number of collectors, without whose loans we should not adequately have been able to represent Turner's full achievement in this field. We offer them all our most sincere thanks.

We are especially grateful to Jan Piggott himself both for his dedicated and thorough work over the last two years and for everything he has done in connection with the exhibition.

Volkswagen yet again has made possible new research into another little studied area. We are so grateful to them for their continuing support.

Nicholas Serota
Director

Sponsor's Foreword

Turner's Vignettes marks the fourth exhibition and publication in the Turner Scholarship series, which Volkswagen is once again proud to support. The Turner Scholarships are offered by the Tate Gallery in association with Volkswagen for important new research related to the works in the Turner Bequest. They are open to students in the United Kingdom proposing original topics in the areas covered by the Bequest, much of which has never been properly catalogued.

Dr Jan Piggott's research into Turner's vignettes gives us a unique opportunity to view an unexplored part of Turner's work. *Turner's Vignettes* examines the exquisite miniature engravings Turner used to illustrate books by writers such as Walter Scott, Byron and Thomas Moore, as well as Milton and Bunyan. Not only does this allow us an insight into the evolution of the vignettes from early sketch to finished watercolour and final engraving, but also a fresh look at the works of literature themselves.

My gratitude and that of my company goes to Dr Jan Piggott for his enthusiasm, effort and research. Our thanks must also go to all involved at the Tate Gallery, particularly Nicholas Serota and Andrew Wilton.

Richard Ide
Managing Director
V.A.G (United Kingdom) Limited

The Turner Scholarships – Sponsored by Volkswagen

The Turner Scholarships were established by the Tate Gallery in 1988, with the support of Volkswagen, to fund original research by visiting scholars into the works contained in the Turner Bequest at the Tate Gallery. The Scholarships provide an opportunity for scholars to work as 'guest curators', and to prepare an exhibition and publication based on their researches.

Awards are made biennially. The first two Scholars, appointed in 1988, were Peter Bower and Dr Cecilia Powell. The results of Peter Bower's researches were seen in the exhibition *Turner's Papers* which opened at the Tate Gallery in October 1990. Mr Bower, a paper historian, examined Turner's use of paper in his drawings during the first half of his working life. He is continuing his research into Turner's later years. Dr Powell's researches resulted in the exhibition *Turner's Rivers of Europe: The Rhine, Meuse and Mosel* which was shown first at the Tate Gallery in the autumn of 1991 and subsequently in Brussels and Bonn. She has now started new research into Turner's travels in Germany.

Two further Scholars were appointed in November 1990: Maurice Davies and Dr Jan Piggott. Maurice Davies's work on the perspective lectures given by Turner at the Royal Academy between 1811 and 1828 culminated in an exhibition and catalogue in October 1992. Dr Piggott's research into the vignettes Turner did for engraving as illustrations to works of literature is the subject of this book and of the exhibition it accompanies.

A further scholar, Gillian Forrester, has recently been appointed and her work on the *Liber Studiorum* will be shown in an exhibition in October 1995.

Acknowledgments

I am profoundly grateful to Volkswagen for their generous and imaginative sponsorship of the Turner Scholarships, and to Nicholas Serota and to Andrew Wilton for their part in the scheme. Thanks to them I have spent many privileged hours in libraries and print rooms and above all at the Study Room of the Clore Gallery, among Turner's sketches, sketchbooks, and finished watercolours. At the Clore I have greatly enjoyed the company of my fellow-scholars, Dr Cecilia Powell and Peter Bower, whose knowledge, enthusiasm and generosity have been an inspiration as well as a boon.

There are many individuals over the three years of my researches who have given me encouragement and practical help, and among them I would particularly like to record the names of Mungo Campbell, James Dearden, Anthony Dyson, John Gage, Luke Herrmann, Nicholas Horton-Fawkes, Evelyn Joll, Nicola Kalinski, Michael Kitson, Marek Kochanowski, Ruari McLean, Dodie Masterman, John Moxon, James Moseley, Virginia Murray, John Newman, Rosalind Turner, Anthony Verity, and Barry Viney. Peter Marlow and Jim Reddaway performed specially gallant and time-consuming services.

At the Print Rooms which I have visited most often I am very grateful to Hilary Williams and Andrew Clary at the British Museum and to Kevin Edge at the Victoria and Albert Museum for their expertise and courtesy. The staff at the British Library, the London Library and the National Library of Scotland were always helpful and patient. Kenneth Dunn at the National Library of Scotland and Richard H. Lewis of the National Library of Wales added initiative and insight to efficiency. I am particularly indebted to those collectors of Turner engravings in fine and 'touched' proof copies who gave their lifetime's collection to institutions, in particular to the Revd George Herbert Woolley and his son the archaeologist Sir Leonard Woolley, who gave to both the Birmingham City Museum and Art Gallery and the National Gallery of Scotland, and above all to Horace Mummery who gave a marvellously full and rich collection to the Victoria and Albert Museum in 1939.

Though I have looked afresh at their source material, I gratefully acknowledge the scholarship of Gerald Finley, Adele Holcomb, Basil Hunnisett and Mordechai Omer, which has been of immense help to me.

I have been perhaps luckier than I deserve in the remarkable kindness of private individuals who nobly agreed to lend watercolours by Turner to the exhibition, meaning that for the public good they would be without their pictures for a long period of time.

An amateur, I have greatly relished the privilege of working among the Tate Gallery staff of all departments whose calm professionalism I so much admire. David Brown and the lively curators of the Clore Gallery made me feel a welcome guest and helped me with information and advice. David Brown and Ian Warrell made very helpful comments on my manuscript. Ian Warrell took seemingly endless care in discussion and in attention to detail. I owe a particular debt to Iain Bain, the Manager of Tate Gallery Publications, for his knowledge and for his interest in the project.

My wife and family have generously encouraged my project, which has taken up so much of my time and thoughts in the last few years.

Jan Piggott

Abbreviations

Roman numerals in brackets (e.g. TB CCLXXX) refer to Finberg's classification of works on paper by Turner in the Turner Bequest in the Clore Gallery.

B&J   M. Butlin and E. Joll, *The Paintings of J.M.W. Turner*, rev. ed., 2 vols., 1984

R   W.G. Rawlinson, *The Engraved Work of J.M.W. Turner, R.A.*, 2 vols., 1908–13

RA   exhibited at the Royal Academy

TB   A.J. Finberg, *A Complete Inventory of the Drawings of the Turner Bequest*, 2 vols., 1909

W   A. Wilton, *The Life and Work of J.M.W. Turner*, 1979

The location of a work is given only when it now differs from that cited in the relevant entry in any of the above publications.

For the full titles of books referred to in the Notes by author and date or volume, see the Select Bibliography.

For the terminology of sizes of volumes (quarto, duodecimo, etc.) refer to the entry under 'format' in J. Carter, *ABC for Book Collectors*, 1952.

?W.B. Cooke after J.M.W. Turner, 'Neptune's Trident',
1825. Vignette on wrapper for the projected series of
Marine Views. Line engraving 108 × 51 (4¼ × 2)
(R 770); based on TB CLXVII C

1 Introduction

Between 1830 and 1839 one hundred and fifty vignettes from designs by Turner were engraved on steel and published in books; under commission from publishers he made many sketches and finished watercolours in the vignette form for the illustration or, in the idiom of the day, the 'embellishment' of editions of his contemporaries – Samuel Rogers, Walter Scott, Lord Byron, Thomas Campbell and Thomas Moore – and also editions of Milton and Bunyan. Approximately one hundred and thirty 'finished' watercolours for these illustrations are known to survive; roughly the same number of unengraved designs, sketches and preparatory studies connected with these vignettes were among the contents of Turner's studio at his death and survive in the Bequest. These vignettes are from the short period which Ruskin considered that of Turner's 'consummate power'.[1] Although they are not well known nowadays, these vignettes spread his fame: Rogers's first biographer wrote that the illustrations to the two volumes of Rogers first made Turner known to 'vast multitudes of the English people'.[2] Ruskin assumes that the two volumes are in the library of every educated household, and frequently uses them as examples for his theories and teachings; he furnished his museums with cases showing copies of Turner's watercolour vignettes made by his assistant, William Ward, and proofs of the engraved vignettes.

This publication aims to increase the understanding of these intense and brilliant small illustrations by relating the images to the texts and by showing Turner's methods in the sequence from sketch to preparatory study to finished watercolour. Turner's involvement did not stop at this point: he strictly supervised the engravers' proofs with 'touching' at several stages of the plate while it was in their hands. In some cases he also made written comments in the margin of the engravers' proofs. Because he insisted on seeing these proofs at several stages and demanded his improvements to the plates before approving them for printing, they may be said to be in a sense his own works; Rawl-inson claimed, 'It is by the *engravings* rather than by the drawings that Turner's vignettes should be judged'.[3] A fair amount of material can also be recovered about the relations of Turner with the publishers and to some extent also about the participation of Rogers, Scott, Campbell and Moore themselves in the commissions; this helps to explain the nature of the images and the differences between the series.

The Development of the Vignette

A vignette – by its etymology a 'little vine' – was originally a small ornamental printer's device of grapes and vine-leaves. There had been vine decorations in medieval illuminated manuscripts, but the great age in book-illustration, when the vignette proper was developed and flourished, was the eighteenth century in France. The wood-engraver J.M. Papillon in his *Traité historique et pratique de la gravure en bois* of 1766, for example, made a vignette showing what was said to be the origin of engraving: Africans incising stone and tree-

fig.1 J.M. Papillon, 'The Invention of Engraving by "les Enfants de Seth"'. Engraving on wood from the *Traité historique et pratique de la gravure en bois*, Paris, 1766

trunks (fig.1). The device was introduced into books printed in England in the seventeenth century and was common by the eighteenth century: for example, Horace Walpole writes in a letter of 1751 of Richard Bentley drawing for him 'vignettes' for the head-pieces and tail-pieces for his edition of Gray's poems.[4] Very fine examples of vignettes may be found alongside the engraved initials and designs from coins in the sumptuous edition of Horace made by John Pine (where even the letter-press was engraved) printed in London in 1733 (figs.2, 3). A vignette may indeed show grapes, tendrils and vine leaves, but had developed by Turner's day to mean an illustration (particularly one used on a title-page) which was not rectangular, had no border, and which might shade away at its edges. The vignettes designed by Henri Gravelot for the edition of the *Decameron* printed in London in 1757 were much admired by one of Turner's most brilliant engravers, John Pye; he called them 'perhaps equal to anything of their kind that has been done since in any country'.[5] Though they have no vines, the subject-matter is still Dionysian: cupidons disport with watering-cans, harps, quivers, torches, garlands and bird-cages; in one image, adapted by Thomas Stothard for a vignette in the edition of Rogers's *Poems* in which he shared the work of illustration with Turner, the cupidons sail in a boat. Stothard's head-piece to 'Jacqueline' in Rogers's *Poems* of a Provençal grape-harvest is strictly a vignette by both form and subject-matter: the vines become the edging to the scene of youths and maidens with their baskets of grapes (fig.4).

It is true that Thomas Bewick, working at the end of the eighteenth century, had already made his wood-engraved vignettes a most poetic vehicle for social comment or for wry and tragic existential statement (fig.5), but it was Turner who was mostly responsible for developing the vignette away from the merely dainty 'embellishment' of books, away from simple anecdote or topographical scene, to become a microcosm of his own imaginative range: we recognise in miniature the 'elevated pastoral' and the 'historical landscape' of the great canvases. The vignettes are still charged, so to speak, with Dionysian sap and pulse, and are concentrated, as if they were Turner's sonnets by comparison with his epics; like a sonnet the narrow confine stimulates Turner in the best of them to reveal and refine some of his most inward states of mind. The studies of

fig.2 John Pine, vignette engraved on copper from *Horatii Opera*, 1733–7

fig.3 John Pine, vignette engraved on copper from *Horatii Opera*, 1733–7

fig.4 William Finden after Thomas Stothard, 'A Vintage', illustration to 'Jacqueline' from Rogers's *Poems*, 1834. Engraving on steel

fig.5 Thomas Bewick, vignette engraved on wood for *British Birds*, vol.I, 1797. Compare the figures with those in Turner's vignette 'A Garden' (cats.10–11)

landscape and architecture and the 'marines' are here; also the cataclysms and the images of the destructive forces of human nature. In certain vignettes to Byron and Campbell there are political statements; in some vignettes to Scott, Milton and Campbell there are intimations of supernatural forces.

The form of the vignette, which by Turner's day was already tending towards the ellipse, allows the viewer to apprehend Turner's image just as the eye apprehends the visible world, without the rectangular conventions of a frame or piece of paper, or today the photograph or television screen. The tondo had done just this in the Renaissance, and Turner paints Raphael on the loggia in 'Rome, from the Vatican', RA 1820 (B&J 228) among the circular images that he has been painting for the easel and in fresco. The whole painting is a complex of circles and ellipses, with an arresting focal point at the tondo, the 'Madonna della Sedia'.

The tondo is exactly positioned from the corners of the canvas as if by compasses, and is central horizontally but not vertically, being equidistant from the two upper corners and the two lower corners. Writing on architecture in the series of articles in the *Spectator* for 1712, 'On the Pleasures of the Imagination', Addison had discussed the circular pleasure given to the eye by the dome and the arch:

> Look upon the outside of a dome, your eye half surrounds it; look up into the inside, and at one glance you have all the prospect of it; the entire concavity falls into your eye at once, the sight being as the center that collects and gathers into it the lines of the whole circumference … For this reason, the fancy is infinitely more struck with the view of the open air and skies, that passes through an arch, than what comes through a square or any other figure.[6]

In 1840 Ruskin (under the pseudonym Kataphusin) contributed a note to J.C. Loudon's edition of Humphry Repton's writings on landscape gardening, in which he speculated on the optical reasons for the superiority of the vignette form to the square, concluding that 'our pictures should all be circular'. He used Turner's vignettes as models of the form, where 'the dreamy brilliancy of light which envelops them extends to their extreme limits, and their edge hardly ever cuts harshly on the paper'.[7]

A view through an arch is a device used by Turner in his paintings;[8] it appears in his vignettes illustrating the Roman Forum and the burning of the Houses of Parliament (App.B, nos.16, 145). The unsquare form does away in his foregrounds with Turner's occasional conspicuous awkwardness with corners – the corners that he advised painters to keep clean; C.F. Bell noted that the engravers' hands made these corners even more clumsy in the rectangular 'landscape' form.[9] The central arena of Turner's pictures is often oval; in the vignette the superfluous burdock, the shrubs or rocks that fill in his lower corners are trimmed away. The vignettes show a chronological development in shape: the series for Rogers's *Italy* are almost square, with rounded corners. Later the vignettes take on more ambitious forms: for example in the Milton series penetrating among the cosmic spheres, or in the Campbell series taking on the shape and movement of conflagration that is his subject in the conquered city of

Warsaw in the 'Kosciusko' (App.B, no.128). His fondness for the form led him later in his career to paint a number of vignette-shaped circular canvases (which also rely on literary, or biblical, allusion) such as 'Dawn of Christianity' (no.57) and 'The Angel Standing in the Sun', RA 1846 (B&J 425).

Within the circle Turner often creates movement in the form of a gyre.[10] By contrast with Turner's vignettes for Murray's seventeen-volume edition of Byron of 1832, those designed by the other artists, such as Clarkson Stanfield, seem markedly static. Critics of Turner's day were aware of the athletic pleasure that his images gave the eye and mind: a commentary by Richard Reinagle R.A., published with Turner's engraved view of 'Brightling Observatory' in the Views in Sussex of 1819 describes how the eye 'turns and winds', and that while the principles of construction of the picture are simple and geometric, the eye is 'drawn into the sweeping lines'.[11] Clouds, water and the contours of Turner's scenes charge the vignettes with movement; for example in 'The Bridge of Sighs' in the Byron series (App. B, no.65) the play of moonlight on stone and water appears to possess movement, and to suggest an amorous latency wholly apt for the sighing Venetian intrigue that Turner places in the foreground.

The engraved images of course present a monochrome world. If it is really true, as Owen Jones said, that form without colour is like a body without soul, to render Turner's images without colour might seem the worst violence that one might do to his work.[12] Turner's friend George Jones wrote, 'his ciiaroscuro is always complete';[13] line-engraving makes the contrasts of light and shade even more dramatic. Without going so far as Sir Frederick Wedmore, who persuaded himself that in the engravings after Turner the subtleties of light and shade 'do suggest and indirectly represent colour to the seeing eye',[14] there is an obvious difference between the engraved vignettes and 'reproduction' by black and white photography: Turner himself supervised the stages of the engravings minutely, and they are capable of conveying extraordinary delicacy, and above all luminousness. An obituary of the engraver John Pye in the Spectator said that Turner's chiaroscuro 'possessed the whole resources of a subtle language in which … to express and to describe the wondrously illuminating quality of light'; 'Mr. Pye maintained that there was a complete scale of light, with as many delicate modulations in it between the two extremes of black and white as there are in a scale of music'. The writer of the obituary recalls Havell's comment that the knowledge of sunlight which Turner and Girtin had acquired was so completely developed in their works that it seemed to have been 'held in hand and thrown into the subject at pleasure'.[15] In the engraved image Turner's chiaroscuro may take on an emblematical meaning of the conflict of light and dark, especially in the designs for Milton, for Rogers's 'Voyage of Columbus' and for some of the Campbell vignettes. An anonymous reviewer of Charles Eastlake's translation of Goethe's treatise on colour, writing in the Art Union in 1840, spoke of 'the boundary line of partition' where 'an angel of light and the prince of darkness may meet on equal terms, and adjust their respective claims'.[16] In Turner's most transcendent vignettes this is exactly what is at work: Apollo confronts the Python.

Pictura and Poesis

'We cannot make good painters', Turner told his Royal Academy students, 'without some aid from poesy'.[17] In Turner's own mind there was a fascinating habitual complex of images, words and ideas. Andrew Wilton and Rosalind Turner in Painting and Poetry have revealed the poetry of his own and much of the poetry of others that filled his head.[18] What Turner told the students about Poussin in discussing how the painter creates horror and gloom in 'The Deluge' by association applies equally to his own art: you find there 'mysterious ties wholly dependent upon association of ideas',[19] in much the same way as in reading a poem. Turner's mind was actually more 'verbal' than Poussin's (which is not to say more conceptual) and he developed during an age of literary illustration. Richard Wilson and Francesco Zuccarelli had painted 'historical landscapes' in Britain for classically educated connoisseurs. Turner's friend Thomas Girtin was also accustomed to devising historical landscapes specifically to accompany poetic extracts, in the days of his association with the Sketching Society. Painters and public knew well the Milton and Shakespeare Galleries in London where academicians such as Henry Fuseli and Stothard exhibited works in illustration of British poets. In Turner's canvases exhibited at the Royal Academy from 1798 with quotations attached to the titles, the association of the landscapes with the lines from a poet such as Milton is not just the elegant or fashionable convention of an epigraph. It is an example of the interrelationship between the abstract and the concrete that Turner eloquently described in his first lecture as Professor of Perspective at the Royal Academy in January 1811, anticipating by his own metaphor the psychologist William James's phrase about the 'stream of consciousness': that process whereby 'Painting and Poetry, flowing from the same fount mutually by vision, constantly comparing Poetic allusions by natural forms in one and applying forms found in nature to the other, meandering into streams by application, which reciprocally improved, reflect and heighten each other's beauties like … mirrors.'[20] With the best of the vignettes, the reader with Turner's illustration in his book experiences a most satisfying intensity bred by text and image: *poesis* and *pictura* marry with more than usual harmony, and the vignettes, in Ruskin's simile, 'bear away the mind with them like a deep melody'.[21] The epigraphs from Milton and James Thomson appended to the frames of Turner's early Royal Academy exhibits in 1798 make the representation of mist or of sober evening numinous, even religious, by associating the Lakeland and Welsh scenes with lines from *Paradise Lost*. 'Norham Castle on the Tweed' (w 225) was also exhibited in that year with a description of sunrise from Thomson as an epigraph. Turner's many later images of the same castle, however, show a sunset behind it, in allusion to the opening lines of Scott's *Marmion*.[22]

Where Turner illustrates literary texts, and especially so where the vignettes form part of a series, such as for Milton's *Paradise Lost* and *Paradise Regained*, for Rogers's 'Voyage of Columbus' and for Scott's *Life of Napoleon*, some of the symbolism is conventional. Thus the vignettes for the Columbus series are unified by the many cruciform motifs, and hope is symbolised by Campbell's own images of rainbows and stars. On the other hand, Turner relished working riddles or askance symbolism into his pictures, using more literary techniques such as puns and emblems. For example, when painting Pope's villa being demolished he introduced the 'prostrate trunk of a willow-tree' (B&J 72), the wil-

low being associated with Pope. John Britton's text that accompanied Pye's engraving of the picture (R 76) in *Fine Arts of the English School* says that this allusion is 'in strict accordance with the subject'.[23] Fuseli had declared that 'all ornament ought to be allegoric'.[24]

Turner and Book Illustration

Turner was fortunate to live in a period when lavishly illustrated books of literature, topography and antiquities were very popular, and when, partly no doubt owing to his own influence, steel-engraving reached its apogee; as Marcus Huish wrote, 'By a coincidence which may in truth be termed little short of miraculous, Turner and the English school of line engravers were contemporaneous.'[25] Though obviously there was some excellent work in book illustration before Turner, he transformed the art from the literal, the narrative or decorative into a vehicle for poetic landscapes. Turner had also in the case of Rogers, Scott, Moore and Campbell the co-operation of the authors in selecting the subjects. Unlike his contemporaries, Turner frequently created an emblem or symbol by his vignettes; through the eye, the mind is 'dilated' and 'exalted' – these are the terms used by the engraver John Landseer, lecturing to the Royal Institution in 1807, to describe the operation of the sublime in expressing a metaphysical meaning through images.[26] Turner's best vignettes may seem to be landscapes, whether topographical or fantastic, but by the end of the decade his confidence with figures, narrative and drama had developed, especially in the Campbell and Milton series. Although they are not in vignette form, the six illustrations for the Waverley Novels made for the publisher Henry Fisher in 1836–7, roughly contemporary with the Campbell vignettes, show how well he could combine drama with landscape in small illustrations.

It is impossible to know exactly how Turner regarded his illustrations. When he tells Lord Egremont that he cannot accept an invitation to Petworth as he is going north 'on a bookseller's commission' (in fact to Scotland for Cadell, to sketch scenes for Scott's *Poetical Works*)[27] there may be a hint of contempt. On the other hand, Turner surely would not be as disgusted as Poussin was when set to design title-pages for books, and such 'bagatelles'.[28] Only one contemporary review of Turner's illustrations that I have seen calls for him to abandon this work: the *Athenaeum*, having described one of his illustrations for Milton as 'positively sublime' in June 1835, in a review of a later volume of the same series in December said that 'the artist might employ his genius in nobler creations than such pretty little phantasmagoria'. The reviewer's parting compliment is presumably disingenuous, calling the books 'the prettiest edition of this poet that could adorn the boudoir and drawing-room table'.[29] Turner had boasted to Rogers that without a copy of Rogers's illustrated poems 'no lady's boudoir would be complete'; he joined in the mockery of publishers' attempts to sell books by 'embellishments', and is recorded as jeering at the fashionable Annuals introduced during this period.[30] These consisted of short pieces of literature with engravings; Charles Lamb called them 'ostentatious trumpery' with 'dandy plates'.[31] However, Turner was not above designing a number of excellent vignettes for the most sophisticated of these productions, Charles Heath's *Keepsake* (App.B, nos.145–8). Scott feared that some of Turner's illustrations to his editions would be on a level with those in 'every Miss's album';[32] writers may perhaps occasionally envy painters. Turner took on commissions for book illustration with alacrity, working on several projects at the same time. These commissions pressed hard upon him, as is illustrated by an anecdote in Thornbury's biography when Turner's Sunday afternoon conversation with Dr Monro at Sandycombe Lodge was interrupted by W.B. Cooke wanting to know when his designs would be ready.[33] A conversation with Turner recorded in Moore's journal, during which the artist proposed to illustrate a collected edition of his works, seems a little calculating on Turner's part: when Turner said to Moore that he had never been to Ireland, but that he would be safe there under Moore's wing, he was no doubt hoping for Moore to finance a sketching tour in Ireland.[34] Indeed, tours were financed by Charles Heath in France for *Turner's Annual Tours*, and by Cadell in Scotland and France for Scott's *Poetical Works* and *Miscellaneous Prose*.

Certainly the editions of Rogers, Byron and Scott were printed and reprinted in very large numbers. Iain Bain has calculated that Turner's editions of Rogers's *Italy* and *Poems* were printed in editions of ten to twenty times the usual issue of a volume of poems, which was more like the number printed for an annual.[35] Lord Macaulay wrote to Rogers saying of his new volume of the *Poems*, 'How the publishers of the annuals must hate you. You have certainly spoiled the market for one year at least.'[36] Finberg regretted the new phase of 'baser metal' that he considered was brought into Turner's art by the influence of his catering to the middle-class reading public and to the dreamy voluptuousness and vulgarities of the contemporary phase of Romantic poetry.[37] Finberg was presumably thinking of Byron and Moore, but Turner's vignettes also include the two sublime illustrations of the War in Heaven from *Paradise Lost* (nos.31, 33).

Turner's vignettes mostly appeared either as the title-pages or frontispieces of volumes, which were small – mostly duodecimo – and which were issued in instalments 'for monthly delivery', in the phrase of the contemporary advertisements, such as the Byron, Scott and Milton sets. These were printed on a fold of heavier paper of better quality than that used for the sections of letter-press; this practice was common in early nineteenth-century printing. However, for the Rogers and Campbell books the vignettes were printed as head-pieces and tail-pieces on the same pages as the letter-press – a complicated and expensive process. The set of Byron volumes had vignettes by Turner and other artists as both frontispiece and title-piece; in the two Scott series each volume contained a rectangular 'landscape' illustration by Turner, printed at a right angle to the title-page, showing a view of a city or a landscape scene. The reader who turns the book through ninety degrees from the frontispiece to return it to its upright position and to focus on the vignette showing a single building or a close-up scene on the title-page has his awareness intensified by the sharper focus on Turner's image; the emblem or symbol takes the form of a meditative mandala.

Philip Hamerton wrote in 1879 of the way in which in Turner's vignettes the objects come out of nothingness into being, and how Turner avoids too much materialism in his treatment of them until he gets well towards the centre. To Hamerton, Stothard's vignettes in the Rogers volumes seemed just patches on the page, however graceful and charming, 'whilst Turner's never seem to be shaped or put on the paper at all, but we feel

fig.6 Henry Le Keux after J.M.W. Turner, 'Loch Coriskin' (R 511), and Edward Goodall after J.M.W. Turner, 'Fingal's Cave, Staffa' (R 512). Frontispiece and title-vignette engraved on steel from *The Poetical Works of Sir Walter Scott*, Vol.x, Edinburgh 1834

as if a portion of the beautiful white surface had in some wonderful way begun to glow with the light of genius'.[38] Laurence Gowing also spoke of the incandescent central axis in many of Turner's pictures after 1840, which he believed was the consequence of Turner's work on the vignettes.[39] Turner surely intended his landscape and vignette folded together in the Scott volumes to be read together as cognates or contrasts, such as the pair made by the formidable 'Loch Coriskin' and the 'Fingal's Cave, Staffa' (fig.6), or that of 'The Field of Waterloo from the Picton Tree' (w 1116; R 539) with the vignette of Napoleon captive on the *Bellerophon* in Plymouth Sound (App.B, no.101).

In the Rogers and Campbell volumes (where the vignettes are printed on the same page as the poems) the paper first received the impression of the engraving, with a large platemark. This was so that the plate-mark would not show on the trimmed page, on which the letter-press was then printed in the normal way.[40] The *Literary Gazette and Journal of the Belles Lettres* commented: 'The very manner in which the prints have been introduced into the text must have been attended with considerable technical difficulty'.[41] Wood-engraved blocks are capable of being 'locked up' with the text, and of being printed in a single impression together with the text, and thus do not need the same complicated, slow and expensive double procedure. The later

quarto *editions de luxe* of Rogers's *Italy* and *Poems* published by Moxon in 1838 did not use the method of being passed twice through the press, but instead had full page illustrations, consisting of vignettes with their engraved titles, printed on India paper and mounted. These are said to be made up from unsold original proof engravings – certainly they bear the dates 1829–30 and 1833 on the publishing line.

There are some very beautiful early nineteenth-century books with wood-engraved vignettes, such as Charles Whittingham's printing (1833) of the *Fables* of James Northcote R.A., with vignettes engraved by John Thompson and others[42] and of the two volumes of *The Gardens and Menagerie of the Zoological Society Delineated* with William Harvey's vignette designs (1830). However, Turner brought up what was in effect a 'school' of line-engravers to execute engravings after his works on copper and steel, realising how well equipped they were to render the subtlety and tonality of his work; he firmly rejected Cadell's proposal in May 1840 to make designs for a new edition of the Waverley Novels to be engraved on wood rather than steel.[43]

Walter Crane, the wood-engraver, expressed contempt for both steel-engraving and the Rogers volumes. His judgment was based on the design of the illustrated page as a whole, and was influenced by William Morris's ideals; in direct contrast to Hamerton, he wrote,

> Such books as Rogers's 'Poems' and 'Italy' … are characteristic of the taste of the period, and show about the high-water mark of the skill of the book engravers on steel. Stothard's designs are the only ones which have claims to be decorative, and he is always a graceful designer. Turner's landscapes, exquisite in themselves, and engraved with marvellous delicacy, do not in any sense decorate the page, and from that point of view are merely shapeless blots of printer's ink of different tones upon it, while the letterpress bears no relation whatever to the picture in method of printing or design, and has no independent beauty of its own. Book illustrations of this type – and it was a type which largely prevailed during the second quarter of the century – are simply pictures without frames.[44]

Turner undoubtedly thought about the total design of the page of an illustrated book, and had seen some early specimens. John Landseer the engraver tells us that Dr Monro, the mentor of Turner's late adolescence, had a collection of early prints, one indeed of the year 1461; at Rogers's house he would surely have seen some of the poet's collection of medieval illuminated manuscripts or miniatures with 'historiated initials' that enclose a vignette illustrating the text within the initial.[45] In designing the vignette for Rogers's poem 'Jacqueline' he uses a medieval convention of illustration by showing us in 'St Julienne's Chapel' two stages of the story in the one image, as in a cartoon without frames (App.B, no.42). The most beautiful of Turner's books with vignettes are the two Rogers volumes, even when found with over-elaborate tooling and gilding. Rogers had a large income from his family bank; it was common knowledge that he helped writers financially, including Moore and Campbell, and also the publisher Moxon. Rogers financed this publishing venture, spending £7,335 on both *Italy* and *Poems,* and still making a profit. The issue was of a thousand copies of *Italy* and most likely the same number of the *Poems*.[46] He also supervised every stage of the production with his aesthete's fastidiousness: the paper, type, and layout, and the printing of the engravings. We hear of him at a later date driving up to the premises of Charles Whittingham at Took's Court and stirring up the printers with his long stick.[47] Rogers's ideal is still that of late eighteenth-century book design: in presenting his own poems to the world he appears to have in mind the edition of *Poems* by Goldsmith and Parnell, printed by Bulmer in 1795 on Whatman paper, and embellished with vignettes by John Bewick and others (figs.7, 8). The 'Advertisement' at the beginning of this book re-

fig.8 Charlton Nesbit, head-piece to 'The Traveller'. Engraved on wood for Bulmer's *Poems of Goldsmith and Parnell*, 1795

ferred to 'the neglected state in which [the art of printing] had long been suffered to continue', pointing to the poverty of eighteenth-century 'Printing, Type-Founding, Engraving and Paper-making'; the reader was promised in this volume 'a complete Specimen of the Arts of Type and Block-Printing'.

A sonnet addressed by Charles Lamb to Rogers pays him the unfamiliar compliment of preferring his text without meretricious ornament:

> When thy gay book hath paid its proud devoirs,
> Poetic friend, and fed with luxury
> The eye of pampered aristocracy
> In glittering drawing-rooms and gilt boudoirs,
> O'erlaid with comments of pictorial art,
> However rich and rare, yet nothing leaving
> Of healthful action to the soul-conceiving
> Of the true reader …

A 'cheap-clad' edition, Lamb concluded, would do better in bringing refinement to the poor man's hearth and would then live 'in the moral heart of England'.[48]

It is remarkable how little Turner repeats himself in his vignettes; on the other hand when they are imitated by other hands they immediately look like imitations, or even parodies. In Samuel Palmer's vignettes to the Revd William Adams's *Sacred Allegories* of 1856 (fig.9) and Birket Foster's vignettes to two series of Hood's *Poems* of 1871 and 1872, engraved by one of Turner's best vignette engravers, William Miller, the sun-bursts and the prospects seen from above with a meandering river below, or the views of the picturesque Continent hallowed by Turner himself, show how potently Turner shaped the illustrative images of other artists and public taste.[49]

In addition to the vogue for the 'Landscape Annu-

fig.7 John Bewick, 'The Hermit'. Vignette engraved on wood for Bulmer's edition of the *Poems of Goldsmith and Parnell*, 1795

fig.9 W.T. Green after Samuel Palmer, 'The Distant and Eternal Hills'. Engraving on wood from Revd W. Adams, *Sacred Allegories*, 1859

als', such as the volumes of *Heath's Picturesque Annual*, *Jennings' Landscape Annual* and *Turner's Annual Tour,* which were topographical, Turner's literary 'landscape' vignettes should be seen in the context of the vogue for volumes of 'Landscape Illustrations' for literature. Those published for Scott, Burns and Bloomfield, for example, were composed of topographical views with a few portraits and were usually published separately from the texts. In addition to his contributions to the set of Finden's well-known *Landscape and Portrait Illustrations* to Byron that was published by John Murray, Turner was, I believe, commissioned to make vignettes and other illustrations for a set of George Crabbe's poems, again under Murray, who announced the publication in 1834, but abandoned it (see p.49, below). He was also approached by Charles Tilt to make landscape illustrations for Scott's poetry in addition to the vignettes he made for Cadell's edition. Murray's correspondence with Moore shows that Murray preferred Turner to design topographical scenes connected with Byron's travels and works rather than dramatised scenes from the poems such as Richard Westall had earlier de-

signed so successfully for him. In preparing illustrations for Scott's poetry for Cadell, Turner surrounded his topographical scenes with a cartouche outside which he drew (in sepia and in line) figures from the poems to which the vignettes were frontispieces. This attempt to have the illustrations serve two purposes was wisely abandoned.

The Studies for Vignettes

Light is thrown on Turner's methods in making his designs for the engravers by study of the series of watercolours in the Bequest classified by Finberg as 'CCLXXX. Studies for Vignettes, mostly Rogers's'. There is also a copy in the Bequest of the 1827 duodecimo volume of Rogers's *Poems* owned by Turner (no.61) in which he began the process of illustration: he made quick sketches in pencil (some of which included tiny figures) in rectangular frames in the margin alongside passages in the text. He put his initials, suggesting sessions of negotiation with Rogers and Stothard, and also lines by the side of stanzas or a cross in the margin where he considered making vignettes.

The sketches in the 'Studies for Vignettes' may be sorted into groups by the type and quality of paper or the thin Bristol board, by watermark, palette, subject-matter and style; two sets are on pieces of very cheap machine-made cartridge paper (see App.A, TB CCLXXX). One group consists of the finished watercolours for both Rogers volumes (complete except for one, 'The Hospice. Great St Bernard (I)' with Landseer's dogs in the margin, which is at Vassar College Art Gallery, Poughkeepsie, USA); there is a group on card with early ideas for the Milton series, including one of 'The Temptation on the Mountain' (no.34). The watercolour previously thought to be a study of 'Satan Summoning his Legions' cannot be part of this series, as it forms part of a sheet that Turner cut into four, and which can be reassembled showing a watermark of 1837 (TB CCLXXX 78). There are also a few interesting early studies for Rogers's *Italy* including some impressive sketches for designs which were not engraved – the Ponte Vecchio at Florence, the Leaning Towers of

Bologna and two piazza scenes (TB CCLXXX 95, 14, 2, 107). For Rogers's *Poems* there is a charming unused design of an eighteenth-century village school scene for Book I of 'The Pleasures of Memory' (fig.18 on p.40). There are some rougher sketches for Campbell, and several unused designs (amidst theatrical Athenian and Egyptian scenery) for Moore's *Epicurean* and *Alciphron*, parcelled up by Ruskin and marked 'Studies of vignettes (Epicurean) – bad'. Some of the latter were obviously ready for an engraver (see TB CCLXXX 113–38). There are studies of details which Turner preserved, such as the sketch of the hill town in the distance at Amalfi with its viaduct, for Rogers's *Italy* (TB CCLXXX 101). Only one study for the Byron series and a possible study for the Scott series were preserved by Turner. There are also a number of roughly vignette-shaped preparatory studies which are hard to identify and some watercolours which are too late to be designs for publishers' commissions, and which are not strictly vignettes.

Finberg also placed in this classification a highly interesting group of landscape-shaped studies connected with Turner's reading of Scott's *Life of Napoleon*, for which he made the remarkable series of sixteen illustrations published by Cadell in 1834. There is an unengraved series of 'Four finished vignettes of fish', which includes 'Cod on the Beach' (no.54). Finberg plainly became impatient with his classification, dismissing thirty-one of the studies as 'all very slight' without separate entries or names. TB CCLXXX 81, for which he misread Turner's inscription as 'Volterra', plainly reads 'Vol.1'. In four series of studies, two each for Rogers and Campbell vignettes, we can see Turner's mind at work as he experiments with groupings and focus: in two sketches for the Columbus series we see him figuring the ominous apparition of soldiers in the sky above the horizon for 'A Vision. Voyage of Columbus' (TB CCLXXX 203, 204) and working alternatives for the procession of cross-bearing Europeans and the foreground figures of the pagan native Americans in 'The Landing of Columbus' (no.25); for Campbell's 'Kosciusko' there are several studies for the multi-arched bridge, the conflagration at Warsaw and the military figures before he works these into the foreground and distance of his final perspective (for example no.46). There is one powerful preparatory study for the Campbell volume which shows in flesh tone the posture of the demented daughter of O'Connor recumbent on her lover's grave and holding his shield (no.48); Turner can convey with a few brush-strokes a powerful sense of evil in the standing figures of her hateful and hating brothers. A few of the designs for Rogers's *Poems*, such as that for 'Traitor's Gate' (TB CCLXXX 93), show the thin red outlines that became a feature of Turner's late watercolours.

Many artists in the latter part of Turner's career were making their designs for engraving in sepia; this was thought to simplify the engraver's task. There is, for example, a highly finished vignette design by Clarkson Stanfield executed entirely in brown-toned colours on pale blue paper for the engraving of St Malo in *Heath's Picturesque Annual* of 1834, bound up in the 'extra-illustrated' copy of Thornbury's *Life of Turner* in the British Library.[50] Turner did an early design for Scott's *Provincial Antiquities* in pencil over grey wash (no.39) but thereafter designed in colour. He presumably had the motive of selling the watercolour designs: Campbell was told by a friend (erroneously, as it turned out) that the watercolours would be like bank-notes.[51] For example, Murray paid Turner twenty-five guineas each for vignette designs for the Byron series, and in 1833 records selling three of the originals for fifteen guineas each.[52] By working in full colour Turner was also giving signals to the engravers for the black and white tonalities of their work. Rawlinson thought that while the drawings Turner made for the engravers were marvellously executed, delicate, highly imaginative and poetical in feeling, the colour was 'strangely forced and extravagant', even in the Rogers series, and that this was indeed connected with the process of engraving.[53] Certainly there is evidence that Turner in his preparatory studies and at later stages of his designs seems to work out the balance of the tonality in his designs and his strong contrasts by opposing blue, yellow and red to work out the distance, the middle distance and the more substantial masses respectively.[54]

The Engravers

The designs for the Rogers volumes were made larger than the engraved image, and were reduced by the engravers. Turner suggested to Robert Cadell in a letter of 1831 that he might design the vignettes the same size as they were to be worked to save the engravers' time and Cadell's expense.[55] Turner must have worked under a lens, as the engraver did, to produce work so fine and delicate as the finished watercolours for Milton (nos. 31, 33, 36) and the finished watercolours for Campbell (National Gallery of Scotland).

Rawlinson thought that the engravings of the vignettes were in many cases more beautiful than Turner's drawings for them.[56] There might truly be said to be a 'School of Turner' among engravers, for Turner trained up a group of landscape engravers – there were specialist engravers of figures and of animals also. This 'School' included the Cookes (William Bernard and his brother, George), John Pye and Henry Le Keux, all of whom he had known from the earliest days of his association with engravers, when he had made designs for John Britton's *Architectural Antiquities* of 1814 (a book which Turner praises for 'good specimens of engraving for depth and well-laid lines') and James Basire's *Oxford Almanacs* (1799–1811).[57] There were also younger engravers, such as Edward Goodall and William Miller: all were 'reared under the eye of Turner', Goodall's son tells us. Studying these engravings, one's admiration of the engravers steadily grows. Hamerton, himself an engraver, wrote in *The Graphic Arts* that Turner's engravers

> reached the high-water mark of landscape engraving, and it will never be surpassed in any way. Nobody will ever translate the tones of water-colours better than they were translated by Goodall, Wallis and Miller, in the vignettes to Rogers. However subtle the distinctions by which Turner separated the pale towers of his distant cities, or the shadowy masses of his mountains, or the vaporous heights of cloud, these men followed him, and in following him they achieved feats of execution entirely beyond the power of all those famous artists who are considered the classical masters of engraving.[58]

Some connoisseurs, on the other hand, despised what they saw as the niggling accuracy and polished smartness of these vignettes, according to the American collector Francis Bullard.[59]

The engravers of the first vignettes after Turner were George Cooke (1781–1834) and his brother W.B. Cooke (1778–1855). George Cooke, who engraved on copper the topographical and emblematical title-page vignettes of Edinburgh for Scott's *Provincial Antiquities* in 1826, was an engraver of the old school who resisted the introduction of steel engraving. An obituary, published in *Arnold's Magazine of the Fine Arts* in 1834 reads: 'He strongly participated in the dislike entertained by nearly all the eminent engravers to the introduction of steel plates, and, as he conscientiously believed that the consequences would be disastrous to an Art which he loved all things beside, he in common with the seniors of the profession, openly declared his determination never to work on the hated metal'. The writer of this obituary declared that most of the earliest steel engravings were 'cheap and trashy ephemera'.[60] It is interesting that John Pye, perhaps the most distinguished and certainly the most articulate of the engravers who have left records of their opinions, says that steel engraving was a great advance, as 'a superior power of exquisite delineation is possessed by the graver, in the same proportion as the needle-point is more delicate than the pencil of the painter'. Pye says that in 1811 the engraver Abraham Raimbach first engraved a steel plate, for the Bank of England.[61] The new process of book illustration on steel developed fast partly because of the need of the Bank to have more and more fine and complex engraving in their banknotes, to avoid forgery. Both William Finden and Charles Heath, engravers of Turner, engraved notes. Among the books belonging to Turner there is an annotated copy of a *Report ... on the Mode of Preventing the Forgery of Bank Notes* (1818), which recommends the use of small vignettes on banknotes.[62] Banknotes (and postage stamps) can even now recall the early nineteenth-century days of steel-engraved vignettes in design and in complexity of line engraving.

Steel engraving differs from copper engraving in that it is made onto a plate of copper that has been coated with the much harder steel. The delicacy of the process of engraving a steel plate meant that work on it took perhaps seven times longer than a copper plate to finish, thirteen weeks being a common time to finish one small landscape plate. The plate was first etched, and then for these extremely fine engravings worked a great deal with the needle-point in dry-point – that is to say without wax and acid – as well as with the burin. To compare the earliest steel-engraved book-illustration with copper-engraved work does not show much difference in style or execution, as may be seen from the illustrations to two books by Campbell, both with designs by Richard Westall, *Gertrude of Wyoming* (1819), which has copper engravings by Charles Heath, and *The Pleasures of Hope* (1822), which has steel engravings by Heath dated 1820, one of which is marked 'Patent Hardend Steel Plate'.

Turner obviously realised the artistic potential of steel for book illustration. 'It is probable', wrote Rawlinson, 'that for extremely delicate engravings, such as the vignettes which were such an important feature in Turner's later work, steel, apart from its superior durability, is even better than copper, as a finer and more certain line can be obtained. It is doubtful if the ethereal beauty and delicacy of the famous illustrations to Rogers's *Poems* and *Italy* could have been obtained from copper. Certainly they would have vanished with the first few impressions printed.'[63] On the other hand it has been remarked that for the *England and Wales* series, a project presumably very close to Turner's heart, he insisted on copper. The commercial possibilities of the new process were recognised by the publishers: a single steel plate could produce a vast number of impressions – the record, in 1851, was said to be 500,000.[64] However, the steel plates were notoriously subject to rust. Horace Mummery, whose meticulous annotated collection is in the Victoria and Albert Museum, has noticed that a number of the Byron vignettes are found in two different states, indicating a second engraving of the plate. This was either because so many copies were printed, and it enabled the printers to print from the two plates for speed, or, as Mummery thought, due to 'wear and tear'.[65] Surely if the former was the case the whole set would have been engraved twice; it is more likely that there was an attack of rust on some of the plates before the second edition of the volumes in 1836, three years after the first edition; at the same time the printing of the text was stereotyped.

In February 1821 George Cooke put on an important *Exhibition of Engravings by Living British Artists* in which Turner's landscapes were well represented, and vignettes designed by Havell and Westall were also shown, engraved by Pye and Finden. Cooke regretted that so many fine engravings were shut up in books: 'A great portion of the time of British Engravers has, of late years, been applied to the illustration of Literature, but the more exquisite performances in this way are scarcely produced before they are locked up in the Cabinets of the Curious, never to be looked at, but by a chosen few.'[66] According to Pye the high price of glass, particularly compared with France, was a determinant in British engravers being more in demand during this period for book illustration than for large plates for the 'decoration of rooms'.[67] Cooke also complains that the preponderance of work on 'book plates' rather than on large plates meant that engravers did not see the work of others. By the time of Turner's principal vignette series, however, this seems to have changed, and there are engraver's proofs of the vignettes in print rooms with inscriptions from one engraver to another.[68]

The publishers of almost all the books illustrated with Turner vignettes made the engravings better known and made more profit by selling portfolios of prints from the plates. These were available in ranks of quality and price: engraver's proofs; on India paper; before and after lettering, and on varying sizes of paper – even on the absurdly large Colombier folio – to satisfy the competitiveness of connoisseurs. As late as 1852, A. & C. Black in the course of their reprints of Cadell's editions of Scott with Turner illustrations offered portfolio sets of impressions of the plates. Advertisements for such sales took prominent places in magazines. Engravers prospered: Pye told a Select Committee of the House of Commons in 1845 that the number of engravers had increased five times since the end of the Napoleonic Wars. Pye was embittered at the exclusion of engravers from the Royal Academy, and the sub-text of his important book *The Patronage of British Art* is a polemic to change the climate of opinion against the inferior status of those 'translators' of the painters' images. Both Turner and Pye referred to the engraver's art as 'translation', to be distinguished from mere 'cold rigid' copying.[69]

The publishers of engravings in this period enjoyed great prosperity: Pye tells us that the turnover of Messrs Graves in 1844 was some £22,000.[70] Turner's involvement, of course also brought him much profit; indeed, C.R. Leslie says in his autobiography that Turner's large fortune was 'acquired very much through the means of engraving'.[71] Pye tells us that Sir Thomas Lawrence was paid £3,000 per year by Hurst and Robinson for the exclusive privilege of engraving his works. Wilkie was paid £1,200 for the engraving rights of 'Chelsea Pensioners' by Messrs Moon, Boys and Graves; the Duke of Wellington had paid the same number of guineas for the painting itself.[72] There is evidence that Turner could command significantly higher rates for his designs for vignettes in projects, such as the Byron and Rogers series, that were done in conjunction with other artists. Rogers, Scott and Campbell all recognised that the illustrations by Turner would sell many more copies of their poems, and Sir Egerton Brydges in his Preface to his edition of Milton says confidently that he knows 'that the illustrations from the rich and incomparable pencil of Turner, will, I doubt not, secure the public favour to it'.[73] As well as payment Turner habitually insisted on a large number of the finest proofs of engravings – these conditions led to quarrels, and there are records of several projects that came to grief over Turner's demands. After his death it was discovered that 'the 30,000 proof impressions that he had wrung from the engravers by so many special arrangements were left to perish by mildew and dirt in portfolios which were never opened'.[74] Turner's letter to the publisher A.J. Valpy of 8 May 1834, gives his terms curtly: '25 guineas each drawing vignette 50 proof impressions of each plate, with a presentation copy of the work (and the drawings and plates not to be used for any other work)'.[75] Turner guarded these rights fiercely, going to lengths such as putting advertisements in the paper saying that certain engravings had not been 'touched' by him, and on one occasion in 1833 taking Tilt before the Lord Mayor of London to stop him re-engraving and publishing on a smaller scale a plate that he had bought.[76] That these measures were necessary to protect the rights of the artist can be shown from a bad experience of Stothard's where Charles Heath broke a contract which had promised him the complete decoration of a book, but for which Heath then commissioned some designs from artists who charged less.[77]

A crucial factor of the engraving process is the stage known as the 'touching' of the engravers' proofs by the artist. We know that Turner was in demand to 'touch' proofs for engravings after other artists, as Thornbury's

printing of W.B. Cooke's accounts proves.[78] After Turner's death it was recalled that 'the engravers found [Turner] troublesome beyond all other painters, by the alterations which he continually made during the course of their plates'.[79] John Thackray Bunce wrote in his Introduction to *The Exhibition of Engravings by Birmingham Men* in 1877 that 'there were few, if any, of the plates engraved from his works upon which there are not traces of his own hand – a bit of dark, a point of light, a new sweep of line, an alteration of light and shade – worked out in consultation with the engraver, and by him translated from rough hints into intelligible and effective shape'.[80] Many examples of the different stages of engravings have survived with Turner's 'touching', showing his use of pencil and white or black chalk. The proof touched by Turner of Goodall's engraving of 'The Fall of the Rebel Angels' (Fitzwilliam Museum, Cambridge; see also App.B, no.114) has been worked on by Turner to accentuate even further the contrast between light and dark, and there is evidence of 'scratching out', probably with Turner's thumbnail. There are sometimes also written comments as well, which are often concerned with the engraver's handling of his chiaroscuro, which had not been contrasted enough for Turner's liking, or (just as in the many touched proofs for the *Liber Studiorum*) showing a passionate interest in the sun as the source of light. He writes, 'I wish the sun's rays to be as brilliant as possible' on a proof of 'The Gipsy' from Rogers's *Poems* (R 375; now in the British Museum), and the proof of Miller's engraving 'An Old Manor House' has his directive to 'burnish into rays' the light falling through the trees to the right-hand side (no.16). Engravers learned to recognise what Turner referred to as 'sparkle' in a print.[81] The Woolley Collection of Turner prints at Birmingham has several important proofs of Goodall's vignettes for the Rogers volumes showing the stages of the improvements made by Turner to the funeral procession in 'The Forum' and abrupt reworking of the figures in 'Leaving Home' and 'Captivity'.[82] In 'St Anne's Hill, 1' Turner has drawn in at the foot of the vignette an open and a closed book (fig.10). This is presumably an allusion to the rival attractions of literature and nature, referring to an anecdote about Rogers's alfresco exchange with Charles James Fox at the statesman's house and grounds shown in the vignette: Rogers said to Fox that lying in the sunny grass would

fig.10 Edward Goodall after J.M.W. Turner, 'St Anne's Hill, 1'.
Engraving on steel for Rogers's *Poems* (R 384). 'Touched' proof
with details drawn in the foreground in pencil by Turner

be '"delightful – with a book"; "but why with a book?"
said Fox, the laziest of men'.[83]

At the sale of engravings from Turner's studio after
his death touched proofs were sold of vignettes from
the Rogers, Milton, Scott and Campbell series.[84]
Turner would insist on the return of most of these from
the engravers, especially those with written comment;
indeed there are anecdotes of him jealously watching
that no scrap of his handiwork went out of his hands.
According to Thornbury, his most bitter quarrel with
an engraver, of which there were many and some of
them in public, was with Edward Goodall over the return of some touched proofs.[85] We have to thank the
great collectors of Turner engravings who competed at
the Turner sale or at sales which included such proofs

after the deaths of the engravers or their heirs for pre-
serving such fascinating records of the process and
detailed evidence of Turner's jealous watch over the
progress of his engravers. There is said to be only one
engraving, Henry Le Keux's desolate 'Loch Coriskin'
(R 511), that Turner did not change at all.[86] The significance of the 'touched proofs' was early recognised; for
example Messrs Graves, who exhibited some of their
own collection for sale at the *Exhibition of Engravings by
Birmingham Men* in 1877, included several. As well as
being visited by Turner or sending proofs to him
through the post, the engravers were visited in the
course of their work by Cadell (for Scott), or by Moore
and Campbell themselves to see their progress.[87]

Bunce quotes in his introduction an anonymous authority (perhaps Henry Graves) on the difficulties faced by Turner's engravers:

> Take a picture or drawing by Turner in his latter time, full of mystery, and apparently with no accurate drawing in it. First a reduction has to be made to scale. The original may be full of the most delicate architectural work, crowded perhaps, with figures – all, at first glance, a shapeless mass, but all requiring, for the engraver's purpose, to be put into order, and to be submitted to Turner's critical eye. When the plate gets well into progress, then comes the question of colour – a bit of bright orange, or scarlet, or blue; how shall it be rendered in black, or white or grey? Turner knows, but the engraver dare not ask him until the plate is in such a condition as to require touching.[88]

Pye describes how Turner would consider an engraver's proof: the artist, he said, 'would turn his proofs, after touching them, from side to side and upside down that the key of colour might be maintained and carried into effect. He was wont to say that engravers have only white paper to express what the painter does with vermilion … The great principle he was always endeavouring to advance was that of the art of translation of landscape, whether in colour or black and white, was [sic] to enable the spectator to see through the picture into space'.[89] Goodall's son said that when his father asked Turner how to translate 'a bit of brilliant red', he was told, 'Sometimes translate it into black, and another time into white. If a bit of black gives the emphasis, so does red in my picture.'[90]

Alaric Watts (1797–1864) founded the *Literary Souvenir* and could be said, along with Rudolph Ackermann, to have introduced the Annuals in England, importing the idea from the Continent, where the *taschenbuch* was all the rage. When describing the 'golden days' of the line-engravers, he said that they would vie with each other for the illustrations which were to be distributed among them, 'like parts in private theatricals, every player dissatisfied and envying somebody else's'.[91] However, their life could be solitary and painful, according to the same anonymous source quoted in Bunce's essay which describes their conditions and their 'almost heroic' skill, perseverance, and endurance:

> Few men have more lacked the sympathy and appreciation of the public than engravers; few men have been less known, few have lived more solitary or more laborious lives. Bending double all through a bright sunny day, in an attic or a close work-room, over a large steel plate, with a powerful magnifying-glass in constant use; carefully picking and cutting out bits of metal from the plate, and giving the painfully formed lines the ultimate form of some of Turner's most brilliant conceptions, working for twelve or fourteen hours daily, taking exercise rarely, in early morning or late at night; 'proving' a plate, only to find that days of labour have been mistaken, and have to be effaced, and done over again; criticised and corrected by painters, who often or always look upon engravers – to whom they owe so much – as inferior to themselves; badly paid by publishers, who reap the lion's share of the value of their work; and treated with indifference by the public – such is too commonly the life of an engraver.[92]

A group of landscape-engravers, principally Edward Goodall and William Miller, was associated with Turner's vignettes throughout the period of his book illustrations; at the same time they might be employed on larger plates after Turner or other artists, with work for the *Landscape* and other Annuals, for the Byron *Landscape Illustrations,* and of course on work after other artists for book illustration. The slow progress of engraving needs to be emphasised: in 1837 Miller was given six months for the etching of a large Venetian painting by Turner, and a further fifteen months to finish the engraving.[93] George Cooke, who engraved one of the topographical and emblematical title-pages for Scott's *Provincial Antiquities* on copper in 1822, has been mentioned as an enemy to steel-engraving; like Henry Le Keux (1787–1868), the architectural specialist, he is associated with Turner's earlier career. His nephew and pupil W.J. Cooke, who engraved the 'Martigny' for *Italy* (App. B, no.8) and 'Newark Castle' for Scott's *Poetical Works* (App.B, no.81), was awarded a gold medal by the Society of Arts in 1826 for improvements to steel engraving. Turner employed Le Keux for Rogers's *Italy* presumably for the stonework and architectural complexities of the 'Aosta' (App.B, no.7) and 'A Villa' (App.B, no.14), in which the light is also marvellously conveyed. Le Keux left the profession in 1838 to join in a crape manufactory.[94]

It is surprising that such an excellent engraver as James Tibbetts Willmore (1800–1863), who carried out a total of thirty-four plates after Turner while the artist was alive, did little work on the vignettes: three for *The Keepsake* and only one other, the 'Lochmaben Castle' for Scott's *Poetical Works* (App.B, no.78). Willmore, a most subtle engraver, was born in Birmingham and studied under Charles Heath in London for three years. According to Marcus Huish, Turner found Willmore's work for the *Rivers of France* series, which is surely among the finest of all Turner engravings, 'soft, spongy and black'.[95] Some of the engravers who executed a single plate for the vignettes were pupils of the principal engravers, such as Robert Brandard (1805–1862) whose plate for the Milton series is found among those of his master Goodall's, or Edward Webb, an assistant of Pye, whose 'Bowes Tower' is alongside one of Pye's engravings in Scott's *Poetical Works* (App.B, no.84).[96] Although all the Byron vignettes are signed 'E. Finden', Redgrave says of both Edward (1792–1857) and his elder brother William (1787–1852) that 'it may be doubted whether [these plates] received more than a few finishing touches from their hands, for the studio of these artists was filled with a number of young men'. The brothers had been taught by James Mitan; they were involved in publishing speculation, and worked for John Murray for fifteen years. Together the Findens published the very successful Byron *Landscape Illustrations*, but they were ruined by the failure of *The Gallery of British Art* in 1842.[97] John Cousen (1804–1880), who engraved two of the three vignettes on the title-pages for *The Rivers of France* series and 'The Temptation on the Mountain' for the Milton series (no.35), was much admired for his 'exquisite taste, artistic feeling and power of execution'; his entry in Bryan's *Dictionary of Painters and Engravers* particularly selects the 'poetic feeling' of these two vignettes for comment.[98]

Robert Wallis (1794–1878) was taught by his father Henry, who had been an assistant to Charles Heath. He followed a long career of engraving after Turner. This included the engraving on copper of the second of the two vignette title-pages to Scott's *Provincial Antiquities* in 1826, and eight of the vignettes for the two Rogers volumes, followed by a single vignette for Scott's *Poetical Works* and two for the Campbell volume. Wallis shows to his best in his larger plates after Turner, such as the ravishing 'Nemi' of 1842 (R 659), and the

'Approach to Venice' of 1859 (R 679), a proof of which he exhibited at the Royal Academy as his final work before retirement. John Pye (1782–1874) was one of the most important engravers of his day, and did significant work after Turner, but is only represented among the vignettes by the 'Tivoli' and 'Temples of Paestum' for Rogers's *Italy* (App.B, nos.18, 22), for which he was paid £35 each, compared with the 20 guineas paid to the engravers of many other vignettes in the book. Ruskin chides him too harshly for his 'feeble' rendering of the dark and furious storm in the 'Paestum'.[99] Pye's obituary in the *Art Journal* claims that much of the excellence of landscape-engraving in the century was due to his example and influence; on him the mantle of the great eighteenth-century engraver William Woollett had fallen.[100] Pye's most original work, perhaps, is the series of very small, exquisite head-pieces for *Peacock's Polite Repository or Pocket Companion* from the 1830s to 1850s, a complete set of which was given by his sister to the Print Room at the British Museum. This series of picturesque scenes of mansions, villas and landscapes after such painters as Havell and Reinagle prolonged the late eighteenth-century and Regency taste in sharp chiaroscuro. Pye, Willmore and Brandard were all originally of the Birmingham School of engravers, which had initially developed so well in response to the demands of the metal industry.

William Miller (1796–1882) and John Horsburgh (1791–1869) were both Edinburgh engravers.[101] Horsburgh, who was well employed by Cadell to engrave vignettes for the edition of Scott's *Miscellaneous Prose*, was a portrait and 'historical' engraver, but his plates for this series are highly successful. He seems to have been given mostly the vignettes involving buildings to engrave, but showed in 'Mayburgh' and 'Calais' (App.B, no.109) that he could compete with Miller in poetic feeling, particularly in the 'Mayburgh' (no.43), which gives the impression of being an interesting optical distortion. Miller was certainly one of the two or three engravers most favoured by Turner.[102] Turner wrote to him in connection with the large plate of 'Modern Italy' (R 658), praising 'the beautiful quality of silvery softness' that Miller had achieved in the water, and asking for the foreground to be 'more spirited and bold'.[103] Miller (fig.11), a Quaker, was of 'an old Scottish family'. He seems to have enjoyed a most happy career, judging from the posthumous private publication,

fig.11 Anon., 'William Miller' (n.d.). Engraving on wood

Memorials of Hope Park (1886) which includes photographs of his house and work-room and a careful list of all his plates, giving the dates of their completion and his fees. He was sent to London to study under George Cooke, and returned to Edinburgh 'after some years'. Miller was also a painter in watercolours.[104] Turner employed him for four plates in Rogers's *Poems*, two of which survive in touched proofs with Turner's written comments (nos.11, 16). At the same time he was at work on the vignette of 'Nantes' for *Turner's Annual Tour* of 1833 (no.28; R 432). Miller's work is both strong and subtle, as is shown by the range of his engravings of Turner's work for Scott's *Miscellaneous Prose*, for example the lyrical 'Rhymer's Glen, Abbotsford' (no.45). Some original steel plates engraved after Turner designs for the Scott series by Miller and Horsburgh have survived (nos.66–9).

Judging by the numbers of vignettes consigned to him by Turner, Edward Goodall (1795–1870) was his preferred engraver of these concentrated and poetic images. He engraved twelve vignettes for Rogers's *Italy*,

twenty-seven for the *Poems*, more than the lion's share of the Campbell, all of Moore's *Epicurean* and much of the Milton. His work spanned fifteen years from his first dated engraving for *Italy* in 1829 to what appears to be the very last vignette supervised by Turner, the 'Lake Nemi' of 1844 (R 638). His best vignettes are highly expressive landscapes with fine skies and some strong figure-work. Ruskin, incidentally, said that the skies are the greatest achievement of the vignette engravers.[105] Goodall was born in Leeds, and according to his son's biography was self-taught, dedicated to engraving and painting from the age of sixteen. He came to London and it was his chief ambition to work for Turner; most of his work was in fact taken up with 'translations' from Turner. Indeed it is possible that but for Turner's praise for his painting of 'North End, Hampstead – Sunset' (RA 1823) and his there and then promising the young man as much of his work to engrave as he liked, Goodall might have continued a painter rather than an engraver. Thus Turner's two most sensitive engravers for his vignettes had experience of painting. For Goodall's strength, study his engraving of 'A Hurricane in the Desert' ('The Simoom') (App.B, no.38) or 'The Fall of the Rebel Angels' (App.B, no.114); for subtlety, look at 'A Villa. Moonlight (A Villa on the Night of a Festa di Ballo)' (App.B, no.24), or the phosphoric water-nymphs in 'Ludlow Castle' (App.B, no.119), the 'Fingal's Cave, Staffa' (App.B, no.85), or each of the Columbus series (App.B, nos.51–7). In spite of their quarrel, Goodall and Turner seemed to have enjoyed most cordial relations: his son's reminiscences give pleasant accounts of his visits among Goodall's artistic children.

The Publishers

Turner's vignettes, especially those in the sets of volumes which have frontispiece and title vignettes, developed from the engravings placed at the beginning of the many volumes of sets of poets. These were mostly in duodecimo size or even smaller, and the engravings were after designs by Westall, Stothard, William Hamilton, Fuseli and many others. They were published in the early nineteenth century by John Sharpe, Suttaby or Bell, together with the particularly elegant volumes issued by F. J. Du Roveroy, the merchant and stockbroker who was also an amateur publisher. By the 1830s they had established a tradition of volumes with a rectangular frontispiece and a title-vignette.

John Murray commissioned Turner's vignettes for the seventeen-volume edition of Byron published in 1832–4, selecting the scenes to be illustrated, and furnishing Turner with sketches from the portfolios of grand-tour artists and architects for him to work up. Longman published the *Rivers of France* series with three title-page vignettes. However, it was mostly the enterprising young publishers rather than the well-established ones who commissioned Turner to embellish their editions. Rogers himself was largely responsible for the enormous capital outlay and the elaborate direction for both of his volumes, the *Italy* of 1830 and the *Poems* of 1834. They appeared under the joint imprint of 'T. Cadell and E. Moxon'. The *New Monthly Magazine* was quick to point out that no publisher could have undertaken the venture on their own.[106] Thomas Cadell was the son of Rogers's earlier publisher; he died in 1836. Edward Moxon (1801–1858) (fig.12) was a protegé of Charles Lamb, whose adopted daughter Emma he married; Lamb introduced him to Rogers, whose literary breakfasts he attended. In 1829 Rogers advanced him £500, and he began business in New Bond Street in the spring of 1830. He was well known as a specialist in poetry, and also published large volumes of Elizabethan plays. In 1835 Wordsworth transferred all his works to him, and for many years he was the sole publisher of Tennyson. The *Dictionary of National Biography* remarks on 'the neatness and delicacy in external details that characterised all Moxon's publications'. His publication of Campbell's *Poems* with Turner's vignettes in 1837 was by the same elaborate process as the Rogers volumes but without the air of luxury and without the vignettes and decorations by Stothard and others which had been a part of the slightly antiquarian charm of the earlier volumes. Moxon's other ambitious illustrated book was the famous 1854 volume of Tennyson's *Poems*, illustrated by the Pre-Raphaelites. In this the lonely vignette by Clarkson Stanfield seems absurdly out of place among the illustrations by Millais, and particularly among those by Rossetti and Holman Hunt: the echoes of

fig.12 Attrib. Samuel Laurence, 'Edward Moxon' (n.d.). Oil on canvas. *Private Collection*

Turner in Stanfield's vignette seem old-fashioned and stale.

Henry Fisher (1781–1837) was a publisher of illustrated books such as *The Gallery of Scripture Engravings*, and his firm had a branch in Paris. In 1836 he published *The Pilgrim's Progress* with Turner's title-vignette (App.B, no.120), and also the *Landscape Historical Illustrations of Scotland and the Waverley Novels*. This included the set of six landscape-shaped illustrations, made for the Waverley Novels by Turner for Robert Cadell, but which Turner had withdrawn when Cadell proposed to reproduce the designs by wood-engraving.

With Robert Cadell of Edinburgh (1788–1849) Turner's relations seem to have been warm, in spite of the loss of the Waverley set of illustrations. Cadell was Scott's publisher, confidant and executor. His remarkably comprehensive archive in the National Library of Scotland with his diaries, account-books, letters and copy letters gives a minute account of his dealings with Turner and the London engravers during his annual trips to London and records their work arriving by post; we are able to feel his excitements and frustrations. Cadell watched eagerly the progress of Murray's Byron edition with the Turner vignettes, well aware of its commercial success; his own three series of Scott editions with Turner illustrations were also issued monthly and in duodecimo size. We learn that Scott was not keen for Turner to illustrate his poems; he had not enjoyed Turner's participation in his *Provincial Antiquities* – they had both, for one thing, lost money in it. Another reason was that Scott, while admiring 'Turner's masterly pencil', did not take to Turner and his manners, in particular his 'itchy palm'.[107] However, he was persuaded by Cadell that Turner's illustrations would increase his sales of the *Poetical Works:* 'With Mr. Turner's pencil I will ensure the sale of 8000 of the poetry – without, not 3,000.'[108] Scott seemed to be reconciled to entertaining Turner on a visit to Scotland to sketch for illustrations, writing in a letter that 'This is in some degree a plague, for Mr Turner though an artist of genius is not so pleasant as such persons usually are'. The reason was that Scott had decided that 'no one but myself perhaps can make him fix on the fit subjects'.[109] Turner came in July 1831 by Cadell's agency to Scotland, staying with Scott at Abbotsford and visiting some of the Border subjects of his vignettes with Scott; then on his own he travelled north, reaching as far as the remote Loch Coruisk on Skye. In September 1832 Cadell helped to finance a trip of Turner's to northern France to sketch for his great series of illustrations for Scott's *Life of Napoleon* which formed part of Cadell's edition of the *Miscellaneous Prose* (1834–6). Turner's final work for Cadell was the design of two vignettes for Lockhart's *Life of Scott* (1839).

John Macrone (1809–1837) was the publisher of Turner's Milton vignettes in 1835. It was his very first venture, and he dedicated the six-volume edition to Wordsworth and Southey. He also negotiated with Moore to publish a collected edition of all his poems with Turner illustrations: Turner's illustrations for *Lalla Rookh* would have been, judging by the illustrations for *The Epicurean*, strange and fascinating. However, Macrone failed to acquire the copyrights from other publishers. By the time that *The Epicurean* was published by his firm (under the direction of his widow and her brother) Macrone was dead from influenza. Moore commented in his journal: 'Poor young Macrone, too – whose death however did not take me by surprise, as I saw, when I last parted from him, that he was not long

for this world'.[110] Macrone was a friend of Dickens: he was originally invited to be best man at Dickens's wedding, and a set of his edition of Milton was his wedding gift.[111] He published *Sketches by Boz* with Cruikshank illustrations in 1836 and also works by Harrison Ainsworth. He emerges from Moore's journals as an intelligent, lively and accomplished companion, who drew well.[112] Macrone was the publisher of the *Monthly Magazine*, but seems not to have been a good businessman, getting into financial muddles and paying Moore too much for the make-weight *Alciphron*, an early version in poetry of the novella *The Epicurean*. This was added as Macrone had forgotten how short *The Epicurean* was. The project of illustrating *The Epicurean* was, from an entry in Moore's journal, presumably in hand by June 1837, but Macrone told Moore he must put the publication off because of the state of the 'money market'; he was, however, 'full of ecstasy at the Letters of the High Priest' *(Alciphron)*. Ainsworth wrote to Macrone wishing him success in his negotiations with Moore and congratulating him on 'adding a princely name to your list'.[113] In August, a few weeks before the death of Macrone, Moore recorded that the publisher 'has got into some wrangle with Goodall, the engraver, about my Epicurean. It appears that Goodall was to have gone half with him, in the speculation, but, taking fright latterly, wanted to be off his agreement – but that Macrone would not hear of'. Turner seems to have felt some residual bitterness about the affair, as in the event he prepared many sketches and some unengraved finished designs for *The Epicurean* (for example, nos.50–3); sitting next to Moore at a dinner at Rogers's sister's house in July 1842, Turner 'talked a great deal to me about the losses he had experienced on the score of the Epicurean – so many of the designs he had made for it being left on his hands &c. &c.'[114] Macrone in his Advertisement to Volume VI of the Milton pays homage both 'to Mr. Turner, whose imaginative genius has never been more brilliantly displayed than in his illustrations of Milton – [and] to the Engravers, whose innate conception of the beauties of this great painter has long stamped them as the first artists in this kingdom'.

The Literary Illustrations for Walter Fawkes, 1822, and the Early Vignettes

Turner's literary illustrations might be said to originate in two Regency milieux: one in Yorkshire at Walter Fawkes's Farnley Hall, with its Library and the Drawing Room hung with works by Turner, the other in London at Samuel Rogers's house at 22 St James's Place (fig.13), the setting of the famous literary circle, the remarkable collections of works of art and the social breakfasts. Writers and painters seemed to know each other better than at other periods: in the literary and social memoirs of the period at meetings of 'choice spirits' the names of Turner, Stothard, Westall, Martin and Landseer occur frequently in accounts of dinners and salons. Rogers's house brought together Turner's modern authors: when Byron came there in the autumn of 1811 to be introduced to both Moore and Campbell, they talked after dinner of Scott.[115]

Turner made a remarkable set of highly finished literary illustrations for Walter Fawkes, only five and a half inches wide and seven and a half inches high, celebrating three poets for whom he later made vignettes. These were for Byron's *The Giaour,* Scott's *Marmion, The Lady of the Lake, The Lay of the Last Minstrel* and *Rokeby,* and Moore's *Lalla Rookh* (W 1052–7). Except for the Moore, they are all illustrations to specific lines, and

fig.13 'Breakfast Room in the late Mr. Rogers' Residence, St. James's Place', *Illustrated London News,* 5 January 1856. Engraving on wood

were presumably chosen by Fawkes. According to the handwritten list made by a member of the Fawkes family, they were 'all drawings of 1822'.[116] In the same year Turner made a small and very beautiful literary illustration, the oil painting for Shakespeare's *Twelfth Night* called 'What You Will!', RA 1822 (B&J 229). Turner also made for Fawkes a frontispiece referring to Byron, Scott and Moore (no.38). This shows a monument with the poets' signatures inscribed on it. On top of this are placed an Irish harp for Moore, and hats – white with a plume for Byron and a highlander's for Scott. On the monument also lies the bugle which plays an important part in the story. Towards the monument climb the huntsman Fitz James (who is James V incognito) and his guide; his horse has died, and the stag he is in pursuit of is shown. In the background there is a view of the snow-clad Benvenue and a Loch Katrine so blue that it must allude to the blue of the eyes of the Lady of the Lake herself: Turner had made reference to this simile of Scott's in his verse letter of 1811.[117] This frontispiece is titled 'Three Poets in Three Different Kingdoms Born', referring of course to the England, Scotland and Ireland of the three poets: it was presumably Walter Fawkes's variation of the beginning of a six-line poem by Dryden entitled 'Under Mr. Milton's Portrait, before his Paradise Lost':

> Three Poets in three distant ages born,
> Greece, Italy and England did adorn.

These illustrations do not seem to have been part of an album with texts in it, such as the albums of cut-up texts and prints for Fawkes's *Chronology* for which Turner made frontispieces (recently rediscovered), but were described as being 'in cases', like Fawkes's set of Turner's 'Sketches on the Rhine'.

Walter Fawkes's interests were literary, as well as political, historical, antiquarian and sporting. This set of illustrations doubtless reflects a literary atmosphere at Farnley of quotation and, most likely, of reading aloud. The image for Byron's *Giaour* (as with certain of the later Byron vignettes) is political in that it refers to the degradation of Greece under the tyranny of the Turks: to illustrate the line "Tis Greece, but living Greece no more', Turner has shown in the foreground a female figure, symbolic of Greece, chained and ogled by a barbarous Turk (W 1055; Vouros-Eutaxias Museum, Athens). The four Scott illustrations picture Norham

fig.14 J.M.W. Turner, 'Melrose Abbey' (w 1056), illustration to Scott's 'Lay of the Last Minstrel', 1822. Watercolour. *Private Collection*

fig.15 J.C. Allen after J.M.W. Turner, title-vignette to *Views in Sussex*, 1819. Engraving on copper (R 128)

Castle (w 1052), a moonlit Melrose (fig.14) with light flooding from the moon which is perched above the mullions and tracery of the great Abbey window with a mysterious solitary figure standing below, the 'hazel shade' of Glen Artney for *The Lady of the Lake* (w 1054) and a 'dismal grove of sable yew' for *Rokeby* (w 1053). The epigraphs are actually written in Turner's hand in the foregrounds, in the Melrose design on fallen masonry, and the 'Rokeby' on a pair of rocks.[118]

For Fawkes Turner had earlier, in 1815, made fantastically detailed trompe-l'oeil frontispieces for the 'Fairfaxiana' album at Farnley, with a device of an opening cabinet door made of card, and with minute writing, surely done under a magnifying glass, on historical documents (see under w 582). Technically these are too large to be called vignettes, but they too lack borders or edges. Ruskin thought that these title-pages were 'in the highest class of Turner's drawings'.[119] They are interesting to the student of the vignettes in that they use configurations of objects such as scrolls, headgear and many items of arms. This semi-heraldic device appears on two early vignettes, the better of which is the title-page vignette engraved by J.C. Allen for his *Views in Sussex* of 1819, with a crown, a crossbow, chainmail, and an arrow piercing Harold's helmet (fig.15).[120] Turner returned to this technique when he again indicated the Battle of Hastings with a group of objects for the foreground of Campbell's 'Camp Hill' (no.46) eighteen years later, but with hardly such a spirited conception or execution. In one of the two vignettes to Scot's *Provincial Antiquities* Turner uses a similar configuration of objects in his foreground, heraldically arranged: for Volume I he shows the Scots regalia, discovered some years before by Scott in a locked trunk in a locked chamber at Edinburgh Castle (w 1058). Turner locates these in the foreground of his depiction of the procession of King George IV with the regalia to Edinburgh Castle. The title-vignette to Volume II (no.39) has an emblem of the clasped hands of the two nationalities, as represented by King George and Sir Walter Scott. Here Turner makes a visual poem about a united kingdom by scene, emblems and heraldry: he shows the King's yacht, the *Royal George*, met by the Scottish barges – one of which carried Scott – and poses the English Garter against the Scottish Order of the Thistle on the sleeves of the clasping hands. In the sky there is a star and the personal emblem of the King, a white horse; it is a bold conception superimposed on the view of the sea and the castellated capital seen from Leith Harbour.

Turner's first published vignette was W.B. Cooke's engraving in Volume I of *Picturesque Views of the Southern Coast of England* (1814–16), 'Martello Towers at Bexhill', (R 103) adapted from No.34 of the *Liber Studiorum*. As a composition this is little more than a reworking on copper of the mezzotint, with the substitution of a brilliant white cloud for the swirling movements in the sky of the original plate. Ian Warrell and Joyce Townsend have suggested that as this was the only vignette among Turner's illustrations for this series, it was originally intended for a title-page.[121] A vignette of a Farnley scene, an illustration for Whitaker's *Loidis and Elmete* of 'The Flower Garden Porch at Farnley Removed from New Hall. A.D. 1814', etched on a copper-plate, was published in 1816 (R 84). Rawlinson thought that the engraving might be the work of a member of the Fawkes family. The vignette is interesting in that it is composed with what is already a recognisable form of Turner's: there is a lateral thrust in *repoussoir* of the dark boughs at the right against the more pliant trees on the left.

The most important vignette of the Farnley era is the frontispiece to the *Catalogue of Mr. Fawkes's Gallery*, 1820, according to Rawlinson etched by F.C. Lewis (fig.16). The marvellously coloured watercolour for this design is at Farnley. This shows a classical tablet with an acanthus base, inscribed with the names of the artists in Fawkes's exhibition, headed by 'Turner, R.A., P.P.'. On the plinth rests a palette marked 'watercolours'; below the plinth is a pool or stream of clear water, the mutable element itself and the vehicle of watercolour, stained here with reflections and thus

fig.16 F.C. Lewis after J.M.W. Turner, front cover to *Catalogue of Mr. Fawkes's Gallery*, 1819–20. Etching

signifying both water and colour. Turner suggests here an almost competitive dialogue between Nature and Art; he does this by visual punning: the lily-pads are palette-shaped; the bullrush is to be seen as Nature's pencil (the common word for brush in the nineteenth century) standing up like the brushes in the palette.

11 Rogers, Byron and the Annuals

Rogers's *Italy,* 1830

The details of the publication of Rogers's *Italy,* and of Turner's commission for half the illustrations for it, are well known; they are best and most interestingly described by Cecilia Powell.[1] These are the most famous of all Turner's vignettes, and were enormously successful, both in spreading his fame and in commercial terms. Frederick Goodall wrote that there was scarcely an educated household in England that did not possess a copy.[2] By 1832, 68,000 copies had been sold. There were five reprints of this edition between 1831 and 1859. At the same time there were other editions of the poem without Turner's illustrations. It is true that the illustrations are more interesting than the text: the *Athenaeum* greeted Rogers's new edition with: 'It may be a little ungrateful to Rogers, but we cannot attend to him now … It is impossible to do anything but turn from picture to picture, from jewel to jewel'.[3] Writers on Turner have, however, tended to dispraise Rogers's poem and to play down the success that it enjoyed on its own. The editions of the poem without Turner's illustrations, both before and after this famous volume, sold well. There was a later duodecimo edition, for example, put out by Moxon in 1839 and printed by Whittingham. This had wood-engraved illustrations after Stothard, Edwin Landseer, Augustus Callcott, Charles Eastlake and Thomas Uwins. At first sight, Turner might seem to have made designs for *Italy* (with the obvious exception of the vignettes of Hannibal and of Napoleon on the Alps) that are contemporary topographical 'landscape illustrations'; they recall the most brilliant of his designs for Hakewill's *Picturesque Tour of Italy* of 1818–20. In no sense are they direct illustrations of Rogers's text, which is a series of personal reminiscences, a versifying of the author's Italian journal, interspersed with affecting stories and meditations on time, history and travel, some of them in prose. This is not to say that Turner was not engaged with Rogers's

fig.17 William Finden after Sir Thomas Lawrence, 'Samuel Rogers', 1834. Engraving on steel

text; indeed the poem was in his mind in 1844 when he gave an epigraph from it to his oil painting 'The Approach to Venice', RA 1844 (B&J 412).

The facility of Rogers's verse has often been remarked. Byron unkindly says in *Don Juan* that the hinges of the doors in the harem were 'smooth as Rogers' rhymes';[4] some of the poetry that Turner is illustrating in the two Rogers volumes is indeed bland and overworked; this is doubtless partly because of his notorious slowness in composition. His *Columbus* took him fourteen years to complete. However, there are some vatic lines and sustained passages in *Italy.* When Wordsworth writes to thank Rogers for the poem his praise sounds faint: there are, he says, as well as some mannerisms of syntax and rhythm that he identifies, 'many bright and striking passages'.[5]

Cecilia Powell has noted that Rogers shows less interest in landscape and nature than in people, and that Turner's vignettes make up this deficiency. Turner's own copy of the edition of *Italy* published by Murray in 1824 (private collection) has asterisks by twenty-six lines as possible illustrations (some of them, as they mark notes to the passages, repetitive). These may be the result of discussion with Rogers. All of these refer to places, and not incidents. Turner eventually designed only four of the marked scenes; two of them were carried out by Samuel Prout. Anecdotal and historical illustrations for the book were designed by Thomas Stothard, 'in that chaste and graceful style which he had brought to such perfection'.[6] Stothard was a friend of Rogers, who had a large collection of his drawings and some oils. The overtly 'human interest' of the poem, focusing on character and incident, is rendered by Stothard in the scenes of the Alpine hunter Jorasse and his Madelaine, or the lady Cristine, who was unjustly walled up alive. In these and in the historical illustrations, such as the jousting in the Piazza San Marco, so finely engraved by Goodall, or the 'Brides of Venice' – an annual ceremony celebrating the twelve brides abducted by paynims and rescued – the emphasis is on the figures, and they show Stothard's elegance and grace; he thought figure drawing the most important part of an artist's training. He was well known by this time for his work in book illustration that had begun in the 1780s, and in particular for his renderings of dramatic scenes from literature; Rogers's *Italy* and *Poems* were his last important commissions.

Only Turner's vignette of 'Banditti' (App.B, no.20) comes near to being an illustration of Rogers's narrative, but the figures are not as menacing as they should be, and the point of the vignette seems more the creation of the sense of space and steepness in the road, mountain and torrent. The figure at the bottom left in the second of the two St Bernard vignettes is actually by Stothard (App.B, no.5), and the dog that was drawn by Landseer in the margin of the same vignette was preferred to Turner's own when the image was engraved – the latter to Ruskin's disgust, since he liked Turner's original couchant dog better.[7]

Turner's vignettes do not fit well with Stothard's; they are obviously much more original and inspired. Adele Holcomb has deplored Rogers's influence on Turner's art in this series of vignettes,[8] but it was actually a fertile conjunction. Turner reworked material

from the sketchbooks of his own tours in Italy, his 'Terra Pictura' as he called it in a letter of 1819. There are certainly reminiscences of Claude, Richard Wilson and J.R. Cozens, and by no means is the stimulus of Rogers's text and his supervision negative. Ruskin thought that the commission was an important stage in Turner's education and development, and that the marriage of the two minds was most productive, in bringing him into contact with modern writers and away from the classic writers who had been his main influence until his middle age:

> But his work under Mr. Rogers brought him into closer relation with modern thought; and now for some seven or eight years he works chiefly under the influence of Scott and Byron, this phase of his mind being typically represented by the 'Childe Harold'. The vignettes to Rogers' *Italy* were simply his own reminiscences of the Alps and the Campagna, rapidly and concisely given in right sympathy with the meditative poem they illustrate. They are entirely exquisite; poetical in the highest and purest sense; exemplary and delightful beyond all praise.[9]

There are references to Rogers's text in Turner's images which obviously involve the reader in the pleasure of recognition. These range from the simple – we identify the boat and its passengers in the first vignette, 'Lake of Geneva' (App.B, no.1), as being the peasants of the poem who take produce to market by 'passage boat'; the tower in 'Amalfi' is the day-mark described by Rogers (App.B, no.23) – to the complex, such as the moonlit shadows of the cypresses that Rogers imagines as the setting at 'Galileo's Villa' for the astronomer's observations with the optic tube (App.B, no.13). By the nature of his commission, or by inclination, Turner is not so much interested in Rogers's dramas of love and death themselves, but he has a way of taking Rogers's ideas and giving subtle references, in the selection of imagery or by clues in the staffage of the foregrounds, that he is also giving his own poetic meditation on the Italian journey. Some allusions become emblematical, such as those relating to death: two corpses are carried. One is the victim of avalanche carried on a stretcher towards the almost submerged 'Death House' (App.B, no.5);[10] as described by Rogers, at the monastery of Great St Bernard corpses were simply laid out in the cold atmosphere and not interred. The other corpse, in

'The Forum' (App.B, no.16), is carried in a coffin by monks . Even the innocent-looking 'Martigny' (App.B, no.8), with its clearly marked hotel name, La Cygne, as well as illustrating the location in Rogers's story probably recalls the death in a deluge of the landlord who was so popular with British visitors, as recorded in *Jennings' Landscape Annual* for 1830; this was Turner's inn, Ruskin tells us, on his way to Lucerne.[11] The vignette of 'The Forum' is a reworking by Turner of details from his oil painting of the same title (RA 1826; B&J 233), but he substitutes a funeral for the festival procession.[12] Rogers makes no reference at all to a funeral in his description of the Forum, but the title of his next section is indeed 'A Funeral'. The monks in the foreground of 'Florence' have an hour-glass (indistinct in the engraving, but clear in the watercolour) as well as an open book (App.B, no.12). Funereal cypress trees are a repeated motif, as if in a kind of defunctive music. The five campaniles shown in separate vignettes (though obviously one could hardly draw an Italian city without them) indicate the passing of time, the tolling for the dead and the pealing for the married. One of Rogers's themes is the enduring presence of the past in the present which the combination of knowledge and imagination makes possible; it is not only from the poem 'The Pleasures of Memory' that he earns his sobriquet 'The Bard of Memory'. Thus, one of his most successful passages in *Italy* is his imaginary peopling of the streets of Pompeii, the 'City of the Dead'. This is, after all, one principal function of literature and art. He addresses his poem to 'those who have learnt to live in Past Times as well as Present'. Into all this Turner enters most significantly with his eye and imagination: the ruined castles and towers are the ruins of time. Italy is not just the haunt of beauty, such as the gardens of the moonlit papal Villa Madama designed by Raphael (no.4), but the country of the days that are no more – the note to Rogers's text indicates that the Villa Madama is also a ruin, which is not clear from Turner's image.

Turner's second study of a moonlit villa, 'A Villa. Moonlight (A Villa on the Night of a Festa di Ballo)' (no.9) shows a scene on the sea near Genoa, illustrating these lines from Rogers:

'Twas where o'er the sea,
For we were now within a cable's length,
Delicious gardens hung; green galleries,
And marble terraces in many a flight,
And fairy-arches flung from cliff to cliff,
Wildering, enchanting; and, above them all,
A Palace, such as somewhere in the East,
In Zenastan or Araby the blest,
Among its golden groves, and fruits of gold,
And fountains scattering rainbows in the sky,
Rose, when ALADDIN rubbed the wondrous lamp;
Such, if not fairer; and when we shot by,
A scene of revelry, in long array
As with the radiance of a setting sun,
The windows blazing.[13]

One would like to be able to show that Turner had also read Shelley's 'Adonais', but the meditations on past grandeur and the rise and fall of civilisations stimulated by Rome in famous passages by Gibbon, Byron and Rogers were a commonplace of the period. The constant reminders of Roman decline and fall – the toppled columns and entablatures, the broken aqueduct and ruined tomb among the desolation in the 'Campagna of Rome' (no.5) – allude not only to the origins of our architecture but to the origins of our civilisation itself. One will never know whether it was Turner or Rogers who selected the two words 'ROMA' and 'VESTA' to be introduced into two vignettes in an architectural cartouche (App.B, nos.16, 18); Rogers's biographer Clayden says 'Everything was done under Rogers's own constant direction and supervision. He chose the subjects, suggested the character of the pictures, superintended their execution, and made the illustrations as much his own as the letter-press they adorned'.[14] Rogers told Ruskin, 'I found [Turner] … ready to accept any hint or suggestion I might have to give him'.[15] In 'The Forum', where 'Roma' is inscribed by Turner, his image seems to assert the foundations of commerce, government and religion; in 'Tivoli' where 'Vesta' is inscribed (doing some violence to the composition) Turner, or Rogers, refers surely to the 'sacred fire' of the City – of Rome, and hence of the civilisation of Western imperial capitals in general – that must not be allowed to go out. Waterfall and temple in this vignette again suggest emblematical meanings. The dramatic representations of Hannibal and Napoleon on the Alps allude to the threat against the *Pax Romana* (App.B, nos.9, 6). The latter shows the stone engraved with 'Marengo', as in the picture by J.L. David which was Turner's source and which he had seen in the artist's studio in Paris in 1802. This was the victory that decided Napoleon's second Italian campaign; it was after Marengo that Pitt said 'Fold up that map', meaning that Napoleon was now the ruler of continental Europe.[16] William Tell's Chapel stands presumably for republican freedom from tyranny (App.B, no.2). The presence of Roman buildings still in use, such as Julius Caesar's bridge in 'St Maurice' (App.B, no.3) and the Roman gate of Augustus at 'Aosta' (App.B, no.7; the name itself a contraction of Augusta) parallels the rhythms of death and renewals, of time past, present and future in Rogers's text. The verso of the title-page of *Italy* carries Flaxman's design of a Roman mother holding a baby:[17] this is the purest symbol of the renewal of civilisation, or that rebirth brought about by looking at landscape, through foreign travel, through historical awareness or through the act of reading itself.

Certainly Turner's illustrations for Rogers seem to be conceived as an artistic unity, in a sequence and without reference to the other illustrations by other hands in the book. This is particularly clear when the series is compared with the separated and less original Byron vignettes, many of which were indeed reworkings of the foreign views of other artists. The Rogers series begins on the brimming waters of Lac Leman; the terraced villa in 'Lake of Como' in the distance on the left-hand shore is the same villa (App.B, no.10) – one can pick out the trees in their pots – from which we take our leave of Italy in 'Lake of Como. 11' (App.B, no.25), indicating how the focus has changed from across a body of water to the foreground and land. These two images of Como are a separation of combined elements in one of Turner's plates for Hakewill's *Picturesque Tour of Italy*, the 'Isola Bella' of 1818 (R 160), involving a transposition of Lake Como for Lake Maggiore. The foreground of formal Italian garden stonework, the balustrades and potted trees, looking towards the lake, forms the 'Farewell' (as the vignette is traditionally called), while the distant view in the Hakewill image of the opening in the mountains at the head of the lake with the ranges of hills to either side and the two villas symmetrically arranged on the shores, now forms the composition of the distance in

'Lake of Como' with its lake-side buildings on the opposite shores. Ruskin was told by Rogers that the 'Farewell' was executed at Petworth where both he and Turner were staying, between breakfast and lunch.[18]

Turner's most interesting emblematical vignette in the *Italy* is perhaps that of the Greek temple at Paestum, engraved by John Pye (App.B, no.22). Turner had sketched the three temples on his 1819 tour, and an early study of the three, which was prepared for Rogers, has survived (no.6). The published vignette was a fairly complex image of Time's ruins, stimulated by Rogers's lines:

> But what are These still standing in the midst?
> The Earth has rock'd beneath; the Thunder-stone
> Passed thro' and thro', and left its traces there;
> Yet still they stand as by some Unknown Charter!
> Oh, they are Nature's own! and, as allied
> To the vast Mountains and the eternal Sea,
> They want no written history; theirs a voice
> For ever speaking to the heart of Man![19]

Rogers's description of his sojourn at Paestum is one of summer skies and of air sweet with violets, but Turner works up the lines just quoted with storm cloud and lightning. Between the watercolour design and the engraving Turner strengthened the lightning in two bold and parallel lines. Rawlinson says that the skies, lacking in most of the coloured designs for the Rogers's vignettes, were added by the engravers, but I do not believe it. Turner made separate designs for skies in the vignettes, and at least one, for 'The Nile' in *The Epicurean* (TB CCLXXX 82) has survived. Turner creates in the 'Paestum' a powerful emblem of the work of man defying the elements through the centuries: Art, in the lines quoted from Rogers, becomes 'as Nature' in the course of time; Rogers says in his note that the temples are two to three thousand years old. Ruskin interpreted Turner's cloud and lightning as signifying 'the power of God ... in scorn of the departed earth-shaker', Zeus; as pagan civilisation punished by the anger of the Old Testament skies.[20] Turner's fondness for this conjunction of pagan buildings and lightning can be seen again in the 'Temple of Poseidon at Sunium (Cape Colonna)' of *c.*1834 (W 497; repr. in col., D. Brown, *Turner and Byron*, 1992, no.28); sometimes the image is accompanied by dead or threatened human beings or by corpses and skeletons of horses, buffalo or sheep. These are figured in a sequence of apocalyptic designs which begin with 'The Fifth Plague of Egypt', RA 1800 (B&J 13; Indianapolis Museum of Art) and its version in the *Liber Studiorum,* and include 'Stone Henge' in the *Picturesque Views in England and Wales* (Wallis's engraving is dated 1829, the same year as Pye's engraving of Paestum). They come to a climax with 'The Field of Waterloo' engraved for Scott's *Life of Napoleon* (R 539). Rogers's lines about Paestum most likely stimulated Turner's mezzotint engraving of 'Paestum' (R 799), from his own hand and possibly on a steel plate in the series called the 'Little Liber', dated by Rawlinson as *c.*1826, just at the time when Turner would be beginning the Rogers project.[21] The mezzotint repeats the motifs of the temples with lightning and an animal skeleton.

The formal qualities of the vignettes for Rogers's *Italy* are less interesting than the later developments. They could be said to be for the most part square images with rounded corners. The shape seems to have become more rounded at the stage of engraving; for example, in 'Martigny' (App.B, no.8) two figures of men pushing the carriage at the bottom left in the watercolour are gone in the engraving, presumably to improve the shape; in 'Banditti' (App.B, no.20) three of them were trimmed off, again at the bottom left.

Rogers's *Poems,* 1834

Although Turner's illustrations to Rogers's *Poems* were published four years later than the *Italy,* and were chronologically the fourth in the series of vignette illustrations by Turner to be published after the *Italy,* they are best considered together. They resemble the earlier series rather than the later ones in that they are still (under Rogers's supervision, no doubt) a touch antiquarian in design, and the thirty-three watercolour designs are highly finished. Together the illustrations for these two volumes were in Ruskin's view 'the loveliest engravings ever produced by the pure line'.[22] Goodall's son thought his father's engravings for 'The Pleasures of Memory' in this book the very best of his father's work.[23] Macaulay wrote to Rogers saying, 'Italy is nothing to the new volume. Everybody says the

same. I am charged with several copies for ladies in India.'[24] The *Athenaeum* saluted this book as a 'volume which, for true elegance and pictorial fancy, is unequalled, in an age remarkable for its love of splendid books'.[25] The volume was also several years in production, and Turner is thought to have been at work on the designs even before the publication of *Italy.* Obviously the sources for the two volumes are different: in place of the echoes of Hakewill's *Italy,* the range of Rogers's writings in his *Poems* gives Turner the opportunity to make use of his English and Scottish sketchbooks from his many tours, and the images recall *The Rivers of England* and the *Picturesque Views in England and Wales.* Rogers's poem 'The Pleasures of Memory' in this volume explores 'the love of our country';[26] we are given images of Turner's beloved river Wharfe with the ash trees at Bolton Abbey and the Strid with the tragic Boy of Egremond, of Petworth, of the church at Grantham, and of booths on the village green; there is May Day dancing, and an old oak is transformed to a ship of the line. There seems a particular emphasis on English waters. Although for a second time Stothard was brought in for certain drawings, Turner seems more confident with his figures, showing Jacqueline and her wild deer (a motif carried over from 'Valombrè') at the cottage door in the Piedmontese Alps (no.18), and there are more vignettes that are full illustrations than landscapes.

Ruskin thought that Turner's illustrations to the new volume lacked (with the exception of 'A Garden' and 'Tornaro'; App.B, nos.26, 34) the sincerity and power of those in the *Italy,* where half the work had produced three times the quality.[27] Although the locus is mainly England, the Atlantic and the Alps figure: Turner's fantasy is engaged, with sublime results, in 'A Hurricane in the Desert', 'The Alps at Daybreak' and above all in the great Columbus series (App.B, nos.38, 48, 51–7). Significantly, the most antiquarian image, the finished image for 'The Pleasures of Memory' (fig.18), showing a dame school, was rejected. This was an appropriate motif, as it illustrated Rogers's own schooldays in Stoke Newington, and it was carried out in a style reminiscent of Westall and even Morland. Even here, however, Turner introduced one of his characteristic punning emblems: in apposition to the school-house there is a grindstone. The Whig sympathies of Rogers and the Holland House circle are

fig.18 J.M.W. Turner, 'Going to School', unengraved illustration for 'The Pleasures of Memory' in Rogers's *Poems*. Watercolour (TB CCLXXX 198)

reflected in the two images of Charles James Fox's house, St Anne's Hill (App.B, nos.37, 50), recalling by the books on the ground the statesman's love of reading Dryden and Shakespeare aloud in the open air. The ironically titled vignette of 'Traitor's Gate' (App.B, no.36), which shows Sir Thomas More and his headsman with an axe in the boat, alludes to the detention in the Tower of Rogers's friend Horne Tooke when he was arraigned for high treason at the time of the French Revolution, and to Rogers's own part in his trial.

Rogers's volume of *Poems* was first published in 1812, 'with vignettes innumerable' by Stothard,[28] and reissued in a duodecimo edition illustrated by the Stothard vignettes in 1827. The reissue with Turner's vignettes includes four long poems; at the beginning is set 'The Pleasures of Memory', which made Rogers's fame in 1792. By 1816 he had sold more than 21,000 copies in nineteen editions, giving him his sobriquet of 'The Bard of Memory'.[29] Byron called this with Campbell's 'Pleasures of Hope', 'the most beautiful didactic poems in our language', except for Pope's 'Essay on Man'.[30]

This is followed by 'Human Life' of 1819, which was said to be Rogers's own favourite among his poems, and which a contemporary estimate called 'warm in colour, deep in feeling, tender in conception'.[31] Then come 'Jacqueline' of 1814, which was published jointly with Byron's 'Lara', and 'The Voyage of Columbus' of 1810. There are also many shorter poems, some of which are illustrated by Turner. One poem, the 'Epistle to a Friend', praises the increased circulation of engravings in Rogers's day:

> Be mine to bless the more mechanic skill,
> That stamps, renews, and multiplies at will,
> And cheaply circulates, thro' distant climes,
> The fairest relics of the purest times.

In the *Poems* Turner develops the more imaginative elements in his designs for *Italy*, such as the 'Hannibal' and the 'Paestum' vignettes, into even bolder conceptions in both image and form, such as the vortical 'A Hurricane in the Desert' (no.17), the ecstatic 'Alps at Daybreak' (no.20) with the chamois-hunters skirting the Mer de Glace, and the sublime supernatural 'A Vision. Voyage of Columbus' (no.22). They stand halfway, as it were, between the more conventional images of *Italy* and the wild inventions of some of the Campbell series. There is certainly a tendency in this volume for Turner to take more licence in treating the text: for example, the 'Venice' (App.B, no.39) with its full moon shining through the arch at the summit of the Rialto bridge over the Grand Canal illustrates a passage describing a piazza in Venice.[32] Architecture does not in general feature so prominently as in the *Italy*, though there are a number of Gothic and Tudor structures and a fine Greenwich Hospital. Turner erects a version of Eton College Chapel on an island for St Herbert's consecrated grove (no.14), which in Rogers's note was 'a small island covered with trees among which were formerly the ruins of a religious house'.[33]

The series begins and ends with emblematical vignettes, which are to a certain extent visual poems by Turner, though they take some motifs from Rogers. 'A Garden' (no.10) and 'Datur Hora Quieti' (App.B, no.58) are both detailed emblems which create a complex of ideas in the reader's mind, in the way Rogers discusses in Part II of 'The Pleasures of Memory', which is concerned with 'every effusion of the Fancy' and the association of ideas. 'A Garden' is an amalgam of Turner's memories of formal Italian gardens such as the Villa Lante at Bagnaia and the Palazzino at Caprarola (which he had sketched in 1828–9 in the *Viterbo and Ronciglione* sketchbook, TB CCXXXVI) as well as the Boboli Gardens and the Villa d'Este. The Villa Lante most likely supplied the detail of the stone horse in the basin with the *jet d'eau*, set in a lap of the hills. Turner instructed Miller on the touched proof to create a mass of light and brightness to the fountain (no.11). Balustrades and arcades, statuary, potted trees on steps and cypress trees form a link with the 'Farewell' vignette of *Italy*, as it is known, the 'Lake of Como. 11' (App.B, no.25). Although 'A Garden' stands as if it was to be a frontispiece to 'The Pleasures of Memory', at the very beginning of the volume, it illustrates two passages in 'Human Life'. Rogers gives the images of groves and fountain, and the contrast between the boy and an 'aged pilgrim' who bends on his staff; the shadow cast by the figures in Turner's image, when read in conjunction with Rogers's text, symbolises our transitory state: we are 'born in a trance'. The boy's careering pursuit of the butterfly is symbolic of man's chase of the 'glorious vision' and 'vain pageant'.[34] Turner adds the rows of potted plants, but the butterfly-net comes from Rogers's description of the child by a fountain-side in his 'May of Life' two pages later. 'Datur Hora Quieti', though loosely echoing the very opening lines of the volume at the start of 'The Pleasures of Memory', forms a symbolic recapitulation at the end of the volume. The abandoned plough is a fit emblem for the poet, and perhaps even for the engraver and the book-binder. There is peace after work, calm after movement, coolth after warmth.[35] The vignette also repeats motifs – glebe, windmill, steeple, river, bridge, ship-masts, a ruined castle on a hill and ash trees – that appeared in the earlier vignettes.[36] The source of life figured in the abounding, glittering jet of 'A Garden' here winds calmly as a river towards the ocean; the sunrises in the earlier vignettes, such as 'Tornaro' (App.B, no.34), are complemented by sunset; the youths are replaced by their elders.

Stothard added to Turner's images for this volume several figures for the Columbus series and the boat and figures for 'Traitor's Gate' (App.B, no.36). Goodall's son also says that the pensioner with his telescope at Greenwich Hospital was a joint creation of his father

and Turner.[37] This practice was less surprising to Turner's contemporaries than to us. The Dutch landscape painters commonly had their figures painted by others, and among engravers it was also acceptable: the engraving of 'Pope's Villa' (R 76) by Pye had the figures put in by Charles Heath.

Byron in his journal for 1813 drew 'a triangular Gradus ad Parnassum' of poets in their hierarchy,[38] which shows how much posterity has stood his judgment on end:

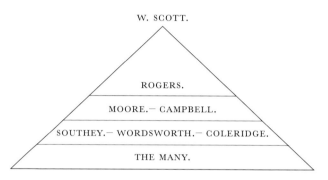

Though artificial, Rogers's 'Voyage of Columbus' seems a work of a higher order than his other poems; Rogers aimed to put into it the 'warmth of colour and wildness of imagery which the old writers employed'. Scott wrote to him of 'your little jewel, the Columbiad'.[39] It is this *epyllion* (or miniature epic poem) which drew from Turner the best work of the volume. The *Athenaeum* reviewer isolated the seven illustrations made by Turner for the 'Voyage of Columbus' as being 'the most truly original' in the whole volume for their 'sublime and awful qualities'.[40]

Rogers's Columbus is the noble epic hero, of extraordinary virtue, piety, courage and 'high thought', the man

> Who the great secret of the Deep possessed,
> And issuing through the portals of the West,
> Fearless, resolved, with every sail unfurled,
> Planted his standard on the Unknown World.[41]

This set of vignettes is narrative and dramatic, and Turner's illustrations point towards those he made for the Milton, Campbell and Moore volumes. Sublimity and awe are created by theme and setting: the sea and sky to which the hero and his ships are exposed are charged with drama and emotion, and Turner rises to

Rogers's theme of Columbus as crucifer, carrying the light of revelation to a New World dominated by primitive malignant spirits. Turner creates a dialogue of symbolic light and dark which is made even more telling by the contrasting black and white of Goodall's engravings. Rogers presents Columbus as a Christian hero, one

> By Heaven designed
> To lift the veil that covered half mankind.

In a new note to this second edition of 'The Voyage of Columbus' Rogers refers approvingly to Washington Irving's famous *History of the Life and Voyages of Christopher Columbus*, published by Murray in 1828. Columbus was becoming a fashionable subject: David Wilkie exhibited 'Columbus at the Convent of La Ràbida' at the Royal Academy in 1835, of which a mezzotint was later published by Moon.[42] By comparison with the plain narrative in Irving's first volume, Rogers's account is fantastic, even bizarre: he adds a supernatural 'machinery' in the mode of Tasso's *Jerusalem Delivered* by inventing an opposition to Columbus from evil spirits, called the Zemi. In a passage which consciously echoes Milton's Pandemonium, Rogers describes the conclave of the Zemi under their leader Merion in a basalt cave in the Andes. These spirits are said to have prevented previous landfalls in the New World, but they now realise Columbus's spiritual superiority. By this *réchauffement* of Tasso and Milton, Rogers all unconsciously follows precisely the directions in Jonathan Swift's mocking 'Recipe' for writing a bad epic poem. However, as Rogers's nephew, Samuel Sharp, wrote in his Memoir, 'The Voyage of Columbus' was written with 'greater boldness' and 'loftier thoughts of creative fancy': 'it aimed at a style very different from his earlier works, which with correctness and delicacy of expression, were marked with accuracy almost minute, and with most careful versification'.[43]

Rogers's abbreviated epic purports to be a translation of a poem written in the Castilian language by a member of the expedition not long after Columbus's death. By his fiction that there was an original Castilian manuscript of his poem decorated with gold leaf and 'gothic portraiture', Rogers seems to draw attention to the derivation from medieval illuminated manuscripts of the mode of illustration by Turner's vignettes in the *Poems*. Perhaps this is an aspect of what

Ruskin had in mind when saying that this series of Turner's had the advantage of being produced 'under the direction of a gentleman and a scholar'.[44]

Turner's first illustration, 'Columbus and his Son' (App.B, no.51), shows the porter at the gateway of the convent of La Ràbida in Spain giving bread and water to Columbus's son Diego at his father's request. They are observed by the Prior, Juan Perez, who, 'struck with the look and manner of the stranger', enters into conversation with the 'desolate and tempest-worn' sea-farer; his zeal subsequently inspired the voyage of discovery. Above the statue of the Madonna and between the towers of the great looming convent church there are crosses, introducing the motif that unifies the series and is to be discovered (in various forms) in all but one of the vignettes. By comparison with Turner's watercolour the engraved figures have lost their cowls and a hat and gained a tender warmth; the wooden postures and spacing of the characters in the watercolour have been much improved in the engraving by the porter's gesture in giving bread and water to Columbus's son, which now suggests a priest administering the sacrament of communion. Stothard's figures are certainly a marked improvement on Turner's own. It is at this convent that the series begins and ends, for Cortes and Pizarro in the final vignette are inside the great church here, standing below Columbus's standard marked with his 'C' and an emblem of his flagship, the *Santa Maria* (App.B, no.57).

'Columbus Setting Sail' (no.21) – not from Genoa, as Rawlinson says, but from Palos in the Gulf of Cadiz – continues the cruciform theme with crosses made by the masts and spars and by the prominent emblematical anchor (a traditional symbol of 'Spes Fidei'); the latter is considerably enlarged in the engraving from the watercolour. The departure from Palos is not described in the poem, but it is likely that Turner is working from Irving. An interesting example of Turner's fanciful elaboration is shown by a comparison of his image in this vignette with the plain church and impoverished main street at Palos in Irving's plate which is his source. Irving tells us that 'a deep gloom was spread over the whole community of Palos at their departure, for almost everyone had some relative or friend on board the squadron'.[45] This is underlined by the mother and son set prominently apart in front of the quayside figures, which in this case are all Turner's own. Columbus's ship is the *Santa Maria* of one hundred tons, and he is accompanied by the two caravels of fifty tons, the *Pinta* and the *Niña*. Turner had probably seen a reproduction of the famous Florentine woodcut of 1493 that showed Columbus's three ships, as his ships and sails are very similar. The blustery day, even more conspicuous in the watercolour, gives an impression of excited impetus and perhaps even the wind of the Holy Ghost.

The awesome 'A Vision. Voyage of Columbus' (no.22), admired by Rawlinson as 'one of the finest imaginative creations of Turner or any other painter',[46] shows Columbus himself cruciform with his extended arms on the high poop witnessing the vision of ghostly warriors from the drowned Atlantis:

> Shrieks, not of men, were mingling in the blast;
> And armed shapes of god-like stature passed!
> Slowly along the evening-sky they went,
> As on the edge of some vast battlement;
> Helmet and shield, and spear and gonfalon
> Streaming a baleful light that was not of the sun.[47]

This vision comes after a night of portents (waterspouts and 'harpy wings') in which the preternatural atmosphere, 'where things familiar cease and strange begin', is finally stilled by Columbus's prayers. Goodall has admirably exaggerated the contrast in engraving from the watercolour, making the weird light show bright from behind the men-at-arms' legs and making the *Santa Maria*, riddled with lights, into a phantasmagoric ship, as if recalling 'The Ancient Mariner'. Ruskin in *Modern Painters* gives this vignette – along with Turner's paintings of the Garden of the Hesperides and of Jason (B&J 57, 19), with their dragons – a profound significance in the history of nineteenth-century art, leading to Watts and Rossetti: he finds here 'the dawn of a new era of art, a true unison of the grotesque with the realistic power'. Ruskin also noted that the 'level flake of evening cloud' in this vignette is 'admirably true to the natural form, and yet how suggestive of a battlement'.[48]

In 'Land Discovered by Columbus' (no.23) both the cross formed by the furled sails of the accompanying caravel and the cross on the flag above Columbus's head oppose a dark cloud, helping to assert Columbus as Deliverer against the as yet unregenerate New World. On the horizon to the right there is the glim-

mering supernatural light, described by Rogers, that was seen at midnight. Rogers's note to this passage helps to explain Turner's symbolism, adducing contemporary accounts to show that it was interpreted in Columbus's day as 'a light in the midst of darkness, signifying the spiritual light that he came to spread there'.[49] That Turner is capable of working in such an emblematical mode can be supported by referring to the predominantly tenebrous vignette he made for the frontispiece to Fisher's edition of the *Pilgrim's Progress* in 1836 (no.60; see p.61 below). Turner's own figure here in the watercolour was unconvincing, in the manner of a toy theatre figure striking a melodramatic pose. However, between them Stothard and Goodall have given the figure more drama and more humility. The *Athenaeum* reviewer points to Flaxman's statue of Michelangelo as a probable source for the actual figure in the engraving.

Reversing the procession of Atlantic warriors seen in the sky prophesying war, the next vignette, 'The Landing of Columbus' (no.26) shows a procession signifying Christian peace: two tall crosses are borne through the surf to the shore of the New World where the Indians, Rogers's 'Children of the Sun', divide to make a triumphal path up a hill towards what the text describes as a royal 'couch of state'. The focus on the Cross, shown at the exact moment of arrival on terra firma, is even sharper in Turner's watercolour. Rawlinson is wrong in noting the sun as setting, since the scene in the poem is specifically matutinal:

> Long on the deep the mists of morning lay,
> Then rose, revealing as they rolled away,
> Half-circling hills, whose everlasting woods
> Sweep with their sable skirts the shadowy floods.[50]

In Turner's image the sun of faith symbolically rises on the New World.[51]

The lower part of 'A Tempest' (no.27) shows Columbus's ships on their return journey in a storm, while in the sky a marvellously figured phantom is seen from the back, who is surrounded by shadowy archers carrying shields. This Angel, as the spirit is called by Rogers, prophesies both war and peace: the globe is to be racked with 'elemental wars' (hence the reappearance of warriors in the sky) but also there is the promise of 'transcendent happiness' to follow, specifically in America: 'Another Nature and a new Mankind'.

Rogers's admiration for America and his many friendships with Americans are well known. His note to this passage endorses his allusion in the following lines to Washington's farewell address to his fellow-citizens which foretold a Christian 'peace without end':

> Here, in His train, shall arts and arms attend,
> Arts to adorn, and arms but to defend.
> Assembling here, all nations shall be blest;
> The sad be comforted; the weary rest;
> Untouched shall drop the fetters from the slave
> And He shall rule the world He died to save.[52]

Turner's winged Dark Angel, who carries a torch and from whose brow there shoots a fountain of light like a firework, is markedly similar in outline and dorsal view to the spirit in the oil painting of 'Shadrach, Meshech and Abednego in the Burning Fiery Furnace', RA 1832 (B&J 346). Anne Tennant has remarked how the Columbus vignettes point towards Turner's religious pictures of the 1840s, and John Gage has illuminatingly discussed the relation of this visionary vignette to 'The Angel Standing in the Sun', RA 1846 (B&J 425), citing the lines from the speech of the Angel of Darkness in Rogers's Canto VI, which Turner used as epigraph to the vignette-shaped painting.[53] Turner gives a double epigraph to the oil painting: the Book of Revelation is quoted first with its call of the Angel to the predatory birds that await the coming carnage, and is followed by Rogers's bell-like pacifist couplet:

> The morning march that flashes to the sun,
> The feast of vultures when the day is done.[54]

Turner's final vignette, 'Cortes and Pizarro' (App.B, no.57), is set in a moonlit chapel. Here Turner rhymes the cross formed by mast and spar on the emblem of the ship, seen on Columbus's standard hanging above the shrine, with the cross formed with the hilt and handle of Pizarro's sword, the sword of the Christian conqueror. Goodall has made this sword conspicuous in outline, as if it also should register as an emblem of the good fight. The statue of the Madonna recalls by a visual pun the name of the *Santa Maria*, Columbus's flagship, represented just to the left of the standard. There was a statue of the Madonna seen to the left of the gateway of the convent in the first vignette; it is repeated here in the manner of a musical motif returning to the tonic at the close of a work. In that it appears at the left-hand bottom corner of the very first vignette of the series, it was almost the first image which had been read by us at the start of the series. In the final chord of Turner's series, so to speak, the eyes of Cortes are raised to the statue of the Virgin as well as to Columbus's standard.

Byron's *Life and Works*, January 1832 – June 1833

Turner's series of vignettes for the seventeen-volume 'pocket' or 'library' edition of Byron's *Life and Works* commissioned by John Murray, for which he contributed exactly half of the thirty-four vignettes, was very successful in terms of the numbers of volumes sold: the last volume of the first impression sold 19,000 copies, according to Murray.[55] He claimed that it was 'a success unprecedented, it is believed, in the annals of British literature, except in the instance of the Waverley novels'.[56] Yet in spite of its commercial success, the series is to a certain extent inferior, in both design and in engraving. (For further discussion, see D. Brown, *Turner and Byron*, 1992, pp.40–56).

Turner's sketchbooks provided him with eight scenes from his Rhine, Swiss and Italian tours. 'The Field of Waterloo' is a variation of his famous oil of the same title, RA 1818 (B&J 138); he designed an Athenian capriccio, 'The Gate of Theseus, Athens' (App.B, no.60), which by its symbolism is a species of *tombeau de Byron*. The remaining seven were reworkings by Turner of three Greek scenes and one of Sta Maria della Spina at Pisa, all said to be by William Page – though the latter attribution to Page on the engraving is probably a (not uncommon) mistake of the publisher, as a drawing of the scene by Turner exists.[57] William Page (1811–1885) was an American who settled in Florence and in Rome, where he was part of the expatriate artistic community recorded by Henry James in *Roderick Hudson* and in *William Wetmore Story and his Friends*; in the latter book he is mentioned by name several times. In addition, even the Venetian scene, 'The Bridge of Sighs' (App.B, no.65), is after a sketch by an architect,

Thomas Little (1802–1859), who designed the chapels at Nunhead Cemetery. The vignette of Sta Sophia at Constantinople (App.B, no.73) is after a sketch by the young Charles Barry, the architect of the Houses of Parliament, but as yet so little known as to be called 'T. Barry' by the lettering engraver. Barry, whose sketches were also reworked by Turner for Finden's *Landscape Illustrations of the Bible,* had made a grand tour to Rome and Greece: Eastlake wrote to B.R. Haydon from Rome in 1818, saying, 'I am accompanied by a young Irishman called Barry, more an amateur than an artist'.[58]

In the archive at John Murray's there is an amusing series of six letters from Barry which confirms Turner's account to the Revd William Kingsley that he had difficulties with Murray and Barry over the imaginative additions he made to Charles Barry's sketches for the *Bible Illustrations.* Turner told Kingsley, 'the publishers thought he was mad, and required him to put nothing into the drawings beyond what might actually be there'.[59] Charles Barry wrote to Murray on 28 January 1833, 'I have seen Turner's Drawings at Finden's this morning – they are certainly very beautiful as works of art but there are some anomalies about them such as the sun & moon being in the Valley together and in the southern view of Jerusalem the sun in full splendour in the north – I intend to call upon the tickleish Gentleman and see whether I can induce him to correct these and some other trifling departures from fidelity by which the character of the country suffers'.[60] Barry and the other grand-tour artists and architects seem to have been acquaintances of Murray's, and the commissioning of illustrations a fairly casual business.[61] Though Turner was capable, in working over White's sketches of India and the Bible illustrations of Barry and others, of producing some marvellous images for the engravers from the sketches of others, the Byron vignettes seem rather cold by comparison with the two literary series so closely supervised by Rogers or the series for Scott's *Poetical Works.* The latter was charged with the feelings generated by Turner's tour to the Borders and his meeting with the declining Scott. It is also possible that Murray and Wright shared Barry's pedestrian approach to the images.

Turner's vignettes for Byron are topographical, with one dramatic exception, 'The Field of Waterloo, from Hougoumont' (App.B, no.69). Although the vignettes

fig.19 J.T. Wedgwood after F. Sieurac, 'Lord Byron', 1828. Line engraving

employ some interesting filaments of meaning from the texts, they are images of the tourist rather than the illustrator. The staffage in the foreground is Turner's rather than Byron's: women launder in the Arno at Pisa and at the School of Homer in Scio; below the Castle of St Angelo there is one of Turner's guignols; in the English cemetery at the pyramid of Caius Sestius there is a burial. The vignettes do not seem Byronic in any real sense; indeed, as illustration of Byron, Murray's 1841 edition of *Childe Harold* with its fifty-nine vignettes and Boyd and Orr's edition of Byron's *Poems and Tales* of 1848, are more interesting. In both volumes the vignettes of Henry Warren, which admittedly derive some of their best motifs or effects from Turner, are particularly effective as illustrations of Byron's incidents; the volumes are also better engraved by the Findens. The engraving of Turner's Byron vignettes by Edward Finden is not as refined or strong as the Rogers or Milton series, for example. Finden was Murray's regular engraver, not one of Turner's 'school' of engravers; apart from one early engraving in an annual and the other series of Murray's, Finden's *Landscape Illustrations of the Bible*, neither of the brothers was used by Turner again.

Having said that there are few thematic connections (and, one should add, except for the 'Waterloo' no dramatic connections) with Byron's text, it should be noted that there are strong political resonances in the Greek vignettes. Turner's sympathy for Greece, now under the Mussulman suppression of political and religious freedoms, had already been expressed in the illustration for *The Giaour* made for Fawkes, ''Tis living Greece no more'. In the 'Corinth from the Acropolis' (App.B, no.64), showing a city where there had been Turkish atrocities, minarets overbear the classical temple; most significant is the image of the island of Chios, 'Scio, Fontana dé Melek Mehmet, Pasha' (App.B, no.70). The public were profoundly aware of the atrocities there in 1822, and Delacroix's oil showing the massacre had been exhibited in London in 1825. Leake commented in his *Outline of the Greek Revolution* about the islanders that 'it would be difficult to find the parallel of their sufferings anywhere but in ancient history'.[62]

A number of Turner's Byron vignettes are connected with *Childe Harold;* it is really only with this text of Byron's, especially Cantos III and IV, that Turner seems to be deeply engaged. One can imagine his sympathy with the apostrophe to 'fair Italy' in Canto IV and to the Rhine in Canto III.[63] *Childe Harold* is, after all, a traveller's poem, and Byron speaks in his Preface of the 'beauties of nature and the stimulus of travel'. As is well known, Turner used passages from these cantos as epigraphs for paintings. That he was engaged with the details of the poem can be shown from the painting on which he was working at the time of these illustrations, 'Italy – Childe Harold's Pilgrimage', RA 1832 (B&J 342) and from 'The Bright Stone of Honour and Tomb of Marceau', RA 1835 (B&J 361). *Arnold's Magazine of the Fine Arts* had called the painting of 'Italy – Childe Harold's Pilgrimage' 'more illustrative of the general beauties of Italy, and the general feelings attached to all her scenes than a hundred written descriptions'.[64]

The very full record of letters between publisher and editor, and the ledgers at John Murray's archive throw much light on this particular commission. The editor of the seventeen-volume *Life and Works* was John Wright (1770–1844), who was Murray's indexer for the *Quarterly*

and the editor of Boswell and of Pitt's correspondence; he later edited Crabbe's *Poems* for Murray, in an edition uniform with the Byron. There is some evidence that Moore, the compiler of the *Letters and Journals* in six volumes with which this edition begins, expected that he would be the editor of Murray's 'new and complete' edition, which was receiving so much publicity. Rogers had assumed that Moore was to be paid extra for the reissue of the *Letters and Journals,* and Moore wrote on 5 February 1832, that 'people fancy [me] to be the editor'. Moore appears to have been involved at the outset, and had suggested an annotated edition, similar to the great Warburton edition of Pope.[65] He also had some say in the choice of illustrations, writing a vapid suggestion to Murray on 30 September 1831: 'I cannot find anything that would at all *se prêter* to the pencil. Byron before the fountain at Bologna would be a pretty subject – but since I wrote last I see, by your list, that it is not your wish to have subjects of this nature, but rather views of places where he had been. Why not Petrarch's Tomb and Dante's at Ravenna'.[66] Murray and Wright made the final list of images to be engraved: a letter from Wright to Murray says, 'I have looked over our list of Engravings, and I do not see how we can improve it. Venice cannot, I think, be left out of the volumes of Dramas'. Wright seems aware that the series may turn out rather hackneyed in its imagery: 'It will, I think, be very difficult to select subjects which have not been touched on before; but they may be so varied as to give them an air of novelty'. He recommends Murray to get Turner to 'take a view from Harrow, for the title-page',[67] but in the event this was done by Clarkson Stanfield.

Turner's first image, for Volume VI, is of the Gothic mariners' chapel, Sta Maria della Spina, alongside the quay of the Arno at Pisa (App.B, no.59). Byron lived in the Casa Lanfranchi on the opposite bank, and from here he wrote the letters in this volume, including one about the 'winding Arno with all her buildings and bridges'. Several of these letters are about religion, including a very witty one about Catholicism.[68] Turner's most interesting design in this series, 'The Gate of Theseus', is a vignette of a different order (App.B, no.60). It stands as frontispiece to Volume VII, introducing the poems in the *Life and Works,* and is surely conceived as a monument to Byron, a triumphal arch as metaphor for the poet's works, in the Horatian convention of *exegi monumentum.* The sections of fallen fluted column and entablature and the wreath of cinerary white smoke from the nearest corner of the Acropolis fortifications suggest death and funerals. The elegiac tone is perhaps a mingled regret for the passing of Byron and of classical times: Byron in *Childe Harold* had used prostrate columns as a metaphor for the decline of Greece.[69] Both the metope sculpture of headless Lapith, or Hercules and a centaur – similar to the cast from the Acropolis frieze that Turner had in his hall at Queen Anne Street – and the carved anthemion appear again in allusion to the death of Byron in the watercolour probably made by Turner at the same time of another architectural feature with Byronic connections, the 'Temple of Poseidon at Sunium' (w 497; repr. in col., D. Brown, *Turner and Byron*, 1992, no.28). The same cart, but without the standing figure, appears in the oil of the 'Forum Romanum', RA 1826 (B&J 233); the so-called Gate of Theseus appears in the massed Piranesian anthology of architectural features in 'The Parting of Hero and Leander', RA 1837 (B&J 370). As David Brown has noted, the seated female figure may be an allusion to the Maid of Athens, who is the subject of the last poem in this volume, which ends with the first poems written by Byron abroad.[70]

The subject of this vignette is not strictly a Greek 'Gate of Theseus' but the Roman Arch of Hadrianopolis at Athens. The Greek inscription on the arch, which is shown by Turner, indeed reads: 'This is the city of Hadrian and not of Theseus'; on the other side was inscribed, 'What you see is Athens, the ancient city of Theseus'.[71] James Stuart's *Antiquities of Athens* says that this was the meeting place, 'or very near to it', of Theseus and Pirithous.[72] Perhaps this vignette and not the 'Sta Maria della Spina' should have had the attribution engraved below it as being from another sketch by W. Page. Finden's *Landscape Illustrations* (Pt. VII, no.1) has an engraving after Stanfield from a sketch by W. Page of 'The Temple of Jupiter Olympus'; at the right are Hadrian's Gate and the Acropolis in the same relation as in Turner's vignette; indeed it is a very similar view to Turner's 'Gate of Theseus'.

Byron was obsessed with the Theseum near to this Gate.[73] Shortly after his death, by 'Colonel Stanhope and others it was suggested that, as a tribute to the land [Byron] celebrated and died for, his remains should be deposited at Athens in the temple of Theseus; and the

fig.20 John Bewick, 'Tomb of Goldsmith' from Bulmer's *Poems of Goldsmith and Parnell*, 1795. Engraving on wood

Chief Odysseus despatched an express to Missolonghi to confirm this wish'.[74] The depiction of a building or tomb in a vignette commemorating a poet, as in Turner's image of Scott's house in Lockhart's *Life of Scott* or the tomb of Goldsmith in Bulmer's edition of his *Poems* of 1795 (fig.20), is a convention.[75] Byron's *Works* in this edition of Murray's begin with Turner's vignette of the Gate of Theseus; the *Life* ended with William Westall's image of Hucknall Church where Byron was buried with his ancestors.

The remaining vignettes consist mostly of illustrations to *Childe Harold*. The vinous Rhine is figured with 'Bacharach' (App.B, no.62), and Rome with the 'Castle of St Angelo' (App.B, no.63); the latter is a sinister design, in keeping with the history of the fortress and prison and its associations with plague and deliverance.[76] As in the vignette of the same subject in *Italy* (App.B, no.15), Turner has enlarged Bernini's statues on the bridge, but his view is significantly more bold and exaggerated than the more conventional view in the earlier vignette. A writer in *Arnold's Magazine of the Fine Arts* found this vignette 'rather too artificial' and the projecting parapet of the castle disproportionate, but he admired the representation of the statues: *'angeli delle tenebre,* a fit threshold to the shades of Hades'.[77]

'The Bridge of Sighs' (App.B, no.65) reverses the conventional view from the Grand Canal, by looking out towards the dome of S. Giorgio Maggiore and a full moon. It illustrates Byron's description of the Carnival in 'Beppo', with a woman at a balcony, or the moonlit scene in *Marino Faliero* with the serenading gallant. The couple may alternatively represent Lorenzo and Jessica.[78] The operatic gestures given by Turner to this pair were no doubt what the reviewer in *Arnold's Magazine* had in mind when describing the 'childish eccentricity' of this vignette. Turner's humour is probably at play, suggesting the replacement of the sighs of the condemned under the tyranny of the Doges by the sighs of the amorous in the carnival city. The vignette of the 'Walls of Rome' (App.B, no.67), tenuously included as it is the named setting for a scene in 'The Deformed Transformed', shows the pyramid of Caius Cestius; it is also made by Turner a suitable figure for those eloquent meditations on the fragile world and the fall of civilisation in Canto IV of *Childe Harold,* where Byron meditated, 'a ruin among ruins'. The Walls were also the scene of Byron's rides with Hobhouse, and, appropriately for Turner's illustration, where they heard the Roman labourers sing the melancholy dirge lamenting the decline of Rome: 'Roma! Roma! Roma! Roma non é più come era prima'.[79]

The 'Parnassus and Castalian Spring' (App.B, no.68), one of the three best vignettes of this series, with the dizzying cleft of Delphi, is included in recognition of Byron's many references to the place and to Parnassus as a symbol of poetic inspiration – Byron uses both 'Parnassus' and 'Castalian' loosely for 'poetry' throughout his poetry and letters.[80] The Castalian Fount, where Turner places women with pitchers, is where the Pythoness bathed to prepare herself for prophesying. Facing this vignette is 'The Field of Waterloo, from Hougoumont' (App.B, no.69), as title-vignette to *Cain, Werner &c.* This is displaced from the volume of *Childe Harold* where Byron describes his own visit and the battle scene with the soldiers in 'one red burial blent'. There was some difficulty over the subject to illustrate this volume, as John Wright's letter of 16 November 1832 to John Murray shows: 'I hope you will abandon the notion of giving *The Ship* as one of the vignettes. Nothing can be less appropriate. Turner should be induced to do something *very striking* for the 14th. volume. This is, I assure you, of great importance.'[81] During a long meditation on St Helena and Napoleon's career in 'The Age of Bronze', Byron had called the battle 'bloody and most bootless.' Here Turner shows the flares and the still flaming Château of Hougoumont where the worst carnage was seen. The foreground has a predominance of French dead, a scattered 'eagle' and sword, and a dead horse; the dead

horse reappears in the same location in Turner's image, reduced to a skeleton, in the view of 'The Field of Waterloo' illustrating Scott's *Life of Napoleon.* The best section of this vignette is the engraving of the chiaroscuro of the blazing château.

Other vignettes in the series are connected with places in *Don Juan.* The island of Scio, or Chios, figures twice in Turner's subjects: no doubt the events of 1822 (when twenty-five thousand islanders were massacred by the Turks and forty-seven thousand sold into slavery) influenced Turner's image of the 'Fontana dé Melek Mehmet' (App.B, no.70). This drinking-fountain is in the main square of the town of Chios and thus was witness to the massacres. Byron's references to the island in the poem are slight, to Scian wine and the Scian muse (of Homer). Turner gives us here in the 'Fontana' a less melodramatic restatement of the design for Fawkes, ''Tis living Greece no more': again there are a dejected Greek lady and luxurious Turks. Eric Shanes has pointed to the emblematical detail of the yoke in the foreground.[82] Volume XV, to which this is a frontispiece, contains the famous lyric 'The Isles of Greece', which expresses the political theme of the spirit and liberty of a noble people crushed by inferior powers, a theme Turner returns to in the 'Kosciusko' for Campbell's *Poetical Works* (App.B, no.123). A passage in *Don Juan,* to which Turner would warmly respond, expresses Byron's hatred of despotism:

> And I will war, at least in words (and – should
> My chance so happen – deeds) with all who war
> With Thought; and of Thought's foes by far most rude,
> Tyrants and sycophants have been and are.
> I know not who may conquer: if I could
> Have such a prescience, it should be no bar
> To this my plain, sworn, downright detestation
> Of every despotism in every nation.[83]

'Genoa' (App.B, no.71) does not illustrate *Don Juan,* but the city from which Byron left for Missolonghi in 1823 on the *Hercules.* 'Constantinople' (App.B, no.73) commemorates Juan's visit, and is where the cupola of Sta Sophia was celebrated by Byron.[84] When Juan travels from St Petersburg to London he passes Cologne, of which Turner gives a vignette.[85] 'The School of Homer, Scio' (App.B, no.74) has no relation to *Don Juan* other than to the reference in 'The Isles of Greece' to the Scian Muse, but Byron visited there. 'The Castellated

Rhine' (App.b, no.75), which closes the series, is titled after a phrase from *Don Juan* at the end of Volume XVI.[86]

The vignettes for the Byron series are best studied either in the portfolios of proofs published by Murray, where they are not cramped by the duodecimo page, or in the large paper copies, with additions, of Finden's *Landscape Illustrations*. By the time that Turner came to embellish the volumes of Scott's *Poetical Works* he had learnt to make the images less detailed and more force-ful. Ruskin's comment that the vignettes in this series were 'like cameo-work and it takes more trouble to look at it than it is worth' is harsh, but it does point to a rel-atively uninspired vision which makes the best among them such as the 'Gate of Theseus', the 'Sta Maria della Spina' and the 'Parnassus' more striking.[87]

Landscape Illustrations to Crabbe's *Poems*, 1834

A puzzling series of three unpublished engraved vi-gnettes that show East Anglian coastal views, 'Lowestoffe', 'Harborough Sands' and 'Orford Castle' (R 305–7) together with five rectangular illustrations, 'Aldborough', 'Dunwich', 'Orfordness', 'Lowestoffe' and 'Whitby' (R 308–12), are, I believe, connected with another scheme of Murray's and the Findens, which was projected in 1834, a further series of 'Landscape Il-lustrations', this time for Crabbe's poems. The *Dictionary of National Biography* gives Edward Finden credit for publishing a book of this title, and Murray announced at the end of Volume IV of his eight-volume edition of Crabbe: 'On the 1st. of July, 1834, will be published, Price 2s.6d., Part I of FINDEN'S LAND-SCAPE ILLUSTRATIONS TO MR. MURRAY'S FIRST COMPLETE AND UNIFORM EDITION OF THE LIFE AND POETICAL WORKS OF THE REV. GEORGE CRABBE'. The edition of Crabbe was published in monthly volumes from July 1833 and was uniform with the Byron edition, being brought out in precisely the same manner, as Murray wrote to Crabbe's son in Sep-tember 1833, but in an edition of half the numbers

printed.[88] This edition had, like the Byron, a fold of two vignettes at the beginning of each volume for fron-tispiece and title, in this case all from designs by Clarkson Stanfield. The artist was paid 20 guineas for each drawing, unlike Turner who had been paid 25 guineas. Findens' proposed landscape illustrations are discussed in correspondence by Murray with the younger George Crabbe, with a list of 'Stories which appear most fit for Graphic Illustration'. However, the younger Crabbe wrote to Murray on 21 December 1835 about the slowness of the sale of the edition and added, 'I hear nothing also of the Illustrations by the Findens – it seems as if there was a stagnation of inter-est in the public, on the subject'.[89] Under 'Illustrations to Crabbe's Life and Works' Murray's ledger for 1835 records payments to William Allen and C.R. Leslie for two drawings each for scenes from the *Tales*. The ledger is balanced up with the outlay of £105 and the com-ment 'not proceeded with'. It is likely that Turner prepared this set of designs originally for this second 'Landscape Illustration' venture of the Findens, from phrases in the advertisement such as that the plates would be 'as nearly as possible on the model' of the Byron series, that 'the most eminent of our painters are engaged to furnish' the illustrations, and that the first group of subjects was to be of 'localities most interest-ingly connected with the details of Mr Crabbe's personal history'. Turner's scenes in this series convey the world of fisher-folk in Crabbe's poems; apart from Aldeburgh, Crabbe gives very few place-names in the *Works*. The activities shown in the vignettes (two of which show fisher-folk in the foreground) and in the five landscapes are just those activities celebrated by Crabbe himself: there are boats, lighthouses, wrecks, and ship-building. This is just such a background, of pier, boat and cottages, as is given by Richard Westall in an illustration to *Tales of the Hall* published by John Murray in January 1822. The sands at Harborough might well have been intended to accompany Letter IX of *The Borough*, 'Amusements', about the fate of a group of people who visit a small islet of sand off the coast.

Further support for this theory comes from the fact that in the catalogue of Munro of Novar's collection made in 1865 just after his death, the watercolour vi-gnettes of 'Orford Haven' and 'Lowestoffe Lighthouse' (W 896–7) are confidently described as 'Two Illustra-tions to Crabbe'.[90] A puzzle is that, according to

Rawlinson, this series was engraved on copper, rather than on the steel which one would expect to be used for a series of landscape illustrations of this date, 'Orford Castle' only reaching an etched state. It is difficult at times to distinguish copper from steel; the vignettes are probably steel engravings.[91]

The Rivers of France, 1833–5, and *The Keepsake,* 1836–7

Three vignettes after Turner were engraved for the title-pages of an Annual known as *Turner's Annual Tour.* The books are usually catalogued (as for the 1833 volume) under their title *Wanderings by the Loire by Leith Ritchie Esq., …with Twenty-one Engravings from Drawings by J.M.W. Turner, Esq. R.A.* However, for this volume and for the other two *Wanderings by the Seine… &c.,* of 1834 and 1835, both the engraved title-page and the lettering on the spine read *Turner's Annual Tour.* This triple publication was part of an unfinished larger European project of the engraver and publisher Charles Heath (1785–1848) which was published for him by Longman, Rees, Orme, Brown, Green and Longman. An advertisement in the *Athenaeum* in 1833 announced, 'GREAT RIVERS OF EUROPE. On June 1 will appear, elegantly bound, price One Guinea, TURNER'S ANNUAL TOUR; or, the RIVER SCENERY OF EUROPE; containing Twenty-one Plates, from Drawings by J.M.W. Turner, Esq. R.A., Engraved by the first Artists, under the superintendence of Mr. CHARLES HEATH, &c.'.[92] Readers of the magazine had already been given this information:

> The Annuals have flourished this season: they have not done much good for art, and we know that they have done very little for literature. The engravers have been crammed with subjects that must be ready to-day, to the exclusion of works of higher claims; and, we believe, they would rejoice at the reign of steel being on the brink of a revolution. Landscape Annuals are, however, yet in vogue … Mr. Watts is about to enter the field into landscape; but what surprises most is the report, that the academician Turner is expected to follow the example.

Stimulated by the success of Mr. Rogers's 'Italy', to which he made such glowing contributions, he is about to engage with Charles Heath in the production of Views on the Loire. We recollect to have heard this eminent artist anathematise the whole race of Annuals, as ruining art, and deluging the public with steel impressions.[93]

The three volumes carried text by Leith Ritchie (1800–1865), a prolific journalist, editor and author of several topographical books and novels; from 1832–45 he wrote the whole text of each of *Heath's Picturesque Annuals.* Ritchie travelled and wrote his text after Turner had submitted his drawings, and he writes with the views in mind, referring to them and identifying details in the engravings. Some of the pictures were evidently already engraved by the time he set out: when in difficulties over a passport he gave the Mayor of Tours 'a few of the beautiful engravings of this volume'.[94] In a fulsome 'Advertisement' to the *Annual* of 1834 he speaks of his pride 'in having his name connected with a work so magnificent in point of art', and he seems to be aware that he will not be able to compete for the reader's interest: we should remember, he says, that 'he did not write with the pencil of Turner'. Rawlinson is wrong in saying that Ritchie 'accompanied Turner in some cases'; a letter from Ritchie to Alaric Watts of 6 December 1852 says, 'My intercourse with Turner, I regret to say, was extremely slight … I could not think of Turner as a companion, one of the most prosaic souls in everything but his art. Heath wanted me to arrange that we should travel together; but I never mentioned the subject, nor did he'.[95] Ritchie's second and third volumes make significantly fewer and colder references to Turner, but in the first volume he seems very conscious of him, and says of the Loire at one point that the water 'was steeped in those gorgeous but delicate hues with which Turner delights to glorify his landscapes'. A rhapsody by Ritchie on the river praises the poetic vision of the artist: 'Here TURNER was in his element; he rioted in beauty and power; and if to the cold in soul and imagination his paintings may seem defective in mathematical accuracy, they will be identified at a single gaze with the original by all who can feel genius, and are capable of seeing in nature something beyond its outward and tangible forms'.[96]

The three vignettes show a stylistic development.

The 'Nantes' of 1833 (no.28) is a highly detailed vignette: it shows the quayside with the bastion and towers of the château, dominated by the square towers of the church of St Peter. The barges and other craft on the river and the figures indicate the energy and prosperity of the city, chief of its Prefecture. Commerce, architecture and the military are shown, along with the Nantaises about whom Ritchie writes with such surprise. The city was also probably given prominence because of its Protestant associations: within the château, Henri IV in 1598 promulgated the famous Edict of Nantes, which gave religious liberty to the Protestant Huguenots; the city had earlier refused to take part in the St Bartholemew's Day massacre. Ritchie's text does not mention the Republican atrocities committed in this stretch of the river at Nantes, but they are graphically described in Scott's *Life of Napoleon*; we know that Turner was making sketches to illustrate this book at the same time as recording the Loire. Jacobin atrocities were committed in the prisons of Nantes, and here victims were roped together alive and thrown into the Loire, or scuttled in ships, these being referred to as Republican Marriages or Baptisms.[97]

The vignette of the 'Light Towers of the Hève' (no.29) lit by the full moon is again elaborate and detailed, though much finer in mood; the engraving by John Cousen, one of the very best pupils from Heath's famous workshop (R 453), is, as Ruskin said, 'a marvel of delicacy'.[98] However, the 'Château Gaillard' of 1835 (no.30) seems more boldly and swiftly designed. These vignettes both give a view dominated by coteau or cliff with medieval castle or the modern light towers constructed by Louis XV. The life of the modern river is shown in the craft, both sail and steam; there are fishermen with nets, and bargees towing a cargo of wine-barrels; a gunboat guards the *embouchure* of the Seine. An unpublished and unengraved vignette (W 1006) shows the château again in the background as 'the Birthplace of Nicholo Poussin', and shows the artist sketching by the river.

When Longman republished the Annuals in 1837 as the *Rivers of France*, Ritchie's text was replaced with cursory and anonymous bilingual descriptions. A good reason would seem to be that Ritchie's description, although he had lived in Normandy, is so patently English in its supercilious eye to French manners and morals, in its descriptions of the cathedrals, for example as 'huge temples of Catholic idolatry', and in its obvious pride in the achievements of Richard Lion Heart, such as the Château Gaillard which he fortified to dominate his conquered lands.

Like *The Rivers of France*, the set of Turner's vignettes in *The Keepsake* of 1836–7 was an enterprise of Charles Heath, who was involved from 1826 to 1838 in the difficult publishing venture of Turner's *Picturesque Views in England and Wales*. The four vignettes which were published here are intensely dramatic, and were commissioned as illustrations to stories and poems, unless, as has been suggested, they were prepared as a series for another publication and made use of here instead. It is likely that the poem by the Hon. Mrs Caroline Norton, Heath's editor, was written to accompany Turner's watercolour engraved with the title 'Destruction of both Houses of Parliament by Fire, Oct. 16, 1834' (App.B, no.145). The 'pale sick moon' is mentioned, and Mrs Norton's description of the way in which the memory of the event will recur is in terms of the image given in Turner's vignette, of that time in the future when

> fancy wanders back through many a day
> And paints again each wild and meteor ray
> Which glow'd upon thy breast, illumined river,
> When the Old Building fell.[99]

Turner shared a boat with Clarkson Stanfield and some Royal Academy students on the Thames on the night of the fire, and the sketches from the occasion survive (TB CCLXXXIV); two large oils of the subject were exhibited by Turner in 1835, the same year as the watercolour was engraved (B&J 359, 364). It is not only because three of the four vignettes were engraved by the accomplished Willmore that they may be thought of as a suite: there are two crescent moons, two fires and two wrecks. In all, human beings are shown as exposed over water and threatened by fire; the final image is of men endangered by both natural and human forces, by simultaneous lightning and naval gunfire. Cumulatively they amount to a characteristic emblematic statement by Turner about man's enterprise at the mercy of lightning and wind, fire and water – a theme of a higher order for which Turner employs the vignette rather than the topographical 'landscape' form of the other illustrations in *The Keepsake*. 'A Fire at Sea' (App.B, no.146) illustrates a narrative by Captain

Frederic Chamier which explains why the escaped but drowning passengers on the rafts and in the cuddy in the engraving are mostly female and undressed, 'just fresh from their cots'. The scene depicted is the sinking of an Indiaman, the *Orontes,* carrying many young women, which caught fire en route for Madras and China, eventually exploding. A drunken brawl had broken out among the sailors, who were arguing about the charms of their mistresses, and a candle had overturned among some straw. Turner in the vignette attends closely to the Captain's narrative: the sinking and shrieking women 'threw up their hands just because they ought to have kept them under the water, if they wished to swim; and they shrieked most horribly when singing out was no use'.[100]

In 'The Wreck' (App.B, no.147), which has the marine motif, characteristic of Turner, of a broken mast to which a drowning figure clings, we can identify the figures in the waves from the poem to which it is an illustration as a mother and her first-born whom the life-boatmen are shortly to save. 'The Sea!, the Sea!' (App.B, no.148) is a homage to the British navy, whose men are seen attending to duty under fire. It appears to illustrate a paragraph in Lord Nugent's story, which is about the death of a gallant young lieutenant, and which describes imperial tall ships of war as a 'grand epitome of beauty, confidence and strength'.[101] The white puff of smoke in the vignette is transposed from the deadly incident in the narrative.

III Scott, Milton, Campbell and Moore

Scott's *Poetical Works,*
May 1833 – April 1834

Thanks to the meticulous Robert Cadell, we know more about this commission of Turner's illustrations than any other. Gerald Finley in *Landscapes of Memory* has treated the subject of Turner's illustrations for Scott in detail.[1] Full and interesting accounts exist of Turner's stay at Abbotsford and the excursions in Scott's company to sketch the Border views; Turner included figures of himself, Scott and Cadell at a picnic in 'Melrose', and in a coach in the '"Presentation" Smailholme Tower' (no.42), an unengraved vignette which he made as a gift for Scott and which Scott received at Naples shortly before his death. There is also the vignette 'Bemerside Tower', which shows the three of them walking in the grounds (no.41).

Cadell visited London, where he had many literary and publishing associates, in 1831; a 'London friend' encouraged him to approach Turner.[2] Cadell wrote to his wife on 7 June that he found the artist 'very common looking, very like some ganger' (i.e. one who goes everywhere on foot). Through Messrs Moon, Boys and Graves he was able, he told her, to secure 'all the leading engravers'.[3] Drawings and proofs passed by coach between Edinburgh and London. At one point he paid Turner's expenses for two map cases. A letter from the Quaker William Miller to Cadell ('Respected Friend') shows that (as is confirmed by the account books) while the letter-press for the edition was printed in Edinburgh, the engraved fold of frontispiece and title-vignette was printed in London: 'I hope with the great superiority of London Printing the effect of the plate will be good'.[4]

In London again Cadell recorded his visit in March 1832 to Moon and Co. He described them as 'poor pinched folk', and said that he 'must watch them, and sharply too'. He travelled in a carriage with Henry Graves to visit the engravers for them to choose their drawings: he visited Pye and Goodall on one day, Pye delegating 'Bowes Tower' to Edward Webb. Webb appears to be an otherwise unknown engraver, but Cadell speaks of him as 'a young man whom [Pye] speaks so highly of and who was bred with him'. The next day he visited Willmore, Wallis and W.J. Cooke, 'a nice good humoured fat fellow'. Cadell wrote to his wife that there was 'but one shout of admiration at Turner's drawings'. Four months later he made a round to see how his engravers were getting on and found them all at home; he was satisfied with Goodall, Willmore and Brandard, but discovered that Wallis had done nothing – rather a doubtful blade this'.[5] Cadell's many anxieties over the monthly production of the *Poetical Works* later seemed nothing to those caused by the public's indifference to the long set of *Prose Works* and the procrastinations of Lockhart in writing his biography of Scott.[6] Turner was also, of course, to design vignettes for both the *Prose Works* and the second edition of Lockhart's *Life of Scott* (1839); Cadell intended them to form a uniform edition which, when combined with his illustrated *Waverley*, was designed to stretch in its duodecimo volumes along eight feet of shelving in a gentleman's library.

Turner was an enthusiastic reader of Scott, and had presumably accepted Cadell's commission gladly, surprising the publisher that he did not charge more for his designs: twenty-four at 25 guineas each.[7] The combination of Scott and Turner produced one of the finest series of vignettes. To begin with, Scott, unlike Rogers, is a very visual poet: 'he saw everything with a painter's eye', the critic Jeffrey noticed.[8] Cadell, in flattering Scott into accepting Turner as illustrator, identified a high common factor in their imagination: 'There is about Mr Turner's pencil what there is in the pen of one other person also, that which renders familiar Scenes more startling than before'.[9] When Ruskin connected Scott and Turner as being 'the principal types and the first fruits of the age', he explained that they were both *seers* rather than thinkers.[10] Added to this affinity, Turner was already inspired by Scotland, which he had visited in 1801 and again in 1818, when he had made studies for Scott's *Provincial Antiquities,* and then again in 1822. He is known to have praised the massy rocks and fine lines of the mountains.[11] The reviewer of this series in the *Athenaeum* found them 'unequalled for beauty, and finished with more care than usually distinguishes the facile pen of the artist'.[12] The engravings are also particularly fine – Marcus Huish considered them (along with those for Rogers, the *Annual Tours* and the *England and Wales*) 'the finest memorials of English engraving'.[13] Miller's work was particularly admired, the *Athenaeum* commenting that his 'fine taste and delicacy of hand must make some of our London artists [i.e. engravers] take another look at a landscape before they lay it before the public'.[14]

In both of Cadell's series, the *Poetical* and *Prose Works* of Scott, the reader opens the book on a landscape frontispiece printed at a right angle to the text facing a vignette title-page. In the *Poetical Works* the contrast is between the modern city scenes in the frontispiece and the vignette where the focus is most often on an historical building. Thornbury noticed that Turner is 'contrasting the feudal and the past as much as possible, and as sadly as possible with the present'. In the vignettes, through the staffage of contemporary scenes and figures, such as the Carlisle coach identified by Thornbury, 'which crosses the bridge over the gorge in front of Johnnie Armstrong's Tower' (App.B, no.77), Turner indicates the enduring presence of the past.[15] Many of these selected scenes lie along the Tweed, Tees or Yarrow, and there is a high proportion of views across water; in more than half of the vignettes the eye is led to tower or castle, mostly roofless. In the illustration made for Fawkes for 'The Lay of the Last Minstrel' in 1822 (W 1052) the roofless Norham Castle dominated over the river and drinking cows; 'Newark Castle' (App.B, no.82) repeats the configuration.

Mists and smoke come from the hills. Apart from the 'Loch Achray' and the 'Mayburgh' (App.B, nos.83, 86), the skies seem to threaten. Scott's poetry had been compared to the flowers of his wild hills, to cloud, stream and gale.[16] As in the Byron series, Turner conveys an elegiac tone suggesting former heroic greatness. In 'Bemerside Tower' (no. 41), as interpreted by Gerald Finley with its symbolic details of the sun-

fig.21 J.T. Wedgwood after F. Sieurac, 'Sir Walter Scott', 1831. Line engraving

dial, the emptied vessel with its stain on the step, and (as in 'A Garden' in Rogers's *Poems*) a finite number of ranged flowerpots, together with a wreath, book, portrait and lute, there are allusions to the coming death of Scott and to his enduring fame.[17] Turner shows himself in this vignette sketching under the great Spanish chestnut in front of the peel tower. Three vignettes commemorate Scott's own career by reference to buildings: there is the obvious 'Abbotsford' (App.B, no.87), appropriately in the final volume of the edition, and at the beginning there is the 'Smailholm Tower' (App.B, no.76), showing the farmhouse where Scott lived for some time when a few years old. Smailholm was at the head of Scott's original list of subjects for the *Poetical Works,* in a letter to Cadell of 13 March 1831; it was here when out-of-doors that the lonely boy first felt the poetic impulse.[18] Turner had accompanied Scott to Smailholm two weeks before Scott left Scotland on his last journey abroad. A note to a plate in Fisher's *Landscape and Historical Illustrations* refers to Scott's 'visible emotion and tears' on this visit; doubtless he was aware of the possibility of its being his last. Scott is recorded in the same source as saying that he loved the farm there well: 'Every gray rock and every green knowe is familiar to me: I have known them from a boy. I was sent out here to die, but Providence had more for me to do'.[19] The vignette of 'Ashestiel' (App.B, no.82) shows the house where Scott composed *Marmion* (rather than a scene of Flodden Field which was first proposed for this volume). Scott was Sheriff of Selkirk at the time when he lived here; the two figures are perhaps meant to recall him and his friend Marriott as they walked along the streamlet and across the lonely downs above the house talking of poetry.[20]

The dilemma as to whether the illustrations should be of places or of dramatic scenes from the poems was resolved by Turner by enclosing the views in his water-colour designs within a cartouche resembling a memorial tablet in a church, with triglyphs and guttae. Outside this cartouche Turner drew in sepia outline figures from the poems, resembling 'penny plain' toy theatre figures completely out of scale with the vignette they enclosed; for example in 'Ashestiel' he drew at the sides the protagonists of *Marmion*, Constance and Beverley to the left and on the right Lord Marmion dying on Flodden Field. This original but rather clumsy device was abandoned when the designs were engraved, but was kept for the 'Abbotsford' (App.B, no.87). Pictured outside the cartouche enclosing the view of the house above the river, the empty chair and desk in the Library with Chantrey's bust of the poet, a suit of armour, and a hound indicate the death of the Master. Scott had complained that Turner overdid the number of highlanders in his designs and put lowlanders in kilts, which may be another reason for the abandonment of these figures.[21]

The series begins with six Border castles or peel towers (App.B, no.76–81). Cadell had written to Scott that there was little difficulty about 'scenes for the Great Poems', but that the four volumes of *Minstrelsy* with which the edition begins 'will puzzle me most'.[22] Earlier, Cadell had told Scott that Turner might have enough stock in his portfolio not to make the journey north. In the event, the sketches that Turner made on his trip to the Borders rendered the first vignettes particularly strong: the whole series has a high proportion of places that carry supernatural or sinister associations. One might include here the 'Rhymer's Glen'

(no.45). This was proposed in one list of subjects for the vignettes for the volume of Thomas the Rhymer's work, 'Sir Tristrem', with the title 'Bridge in Small Glen', but was not used until the volume of 'Periodical Criticism' in the *Prose Works*. This shows Scott's favourite mossy seat for contemplation and composition, 'near a little succession of water-falls' at Huntly Bank on his estate, where 'from immemorial tradition' Thomas the Rhymer saw the vision of the Queen of Elfland and was 'away' for seven years.[23] Turner renders the sinister atmosphere of Scott's Borders, the 'Debatable Land' with its treacheries and robberies, by showing the Border towers where the ballads dear to 'savage virtue and feudal rage'[24] were composed and sung. At Johnnie Armstrong's Tower the 'unfortunate hero' who inspired the ballad about the King's deceit was hanged by King James on the nearest trees, together with his retinue of thirty-six men, after his own long history of hangings, marauding and neck-breakings.[25] Scott wrote a significant note about these towers: 'The situation of a Border house, encompassed by woods, and rendered almost inaccessible by torrents, or rocks, or by morasses, sufficiently indicated the pursuits and apprehensions of its inhabitants'.[26] 'Lochmaben Castle' (no.40) shows the ruined seat of Robert the Bruce. Scott had described Hermitage Castle as having 'darksome strength' in its 'retired situation'; Thornbury compared this vignette to 'a glen in the Inferno'.[27] Turner pictures the 'ruins regarded by the peasantry with peculiar aversion and terror', the former abode of the warlock Lord Soulis, who boiled his victims in cauldrons. His Northumbrian adversary, the chieftain Cout of Keeldar, perished in the pool overlooked by the silver birches in the foreground. The *Descriptive Catalogue* of Messrs Moon, Boys and Graves who mounted an exhibition of a dozen of the watercolours from this series and some from Turner's *Views in England and Wales* in June 1833 quoted this stanza to accompany the image, from J. Leyden's 'Ode on Visiting Flodden':

Rude Border Chiefs, of mighty name,
And iron soul, who sternly tore
The blossoms from the tree of fame,
And purpled deep their tincts with gore,
Rush from brown ruins, scarr'd with age,
That frown o'er haunted Hermitage;
Where, long by spells mysterious bound,

They pace their round, with lifeless smile
And shake with restless foot, the guilty pile,
    Till sink the mouldering towers beneath the burden'd
        ground.[28]

'Mayburgh' (no.43), which is also referred to as 'Penrith Table', is an astonishing composition in which the vortical scene of the clearing and its standing stone seems mediated through an irregular lens or in a slightly convex mirror. Turner illustrates Scott's lines:

Mayburgh's mound and stones of power,
By Druids raised in magic hour.[29]

Two vignettes, however, do not fit into the general patterns outlined above: the 'Loch Achray' (App.B, no.83) and 'Fingal's Cave, Staffa' (no.44). The former with its 'sweet strand' and 'bosky thickets' is more suitable to the mood of *The Lady of the Lake*, which it illustrates. Turner found this poem particularly interesting, and there was an abandoned plan for him to make twenty illustrations for a separate edition of this poem for Cadell in 1838.[30] 'Fingal's Cave, Staffa' is perhaps the masterpiece of the series: Turner parallels the architectural language in Scott's description of Fingal's cave, the natural temple and 'Minster' facing Iona, by creating a design where the architectural arch formed by nature encloses a world of eternal flux: the ebb and swell of the tide, the rise and fall of the sun.[31] Turner, as Ruskin noted, shows an interest in the columnar basaltic structure; he had written in a lecture of 1818 that, 'The cell of the Bee and the Bysaltic mass display the like Geometric form, of whose elementary principles all nature partakes'.[32]

Scott's *Miscellaneous Prose*, May 1834 – August 1836

To complete Cadell's edition of Scott's *Works*, the *Miscellaneous Prose* in twenty-eight volumes was published in monthly sequence, immediately following the issue of the *Poetical Works*. The most important item was the *Life of Napoleon* in nine volumes, for which Turner created one of his most important series of illustrations, half 'landscape' frontispieces and half vignettes. The earlier book, *Paul's Letters to his Kinsfolk*, which included Scott's account of a visit to the Field of Waterloo, was also given two Napoleonic illustrations. The rest of the series consisted of Scott's biographies and contributions to periodicals, the *Tales of a Grandfather* – five volumes of Scottish history and two of French – and the *Provincial Antiquities*, the original edition of which in 1819 had carried elaborate large engravings after Turner.

Three vignettes celebrate writers admired by Scott: one for the 'Life of Dryden', showing his monument in Westminster Abbey (App.B, no.88);[33] one for Shakespeare to accompany Scott's panegyric in the volume containing the Drama (App.B, no.92);[34] the third pays homage to Smollett, in a rather tenuous link by Dumbarton Castle with the town where Smollett had been to grammar school, and by the river Leven, to which he was attached in his boyhood (App.B, no.89).[35] Two scenes from the Abbotsford estate celebrate Scott himself: the 'Rhymer's Glen' (App.B, no.103), and 'Chiefswood Cottage' (App.B, no.102), which was the summer residence of Lockhart, his son-in-law and (as editor of the *Quarterly*) a publisher of Scott's journalism. In the 'Rhymer's Glen' the woodland path and stream in its deep channel create an open-air setting for a moving elegy for the poet of the Scottish landscape: the walking stick and open book show the glen dispossessed of the rhymer. As with the 'St Anne's Hill, 1' in Rogers's *Poems* (App.B, no.37) which alludes to the deceased Charles James Fox (see p.40, above), the detail of the open book is a device to indicate the legacy of the printed word, now that the voice is dead. A gyratory rhythm is set up by the path curving upwards and the downwards twisting stream; there is a strong sense of the play of light, air and water.

Two further drawings made for Cadell commemorating places associated with Scott were used as title-vignettes for Lockhart's *Life of Scott*, and were engraved by William Miller, who records finishing them in December 1838 and January 1839.[36] 'Sandy Knowe, or Smailholm' (App.B, no.111) shows the lame young Scott pictured with walking stick and nurse among twilight scenes of milking. The bright evening star is reflected in the tarn below the familiar outline of the peel tower. The other vignette, of Scott's residence, 'No.39, Castle Street, Edinburgh' (App.B, no.112), also shows a star, with a biblical suggestion that it has positioned itself over where the young man was. In this vignette the darkening street leads to the faintly luminous castle, while light in the chiaroscuro is also created by white smoke from the road-menders' brazier and from lit-up windows.[37]

Among the Scottish scenes for the *Provincial Antiquities* is a vignette of 'New Abbey' (App.B, no.91), which is not mentioned in the text, but was a design unused from the *Poetical Works*;[38] the scene is typical of the Border ruins. 'Dunfermline' (App.B, no.104) for *Tales of a Grandfather* was the seat of King Malcolm. 'Craigmillar' and 'Linlithgow' (App.B, nos.105, 106) show palaces and abbeys, the roofless settings of the turbulent past with their history of liaisons, intrigues, and treacheries. 'Fort Augustus' (which Turner sketched en route to visit Munro of Novar at Evanton) shows the Caledonian Canal with a steamboat and Loch Ness beyond (App.B, no.108). The baleful 'Killiecrankie' features burning cottages with a corpse to the left and a storm and torrent to the right (App.B, no.107). Although the massacre is described in Volume XXIV, the vignette makes an obvious pair of atrocities together with the frontispiece 'Glencoe' (R 549) in Volume XXV.

The two French vignettes, 'Calais' and 'Abbeville', end the series. In 'Abbeville' (App.B, no.110) there are four alternating dark and light horizontal planes from the front, like stage flats or foot-pieces, in an unusual scheme; in the market-place peasants in Normandy hats sit cross-legged, with a dark diligence behind them; at the rear the lofty church is in shade. The 'Calais' (App.B, no.109) is a supreme nightpiece: the lighthouse casts its light on the Hôtel de Ville and on the English packet boat, which is arriving on the oily-looking harbour waters.

More than other series, the title-vignettes for the *Life of Napoleon* should be considered alongside their landscape frontispieces. Taken together, they demonstrate Turner's response to Napoleon: they give a narrative and a critique, based on Turner's response to Scott's interpretation of the former Emperor, and they shed light on Turner's dramatic images on canvas of 'The Field of Waterloo', RA 1818 (B&J 138) and 'War: the Exile and the Rock Limpet', RA 1842 (B&J 400). Scott's view of Napoleon was of a 'strangely mingled character', capable of splendour and tyranny. A recurrent theme is his hubristic belief in the 'force of his own destiny'.[39] Scott admired Napoleon for leading France out of the

Terror, the unthinkable anarchy and atrocities of which Scott does not spare his readers. The Revolution, he says, 'resembled one great bedlam, set on fire by the patients, who remained dancing in the midst of the flames'.[40] Power and pride carried Napoleon away, however, and Scott's view of his fall is that of divine punishment and the restoration of Nature. Turner follows this in his imagery.

Napoleon was commonly seen as a fallen angel by contemporary writers. Byron compares him to Lucifer:

> Since he, miscalled the Morning Star,
> Nor man nor fiend hath fallen so far.[41]

The analogy is also used by both Southey and Scott in their poems on Waterloo. In defeat, Byron says, the Desolater was desolate. In indicating Napoleon's fall in the final volume of the Napoleon illustrations it is obvious that Turner connects the violent storm and lightning in 'The Field of Waterloo from the Picton Tree' (R 539) with Nemesis.

Turner's subject is peace and war: illustrations of cities or palaces alternate with battlefields or places of execution. The series is unified by recurrent motifs: columns of soldiery or horsemen cross landscapes at speed; corpses or skeletons of men and horses lie in the left-hand corners of the views; storms and skies convey judgments; crescent moons rise and set; suns mostly set. The series has integrity, particularly when compared with the conventional series of battlefields and portraits originally envisaged by Cadell.[42] Turner illustrates buildings significant in the drama, presenting Napoleon finally dwarfed on the steps of Fontainbleau (App.B, no.100); likewise he is shown a minute figure captive on the deck of *HMS Bellerophon* at Plymouth (App.B, no.101). In both cases he is numinous even in defeat, lit from behind by torchlight or irradiated by his white uniform. The series culminates with the desolation and horror of 'The Field of Waterloo' (W 1116; R 539), signifying both the mass destruction of the fine flower of European manhood and the divine punishment of Napoleon. Peace and justice are restored, as with the authority of the heavens: one almost expects to see in the sky a shadowy Old Testament figure with raised hand from where the lightning emanates, as is pictured by Turner in 'Sinai's Thunder' from the Campbell series and in the Miltonic 'Fall of the Rebel Angels'.

The vignette of 'Hougoumont' for *Paul's Letters* (App.B, no.90) shows the château on the battlefield, which the Guards defended, killing ten thousand of the enemy and losing twenty-eight of their officers and eight hundred rank and file. Here the valour of the British – not forgetting the Scots officer who, Paul writes proudly to his kinsfolk, closed the gates – might be said to have saved Europe, as the 'GR' (King George's monograph) on the baggage-cart and the neat pile of cannon-balls remind us. Hougoumont (whose real name was Château Goumont, but being garbled by Wellington, was officially renamed for history) had emblematical features – dove-cote, chapel and garners – which are all described in detail by Scott, and also by Southey in *The Poet's Pilgrimage to Waterloo* of 1816; it presented the ideal of that agrarian and cultivated aristocracy so much admired by Scott. Here the gathered hay was set fire to by the French, while the wounded were trapped inside the courtyard, providing the holocaust that seems to be hinted at in the apparently innocent but proleptic wisp of smoke in the distance. The same roofed gateway to the château appears in the oil painting of 'The Battle of Waterloo' of 1818, and in the vignette of Waterloo for *Childe Harold* (App.B, no.69) as a mouth of Hell, in both strengthening the hideous foreground image of the corpses in 'one red burial blent'.

For the first vignette of the *Life of Napoleon,* Turner illustrates the Hôtel de Ville at Paris (App.B, no.93). The building, erected by the citizens in the reign of Henri IV, was the scene of important Revolutionary events, such as the attack on Robespierre and his Terrorists (who mostly committed suicide inside) by fifteen hundred men, when cannon were turned on the doors. The same sketchbook, *Paris and Environs* (TB CCLVII) shows sketches for this vignette and for the side-angle view of the Hôtel and the suspension-bridge in 'Hôtel de Ville and Pont d'Arcole' in *Turner's Annual Tour, The Seine, 1835.* Rawlinson quotes from a touched proof of this vignette on which Turner wrote to Horsburgh that his first efforts at the architecture were not rich enough in ornament – 'it looks in Nature like Lace; … I fear I must ask you to send it to me again'.[43] 'Napoleon's Logement, Quai Conti' (App.B, no.94), is where the hero arrived in Paris at the age of twenty-six, and left a 'favourite of Fortune'.[44] The reader is directed to identify Napoleon's window with its parted curtains (which

resemble a nineteenth-century stage curtain about to open on a play) by a *remarque* or etched marginal sketch of the dormer, on the publication line of the engraving. Above is a crescent moon which hints at Napoleon's rise and perhaps his fall – the star placed over Scott's house in Edinburgh, in Turner's vignette for Lockhart's *Life of Scott,* is a similar, more optimistic, device. In 'Venice' (App.B, no.95) the Campanile and Duomo of San Marco indicate a devout civilisation. The view into the Piazzetta from the Bacino presents Venice as a place of unity and wholeness in terms of repeated circles, domes and arches and a generalised symmetry and balance; the central image is a man and woman standing on a gondola and holding hands. In the oil 'Venice from the Porch of Madonna della Salute', RA 1835 (B&J 362) this same couple (still holding hands) has arrived on the other side of the canal. Wings and a halo gesture towards a clear ether. Napoleon's threat to the city was that he would be an 'Attila' to it. It surrendered in 1797, when three thousand French soldiers took possession of the Piazza San Marco.[45] Turner here and in the watercolour for this vignette (W 1105), leaves out the famous horses from Constantinople in their proud position on the Duomo: Napoleon had removed them to Paris. However, he does show the Lion of St Mark, which Napoleon had also taken to Paris. The Emperor intended the horses to be put on the top of a triumphal arch and harnessed to a gilded chariot conveying an image of himself. Scott painfully describes the subjugation of the 'city of lofty remembrances and independence' to Napoleon, who later surrendered it to the Austrians.[46]

A central image in the series is the 'Vincennes' (App.B, no.96), which shows the execution of the Duc d'Enghien. This execution, which Scott called 'the deepest stain on the memory of Napoleon', showing 'the vindictive spirit of a savage',[47] is given a sinister setting by Turner as taking place below a barbican; it makes an ironic contrast with the delicate Gothic tracery of the church, which looks down on the scene. This episode of 20 March 1804 – in which Napoleon had the Bourbon Duc d'Enghien abducted from Baden, which was not even in French territory, interrogated at night and then shot and placed in the grave which had been dug before the trial (pickaxe and spade lie between the firing-squad and the murdered man) – deeply shocked Scott; it is the climax of this volume of his biography.

The Duke was the grandson of the Prince of Condé, and was described by Scott as 'in the flower of his youth, handsome, brave and high-minded'.[48] Most sinister of all is the small figure on the parapet just to the left of the moon, which represents Savary, Napoleon's Chief of Police. That this is a human figure, and not an architectural finial, is proved by Turner's sketch in the *Paris and Environs* sketchbook for the upper and architectural part of this vignette (no.65). In this a figure is clearly shown, also proving that Turner was thinking of illustrating the drama as well as the setting when he was on the spot and making his sketch. Vincennes, a mile outside Paris, figures again in the biography several times as the precursor of all secret service prisons where the 'victims of political suspicion' lay without trial during the Napoleonic regime.[49]

The following vignette, 'Mayence' (Mainz) (App.B, no.97), is placed opposite the frontispiece of St Cloud for a contrast between the damaged city (including, as Cecilia Powell has noted, the loss of the dome of the cathedral at the eastern end)[50] caused by Napoleon's warring over the Rhine boundary, and an artificial and insecure-looking refuge, the palace made for Napoleon and his court as a part of his megalomaniac building programme. 'The Simplon' (App.B, no.98) with its variation on Turner's giddy Alpine passes, clefts, torrents and peaks, represents the gateway to Italy and shows the pass wrested by Napoleon from the mountaineers of the Valais. The ant-like columns of soldiers seem ironically placed among the falling waters and the vast peaks. The subject recalls the heroic early crossings of the Alps made by Napoleon and his troops, which are so eloquently described by Scott. In 'Malmaison' (App.B, no.99) Turner creates an image of the Seine from on high, similar to the glimpses of serpentine river in the vignettes for Milton; it is a summary of those consummate views of the Seine from on high in Turner's *Rivers of France*. However, the mood, with the setting sun and the palace in the shadows at the bottom right, in addition to the melancholy associations of the palace and even its name, makes it an elegiac image. It was here that Josephine lived when Napoleon dissolved their union, and here that she died shortly after Napoleon was exiled to Elba. The Emperor himself was brought here under guard after Waterloo.

In 'Fontainbleau' (App.B, no.100) Turner has created an intensely dramatic image lit by full moon and torchlight. This is the scene of Napoleon's first fall on 20 April 1814, where he took leave of the Imperial Guard having embraced or kissed their 'eagles', or standards. Scott remarks on what a fine historical painting this scene would make, and Turner's watercolour sketch (TB CCLXXX 29) marked 'Adieu Fontainbleau' would seem to suggest that he contemplated painting a canvas on the subject.[51] Turner creates his dramatic image in the Scott illustration by isolating the Emperor in the exact centre of the horizontal line and dwarfing him by the architecture of the Cour du Cheval Blanc, lighting the outline from the torchlight behind him and in the bottom left placing the ominous waiting black carriages.

The most powerful image in this series is the landscape frontispiece, the 'Field of Waterloo from the Picton Tree' (W 1116; R 539), to which Turner gives his characteristic apocalyptic motifs, but indicates at the same time a spray of greenery on the blasted Picton tree, signifying perhaps the immortality of the gallant slaughtered officer, Sir Thomas Picton, and an indication of renewal. This is placed opposite the final vignette, a more obvious political image of Napoleon on *HMS Bellerophon* (App.B, no.101); the small white figure on the deck as the sun sets, the prisoner of Captain Maitland, is no longer a threat to Europe and to civilisation. Justice and freedom are defined in terms of the British ship, the flag, and the jolly tars and their women who crowd the foreground in small craft.[52] Thus the Napoleon commission gave Turner the opportunity in a sequence of vignettes for a sustained meditation on Napoleon's fall. The Cadell papers reveal the discussion between Lockhart and Cadell over the subjects, Lockhart being familiar with Turner's great painting of Waterloo, and urging Cadell to trust to Turner: 'he will judge best'; and 'no fear for his tact'.[53] Cadell and Lockhart must have been delighted with Turner's designs, as at one point later on they discussed the possibility of publishing *Landscape Illustrations* for the *Life of Scott* in the manner of the Byron series.[54]

Milton's *Poetical Works,*
May – October 1835

Turner's style in his vignettes changed markedly in the last part of the decade with the Milton and Campbell series, the four designs for Moore's *Epicurean* and the title-vignette for *The Pilgrim's Progress.* Not only did Turner handle figures with greater confidence, but his devices became bolder; the effects may strike one as highly original or, in a few cases, as clumsy. The human figure takes the centre of five vignettes, the 'Temptation on the Pinnacle', 'Lochiel's Warning', 'The Last Man', 'The Death Boat of Heligoland' and 'The Ring' (App.B, nos.117, 127, 132, 138, 142); otherwise the focus is still on landscape. Turner is free from the influence of Rogers's fastidiousness, and his imagery is more fantastic and sublime.

The War in Heaven in the Milton series inspires Turner to perhaps two of his greatest vignettes, images which Hamerton, usually a subtle critic, dismisses as 'a mixture of unaccountable astronomy and bad figure-drawing'.[55] In his preface to the six-volume edition, Sir Egerton Brydges wrote that Turner 'has entered upon the work with the enthusiasm and fellow-feeling of a highly-endowed poetical mind, and in his daring flight has reached a level of imagination, which no rival, ancient or modern, has surpassed. – He is worthy to illustrate MILTON'.[56] Turner was worthy to illustrate Milton also in that he had read Milton for many years, as is shown by the six epigraphs that he takes for oil paintings from Milton, three of them made before 1800, and also by the Miltonic quotations in the Perspective lectures.[57]

The frontispiece to Volume I was 'Mustering of the Warrior Angels' (no.32). Macrone's 'Index of Illustrations' gives the quotations from which the illustrations have since become detached. Lines are quoted from Book VI of *Paradise Lost,* where the voice of God is exhorting Michael and Gabriel along with the celestial armies and the bright legions 'by thousands and by Millions ranged for fight'.[58] Turner is inspired by Milton's description of light alternating with darkness and the angels mustering in the symbolic orient beams of the dawn to triumph over evil. With great imaginative boldness he locates Milton's Plain and the 'sacred Hill'

(where the Warrior Angels muster in response to God's order to drive the Rebel Angels through Chaos into Hell) actually among the spheres: they walk through space – 'the passive air upbore their nimble tread', as they march 'to the sound of instrumental harmony'. The two angels on the sun anticipate the late oil painting 'The Angel Standing in the Sun', RA 1846 (B&J 425), which pictures Gabriel again. John Gage has demonstrated Turner's interest in cosmology and has shown how the globes in this vignette may well derive from the diagram of Galileo's solar system in a rejected earlier design for 'Galileo's Villa' from Rogers's *Italy.*[59] The subject of the 'Mustering' in Turner's hands is another working of the theme of the triumph of light over darkness: the archangels stand on the sun itself while the muster takes place in serried ranks on the hill, and columns of angels sweep across the interstellar spaces. A figure among these columns makes a conspicuous posture of crucifixion. The scene is played out among a series of globes, and radiations of light among the stars and moon. Turner probably also had in mind in this vignette the passage about the creation of the two great lights, the sun and moon – the stars that rule by day and night in the same Book VI of *Paradise Lost.* The porous sun, Milton writes, had 'liquid light' instilled into it by God as a 'Palace' of light, from which the stars in turn draw light in 'golden urns'. Turner has combined the narrative of the mustering of the angels of light with the representation of the primordial separation of the sun from the 'globose' moon and the stars – 'et deviderent lucem et tenebras'.[60] The *fiat* creates chiaroscuro, a duality of the utmost significance for Turner and his engravers.

In 'The Fall of the Rebel Angels' (no.33) the falling star, the phosphorescent Lucifer, parallels the headlong Rebel Angels on the right. Out of the heart of light there issues the Hand of God. The blues and reds of the watercolour create a particularly lurid image of terror as the bodies of the damned fall like inverted flames. The quotation given in the Index is the famous passage in Milton's exordium:

> Hurl'd headlong flaming from the ethereal sky
> With hideous ruin and combustion, down
> To bottomless perdition.

In the upper portion of the vignette Goodall was told by Turner to 'put me in innumerable figures here'.[61]

The glimpse of lost Paradise in 'The Expulsion from Paradise' (App.B, no.115) is pictured as a meander of river among a forest with our 'lingering parents' turned away as from a demesne beyond aristocratic pier-gates of the early nineteenth century. 'The Temptation on the Mountain' from *Paradise Regained*, Book III, shows the created universe as a meander again, illumined by the sun (App.B, no.116). The snake on the rock is a quotation from Poussin's 'Deluge'. Turner's paintings of 'The Holy Family', RA 1803 (B&J 49), 'The Deluge', RA 1813 (B&J 55), 'The Vision of Medea', RA 1831 (B&J 293) and 'The Golden Bough', RA 1834 (B&J 355) all have a snake to indicate the presence of evil, the first two showing, as in Poussin's original and here, the snake slithering on a rock.[62] An important touched proof has pencilled notes by Turner identifying the various cities looked down upon by Jesus and Satan: the Cities of the Plain, the City on the Rock, the 'City not wall'd'.[63] The nearest city is intended as Nineveh: 'domes and towers of Nineveh, and wall'd round'. Turner perhaps had in mind the prophecy that Nineveh would 'become a desolation'; he had worked up a sketch of Nineveh by C.J. Rich for Finden's *Bible Illustrations* concurrently with the designs for the Milton series.

For the 'Ludlow Castle. Rising of the Water-Nymphs' (no.37), an illustration to *Comus*, Turner pictures the phosphoric nymphs whose aid is invoked in summoning the goddess of the local river, Sabrina, spirit of purity, who alone can lift the spell put on the Lady by Comus. Sabrina represents the river Severn, on the tributary of which lies Ludlow Castle, the seat of the Egertons. Turner seems to connect these water-sprites with the Nereides that figure in 'Ulysses Deriding Polyphemus', RA 1829 (B&J 330) and 'The Parting of Hero and Leander', RA 1837 (B&J 370). They seem here to rise on a wave. The lines quoted to accompany this vignette given in Brydges's Index are these:

> By all the nymphs that nightly dance
> Upon thy streams with wily glance,
> Rise, rise, and heave thy rosy head
> From thy coral-paven bed,
> And bridle in thy headlong wave,
> Till thou our summons answered have.[64]

Turner's depiction of Ludlow Castle repeats a device

recalled from Rogers's *Poems*, where mullions in 'St Herbert's Chapel' are illuminated by the full moon or by candles (App.B, no.32).

In 'The Temptation on the Pinnacle' (from *Paradise Regained*) (no.36) and the design for *Lycidas*, both for the final volume, Turner figures Jesus and St Michael as emanating from light, referring back to the angels shown in this way in the first vignette. The upper part of the 'Temptation on the Pinnacle' with the representation of Jesus and the angels hardly seems sincere or inspired; the lower part, however, is a complex architectural caprice of spires, domes and roofs of Turner's own day to represent the Temple in Jerusalem. Turner adds the epigraph:

> He said and stood:
> But Satan, smitten with amazement, fell.[65]

In the fantastic 'St Michael's Mount – Shipwreck of Lycidas' (App.B, no.118), Turner responds melodramatically, combining a favourite Cornish scene with a disaster that gripped his imagination. The waters and lightning play in a realistically impossible configuration; St Michael stands with spear in a posture surely intended to recall his figure in the vignette of the 'Mustering'. The original title given in Macrone's edition, 'The Death of Lycidas – Vision of the Guarded Mount', is a better title, in that it draws attention to the figure of the archangel on the pinnacle; the forlornness of the drowning figure, merely an arm and an outstretched hand, is accentuated by the lines quoted in the Index:

> Where were ye nymphs, when the remorseless deep
> Closed o'er the head of your loved Lycidas.[66]

In the title-vignette for Fisher's *Pilgrim's Progress* of 1836 (no.60) Turner uses for the Celestial City, above the Delectable Mountains and at the crown of the elongated vignette, contemporary entablatures, domes and porticoes similar to those in the 'Temptation on the Pinnacle'. St Paul's Cathedral appears to be in the centre of the city.[67] The dark, rocky, barren and gloomy ways of the Progress are strongly expressed in Turner's vignette, another dialogue of emblematical dark and light. The foreground image is that of the Evangelist saving Christian from the River of Death; Turner wrote in the margins of a proof now in the Mummery Collection at the Victoria and Albert Museum (EL 123) identifying 'C. & A. in the Valley' to the right, that is to say, Christian and Apollyon in the Valley of Humiliation, and the 'City of Desolation' to the right of the Madonna and Child. He also identifies the more obvious symbols of Fire and the 'Bow of Hope', also to the right.

Campbell's *Poetical Works*, 1837

Moxon followed his edition of Rogers's *Poems* three years later with an edition of Thomas Campbell's poems printed by the same elaborate method that he had used in both Rogers volumes, passing the pages engraved with the vignettes twice through the press (see p.19, above). The first we hear of the project is in a letter of Campbell's as early as 6 July 1831: 'Turner, the Painter, has promised to illustrate, with his powerful pencil, "The Pleasures of Hope". I came to this place [Maidstone] in order to ascertain the price of paper for a new and splendid edition like Rogers' "Italy", at one of the papermills'.[68] Campbell was familiar with the milieu of the writers and publishers who had employed Turner. He was well known in Whig circles, and was a frequent guest at Holland House (see p.39, above). Campbell made his reputation young with *The Pleasures of Hope*, begun on Mull when he was still a student, in reply to Rogers's *The Pleasures of Memory*. It was Campbell who in 1824 made the first proposal for the new London University in a letter to the Prime Minister, Lord Brougham. To his dinner parties at Sydenham came Moore, Rogers, and on one occasion Byron himself.[69] He was also known to Tories such as Scott, and to John Murray. Of Murray's drawing room at Albemarle Street he wrote that, 'I have met more noted men of talent under his roof than any other, except that of Lord Holland and Rogers'.[70] Although Campbell has left no record of admiration for Turner, they were certainly acquainted: Campbell and Turner exchanged toasts at a formal dinner 'with a large party'; Campbell, in compliment to Turner, proposed the health of 'the painters and glaziers'; this was capped by Turner's reply, a health to the 'paperstainers'.[71]

Campbell spent well in excess of £800 on Turner's

watercolours and on the engravings, paying Turner 25 guineas each for twenty vignettes. Under the threat of organising a lottery for the drawings, Campbell, as he had been told he would, stirred Turner to offer 200 guineas for them. Campbell wrote dyspeptically to a correspondent, 'How could I propose to extort from your brother three hundred, or even two hundred guineas for bits of painted pasteboard, which my adviser told me, when I showed him Turner's money, were purchased from me at twice their intrinsic value'. By June 1838 Campbell reported that Moxon had sold 2,500 copies of the edition.[72] All the finished drawings, a few of them as fine as any for Turner's vignettes, survive, appropriately in the National Gallery of Scotland. There are in the Bequest also some thirty or so preliminary sketches on very cheap paper, some of them for details, such as the bridge in 'Kosciusko'. Two sketches, for the landscapes to 'O'Connor's Child' and to 'Gertrude of Wyoming – The Waterfall' are in a tiny sketchbook of amorous scenes, thought to have been used at Petworth (TB CCCI b; f.51v. and f.52v.). The latter sketch shows some figures, the castle and the moon. The vignettes were engraved by Edward Goodall, with

fig.22 Edward Finden after Sir Thomas Lawrence, 'Thomas Campbell', 1834. Line engraving

the exception of two that were engraved by Robert Wallis, 'Hohenlinden' (App.B, no.129) and 'Lord Ullin's Daughter' (App.B, no.130), and one, 'The Dead Eagle – Oran' (App.B, no.140), by William Miller. Campbell called frequently at Edward Goodall's house to see the progress of the engravings.[73]

Campbell's imagination was more vigorous and ambitious than Rogers's, and he inspired Turner to some strange and dramatic images, a few perhaps rather contrived. 'The Beech Tree's Petition' (App.B, no.136) and the lower panel of 'The Soldier's Dream' (App.B, no.131) (an unsuccessful attempt by Turner at a double-yolked design) are, however, in the nostalgic antiquarian countryside style of Turner's designs for Rogers's *Poems*. In general the designs are detailed and crowded with incident. Turner's skies were never so populated with beings or with phosphoric men, or filled with abstract crosses and triangles; in this series baleful sunsets and what Campbell calls, in 'Lord Ullin's Daughter', 'the scowl of heaven' abound. For a poet known as 'The Bard of Hope', Campbell's poems are so full of cataclysms, blighted passions, drowned daughters and dispossessions; Turner responds to these images of fallacious hope. The vignette to 'O'Connor's Child' (App.B, no.126) has as part of its central image a man's grave, that for 'Theodoric' (App.B, no.125) a woman's grave. Turner creates the violently emotional dramatic scene for 'O'Connor's Child', and also the unearthly 'Death-Boat of Heligoland' (App.B, no.138), the latter in the manner of Cruikshank. 'O'Connor's Child' is even more dramatic in the watercolour design where the life-blood oozes red from the grave of Connacht Moran, and his lover carries a piece of the dead man's bright yellow garb.

Campbell had profound political concerns, such as his sympathy for the Poles suppressed by the Russians: this was, his biographer says, feverish, and he was President of the Association of the Friends of Poland. These concerns stimulated Turner to create another political vignette in 'Kosciusko', celebrating the romantic Polish hero (App.B, no.123). This is an eloquent emblematical protest against tyranny, at the moment when Poland lost its liberty and its name, being 'obliterated from the list of nations' and suffering partition by Russia and Prussia: he pictures the massacre and the great and historic capital of Poland put to flames, with the fall of the hero and 'Samartia' – or Poland – on her knees. At

fig.23 Francis Engleheart after R. Cook, 'Gertrude of Wyoming'. Engraving on copper for Campbell's *Gertrude of Wyoming and Other Poems*, 1812

Campbell's funeral in Westminster Abbey, 'a Polish exile threw some of the dust from the grave of Kosciusko upon the coffin' as it was interred at Poets' Corner.[74] Campbell's European travels and awareness are illustrated by Turner with some of the finest vignettes in the book: for 'Hohenlinden'; for the 'Ehrenbreitstein' to accompany the 'Ode to the Germans', which calls the fortress 'still the camp of slaves', and the 'Rolandseck' (App.B, no.135). Campbell's Algerian visit is commemorated by Turner in 'The Dead Eagle' (App.B, no.140). 'Sinai's Thunder' (App.B, no.124; which surely derives from John Martin's 'The Giving of the Law') and 'The Last Man' (App.B, no.132), where the figure was much improved, if made more conventional, by Goodall, are apocalyptic images, the latter particularly successful. However, Turner seems to miss an opportunity to express drama in the two vignettes for *Gertrude of Wyoming* (App.B, nos.133, 134), providing some scenes of 'Wyoming', seen by Campbell as 'terrestrial paradise', which are as unlikely as Campbell's own panthers, flamingoes, aloes and palm trees which he misplaces in the Golden West; Campbell's Wyoming, wrote Byron, was 'grossly fake scenery', having 'no more in common with Pennsylvania than with Penmanmaur'.[75] When Turner pictures Gertrude reading Shakespeare out-of-doors at the moment when she is unexpectedly surprised by the arrival of her former childhood friend, Henry Waldegrave, now a kilted adult, he adds to the scene a magnificent cascade and a prospect of a widening river, while the actual scene in Campbell is a 'deep untrodden grot' (App.B, no.134). He appears to be following the deployment of the figures in the frontispiece to the fourth edition of *Gertrude of Wyoming* of 1812, engraved after R. Cook (fig.23), but does not create drama: the figures, unlike those in 'O'Connor's Child', are subsidiary to the landscape.

The first two vignettes for 'The Pleasures of Hope' present Campbell's idea by the symbols of rainbow and star. 'Summer Eve – The Rainbow' (App.B, no.121) shows the mountains from which the river flows through multi-arched bridges. The famous line to which the landscape is an illustration is of course a particularly apt idea for Turner,

> 'Tis distance lends enchantment to the view.

It is possible that Turner had read Hazlitt's essay on 'Mr. Campbell and Mr. Crabbe' in *The Spirit of the Age* where the rainbow Turner uses on the first page of Campbell's poems is used by Hazlitt for a symbol of those poems themselves: 'Mr. Crabbe presents an entire contrast to Mr. Campbell:– the one is the most ambitious and most aspiring of living poets, the other the most humble and prosaic. If the poetry of the one is like the arch of a rainbow, spanning and adorning earth, that of the other is like a dull leaden cloud hanging over it.'[76] In 'The Andes Coast' (App.B, no.122) Turner is illustrating the idea that even in 'Earth's loneliest bounds' and on 'Ocean's wildest shore' Hope recalls home, bringing thoughts of the English (or properly the Scottish) landscape. Turner here uses Campbell's own emblem of Hope in this passage, the 'starry pole', clearly seen to the left.

For 'Kosciusko' (colour plates 12–14) Turner pictures what Campbell calls 'the bloodiest picture in the book of Time', when the earth shook in outrage. Turner seems to have prepared more studies for this vignette,

judging from the number which survive in the Bequest, than for any other. Turner has combined two incidents of 1793 from the career of Thaddeus Kosciusko. In the second foreground he has pictured two fallen patriots, who wear the peasant costume adopted by Kosciusko and are tended by Polish ladies. They are probably intended to recall an actual fall of Kosciusko at the battle of Maciejowice earlier in the year when he was dangerously wounded in the head and neck and pierced in the back with a lance. 'Falling senseless from his horse, he was on the point of being put to death by the barbarians, when one of his officers, who lay bleeding on the ground, saved him by disclosing his name'.[77] Centre stage is placed Kosciusko himself, together with the allegorical figure of Poland on her knees, the sword in her 'nerveless grasp' indicating defeat. He holds in one hand the crown of Stanislaus, who was forced to abdicate after this defeat, and in the other is doubtless the famous scimitar that had been blessed by a Capuchin at the time of his vow of 'victory or death'. At his feet lies a Polish lancer's cap. Campbell at this point in 'The Pleasures of Hope' has the hero repeat this patriotic vaunt on the 'rampart-heights' at the scene of the massacre. Campbell's note to this passage describes 'the triumphant entry of Suwarrow into the Polish capital, and the insult to human nature, by the blasphemous thanks offered up to Heaven, for victories obtained over men fighting the sacred cause of liberty, by murderers and oppressors'. Turner has written out below his watercolour design Campbell's line,

> The sun went down, nor ceased the carnage there &c.

Turner shows the resistance of the patriots at the bridge of Prag over the Vistula at Warsaw, where very many of them were drowned, against the colossal Russian force of 15,000 men sent by the vindictive Catherine the Great under Suvárov. Kosciusko, an ardent Republican, had fought on the American side in the War of Independence, and was well known in London. Byron had written in 'The Age of Bronze' of

> That sound that echoes in a tyrant's ear –
> Kosciusko!

Turner probably knew that the hero was known (because he was also a painter) as the artist–soldier.[78] Campbell's passage is not just about Kosciusko, but also about the crimes of tyranny and despotism, the fall of civilisation and the suppression of truth, mercy and freedom. Turner adds the ramparts and the magnificent massed architecture, and stresses what Campbell does not, the churches silhouetted or balefully lit by the flames. The final shape of the vignette seems of itself to flame with the city. A feature of the watercolour design is that the setting sun clearly shows the outlines of large predatory birds awaiting the carnage of the apocalyptic massacre; these were not shown when the design was engraved, but were recalled by Turner when he came to paint 'The Angel Standing in the Sun' (B&J 425).

'Hohenlinden' (App.B, no.129), for which a preliminary study showing the outlines of horse and cannon survives (TB CCLXXX 5), illustrates the famous poem about the blood-stained snow of the field where in 1800 General Moreau defeated the Austrians at the meeting of 'furious Frank and fiery Hun'. Campbell himself described the poem as a 'damned drum-and-trumpet thing'; it was only published at Scott's insistence. Both Campbell and Scott picture the river Isar as if it was next to the field of battle when in fact it was twenty miles away; Turner probably shows Munich in the background.[79] The experience of Campbell's which contributed to the horror of the poem was his crossing a battle-field near Vienna:

> On emerging from a pine-wood he came upon open ground, where the ravages of war were horribly visible in the bodies of men and horses strewed on the bloodstained ground. Nothing impeded his route, yet he perceived the vehicle stop, and missed the postilion, who left him full three-quarters of an hour alone. 'I had enough around me to meditate upon,' observed Campbell …'that is if the weather had not been unbearably chill. I had lost all patience, when the Bavarian scoundrel came up loaded with horse-tails. He had been cutting off the tails of the horses that lay dead around, then piling up a goodly number of them behind the carriage, he resumed his tardy pace.'[80]

Moore's *The Epicurean*, 1839

Macrone's commission for four vignettes for his edition of Moore's *The Epicurean* produced the strangest of Turner's designs. The element of fancy in the Columbus series, the Milton series and some of the vignettes for Campbell's poems becomes here truly fantastic, some would say even theatrical. Moore's novella is an oriental fantasy, an absurd pseudo-Egyptian farrago: a love-quest ending in the death of the heroine from a poisoned coral chaplet as is pictured in Turner's last vignette; ordeals by fire and water; initiation into Heliopolitan mysteries; tombs, subterranean passages and moonlit Nile journeys; escape from evil priests. At the same time, as is suddenly revealed at the close, it is a Christian morality and cautionary tale. It is as if the imagination is licensed to play truant among bizarre dreams of the ancient world by the conventional Christian about-turn in the last chapter. As usual with

fig.24 J.T. Wedgwood after F. Sieurac,'Thomas Moore', 1829. Line engraving

Moore, much of the writing is maudlin, but there are interestingly freakish visual details or phrases. Moore's journal conveys the fashionable Regency milieu of this oriental novella: 'Ellis told me before dinner that while he was writing a letter this morning, he heard a violent sobbing behind him, & on turning round, found it was Lady Georgiana over "The Epicurean" – Sang in the evening'.[81] *The Epicurean* was first published in 1827, and was written following the Napoleonic vogue for things superficially Egyptian, and after the exhibition of 1821 in London by Giovanni Battista Belzoni of the Egyptian antiquities that he had excavated.

Turner and Moore had met as long ago as November 1819, in Rome, when Canova, Thomas Lawrence, and Francis Chantrey were at dinner with the two of them after a visit to the Venetian Academy of Painting.[82] Moore wrote in his diary on 31 July 1836, 'Received a letter from M[oran] of the Globe, considering a proposal of a plan from Macrone to publish a new Edition of all my work on the following terms – one thousand pounds for an edition of your works, prose and poetical Complete to be published by him – say 8000 copies in monthly numbers commencing with the ensuing year. If they go to 15 volumes, he makes his offer 2000 guineas. Turner to embellish the volumes with his best style of illustrations, going, if necessary to Ireland for the purpose.'[83] There were many copyright difficulties, and the complete edition was abandoned. Meanwhile, Macrone became ill, and *The Epicurean* was the only remnant of this scheme. Moore writes again in his diary about the scheme on 30 April 1837, 'Had some talk with Turner about his task, and in referring to the subjects I had marked for him, he said, "There is one you have done yourself" – meaning, as he added, the incident of the Epicurean hanging by the ring'. Moore, oddly enough, took against Turner's rendering of his description, which is the best vignette of the set (App.B, no.142); it is a subject that Gustave Doré illustrated in the edition of the novel published in Paris in 1865. Two months later Moore inspected the engraving at Macrone's and concluded that Turner had misunderstood his prescriptions that the artist should attempt only scenes where Moore himself had been 'vague and unparticularised'; 'his conclusion on the contrary was that as I had so much brought out and elaborated this extravagant scene it left him an easier task in extravagising also – a lame conclusion'. The

fig.25 Edward Goodall after J.M.W. Turner, 'Lake Nemi', *c*.1844. Engraving on steel (R 638)

next day he called on Goodall to see the drawings and the engravings, and found some beautiful, but the gentleman with the ring on his finger as bad as it might be expected to be'.[84] The vignette shows a falling figure in a dream image, with a collapsing balustrade and ghouls and grotesque faces in the darkness. A crude variant of this design, enclosing the title in the ring, was blocked on the cloth spine of the book.

As has been mentioned earlier, Turner prepared more finished drawings than were used for the novel, some of them illustrating details in *Alciphron*. Six of them are now in the Bequest (see nos.50–8); another, entitled 'The Garden' in the Victoria and Albert Museum (W 1212) is of the Epicurean academy at Athens, showing an amorous couple, a winged statue of Mercury in the style of Canova, and in the distance the Acropolis. There are also a number of preliminary sketches, including a fine sky-study for 'The Nile' (TB CCLXXX 82). This can be identified by its architectural outline and by comparing it with the engraving – this is the sky that Rawlinson thought the interesting feature of the whole otherwise worthless series.[85] The frontispiece of *The Epicurean*, 'The Garden' (App.B, no.141), pictures the hero, Alciphron, on the left, meditating under a statue. Scenes of Epicurean luxury are played out in the foreground; the Acropolis forms a kind of apex to the design. Turner introduces a circular motif, independent of Moore's text, by having an Athenian lady hold up a ring or chaplet that appears again twice in the series. The final vignette, 'The Chaplet' (App.B, no.144), looks very much like an elaborate 'Egyptian' theatre set of the 1830s. These illustrations seem to have influenced his oil paintings of this period, for the motif of a ring appears again in 'Undine Giving the Ring to Massaniello, Fisherman of Naples', RA 1846 (B&J 424). More interestingly, 'Phryne Going to the Public Baths as Venus – Demosthenes Taunted by Aeschines', RA 1838 (B&J 373) is a restatement of the debate in Moore's novel between the pleasures of the senses and stoical renunciations; the Athenian cityscape resembles the garden in the Moore frontispiece.

The vignettes for *The Epicurean* were the last plates for a book to be published in Turner's lifetime. After his death a most lovely vignette was published in *Art and Song* of 1867. It was said to be among the last group of engravings supervised and touched by Turner himself, for a volume to be called 'Dr. Broadley's Poems', which turns out to have never been published.[86] This was 'Lake Nemi' (fig.25). Turner's imagination brooded over this lake, which he sketched and painted many times. He was no doubt stimulated by Byron's lines in *Childe Harold*:

Lo, Nemi, navelled in the woody hills
So far, that the uprooting wind which tears
The oak from its foundation, and which spills
The ocean o'er its boundary, and bears
Its foams against the skies, reluctant spares
The oval mirror of thy glassy lake;
And, calm as cherished hate, its surface wears
A deep cold settled aspect nought can shake,
All coiled into itself and round, as sleeps the snake.[87]

This seems an ideal image in conclusion of his vignettes. It possesses the formal qualities of his designs for vignettes that other artists could never really match. This most poetic image, in Goodall's engraving, seems a quintessence of the form: the oval mirror of the lake reflects its steep volcanic sides. The eye is led by way of a ruined tower seen across the lake to the cloud which extends the hill on the left, and recoils in response to the repoussoir of the stone-pine on the right. As in the great watercolour of 'Lake Nemi' in the British Museum (W 1381), of which it is a summary in miniature, a woman cradles her child; the women protect their children, symbolising maternal Nature. On the ground lies a fallen entablature with egg and dart moulding, a quasi-iambic way of representing the union of male and female. The vignette seems a perfect union of song and art, a painted *poesia*, an elegiac restatement of Rogers's *Italy* and Byron's poems of European travel, and indeed (as an image worthy of Keats's 'Ode on a Grecian Urn') an elegiac restatement of the English Romantic movement.

[67]

Notes

All books published in London unless otherwise stated.
For abbreviated references, see Bibliography.

1 Introduction

1. Ruskin XIII, p.169.
2. Clayden 1889, II, p.5.
3. Rawlinson I, p.lviii.
4. *Designs by Mr. R. Bentley for Six Poems by Mr. Gray*, 1753; *Letters of Horace Walpole*, ed. P. Cunningham, 1857, II, p.257.
5. Pye 1845, p.56.
6. *Spectator*, 26 June 1712, new ed. 1822, vol.V, p.53. Andrew Wilton discusses the possible influence on Turner's vignettes, in shape and figures, of the painted cupolas of the Italian Baroque. See Wilton 1979, p.216, and also A. Wilton, *Turner and the Sublime*, exh. cat., Yale, Toronto and British Museum 1980, p.140.
7. Ruskin I, pp.236–7, 240.
8. For instance, 'Venice: The Rialto' (W 725) and Turner's copy, 'Lake Albano, after J.R. Cozens' (sold Sotheby's, 7 July 1983).
9. C.F. Bell, 'Turner and his Engravers', in *The Genius of J.M.W. Turner*, ed. C. Holmes, 1903, p.E xvi.
10. Or 'vortex'. See J. Rothenstein and M. Butlin, *Turner*, 1964, p.19.
11. *Views in Sussex*, p.32. See also p.26 for Reinagle's comment on 'Battle Abbey': 'The knowledge of geometrical connection and propriety of lines, angles, curvilinear forms and parallels of unequal proportions, with various scientific variations and contrasts of shape, the drawing affords, and at the same time offers one of the finest tests of Academic Professorship, to be referred to and quoted as a model of judicious and perfect composition'.
12. Speech at Fishmonger's Hall. Quoted in M. Darby, 'Owen Jones and the Eastern Ideal', unpublished Ph.D. thesis, University of Reading 1974, p.432.
13. *Recollections of Sir Francis Chantrey*, 1849, p.106.
14. 'Turner Prints', *Pall Mall Gazette*, vol.19, 1899, p.451.
15. 'John Pye and Chiaroscuro', *Spectator*, no.2382, 28 Feb. 1874, pp.268–9.
16. *Art Union*, vol.II, 15 July 1840, p.18.
17. B.Lib. Add Ms 46151 BB f.22v.; quoted Gage 1987, p.205.
18. A. Wilton, *Painting and Poetry: Turner's Verse Book and his Work of 1804–1812*, exh. cat., Tate Gallery 1990.

19. Quoted by J. Ziff, 'Turner and Poussin', *Burlington Magazine*, no.105, July 1967, p.319.
20. Quoted by J. Ziff, 'Turner on Poetry and Painting', *Studies in Romanticism*, III, Boston 1964, p.203.
21. Ruskin III, p.435.
22. For instance, 'Norham Castle' (W 1052) of 1822 for Fawkes.
23. J. Britton, *Fine Arts of the English School*, 1811, p.20. See also L. Gowing, review of *Turner and the Sublime*, *Times Literary Supplement*, 10 July 1981, p.781: 'The nature of Turner's use of poetry, the mingled dependence on it and ruthlessness with it, is worth study if the elusive, private man is to emerge.' Thus 'Oberwesel' (W 1380) employs a pun on 'Liebfraumilch' – the vinous Rhine, Byron's 'maternal Rhine' of Canto III of *Childe Harold*, is to her sleeping children as the mothers are to their suckled infants. See C. Redding, *A History and Description of Modern Wines*, 1833, pp.202, 208 on Rhine wines and liebfrauenmilch.
24. No.166. J. Knowles (ed.), *Life and Writings of Henry Fuseli*, 1831, p.127.
25. *Notes by Mr. Ruskin on his Collection of Drawings by the Late J.M.W. Turner*, 13th ed. 1878, p.149.
26. J. Landseer, *Lectures on the Art of Engraving*, 1807, p.167.
27. According to Constable; quoted Finberg 1961, p.348.
28. W. Friedlaender, *Poussin*, 1966, p.60.
29. No.398, 13 June 1835, p.446; no.423, 5 Dec. 1835, pp.902–3.
30. Goodall 1902, pp.4–5; to E. Goodall, Gage 1980, p.138.
31. W. Macdonald (ed.), *Letters of C. Lamb*, 1903, II, pp.180, 212.
32. Scott to Cadell, 22 March 1831. National Library of Scotland, Ms Acc 5131, f.49.
33. Thornbury I, p.409.
34. Moore IV, p.1670, 1 March 1835.
35. F.W. Faxon (ed.), *Literary Annuals and Gift Books*, 1973, p.25.
36. Clayden 1889, II, p.88.
37. A.J. Finberg, *Turner's Sketches and Drawings*, 1910, p.87.
38. Hamerton 1895, p.229.
39. L. Gowing, *Turner: Imagination and Reality*, exh. cat., Museum of Modern Art, New York and Tate Gallery, London 1966, p.27.
40. The size of the platemarks can be seen from their imprints: for Rogers, in Moxon's quarto ed. of 1838, 10½ x 5½ inches; for Campbell, in Moxon's portfolio of engravings, 11 x 6½ inches.
41. *Literary Gazette and Journal of the Belles Lettres*, no.710, 28 Aug. 1830, p.564.

42. Second series. Turner or Harvey has plagiarised the main features of the design of the gypsies with a windmill, p.177, which is reversed in Rogers's *Poems*, 1834, p.12.
43. Cadell's Diary of 1841; Turner's letter has not survived. Finley 1980, p.187.
44. W. Crane, *Of the Decorative Illustration of Books Old and New*, 2nd ed. 1901, p.146.
45. J. Landseer, *Lectures on the Art of Engraving*, 1807, p.192; 'Reminiscences of Samuel Rogers', *Quarterly Review*, no.334, 1888, p.509.
46. W. Maginn (ed.), *The Maclise Gallery*, 1873, p.16; H.G. Merriam, *Edward Moxon*, Columbia 1939, p.18; Clayden 1889, II, p.7.
47. C. Warren, *The Charles Whittinghams*, New York 1896, p.144.
48. See C. Powell, 'Turner's Illustrations to Poetry', *Turner Society News*, no.52, June 1989, pp.10–14.
49. The first of the two Birket Foster volumes is particularly derivative.
50. Vol.VII, frontispiece. See also the half-tone sepia and blue-grey design by R. Westall for *The Lay of the Last Minstrel*, Vol.VI, p.56v.
51. Beattie 1849, III, p.237.
52. John Murray ledger, 31 Dec. 1833.
53. W.G. Rawlinson, 'The Water-colours of J.M.W. Turner', *The Studio*, special number, Spring 1909, p.19.
54. Gage 1969, p.111.
55. Gage 1980, p.146. Even so, they were designed slightly larger than the engraved images.
56. Rawlinson I, p.li.
57. Gage 1980, p.62.
58. P.G. Hamerton, *The Graphic Arts*, 1882, pp.363–4.
59. F. Bullard, *Handbook to Exhibition of Line Engravings after Water-Color Drawings by J.M.W. Turner*, Harvard 1906, p.5.
60. *Arnold's Magazine of the Fine Arts*, N.S. III, April 1834, p.560.
61. See Pye 1845, p.210 and p.372n.
62. T.C. Hansard, p.5. Private collection.
63. Rawlinson I, p.xli.
64. Dyson 1984, p.137.
65. Note inside folder EL 127, V&A Print Room.
66. G. Cooke, *Exhibition of Engravings by Living Artists*, exh. cat., Cooke's Gallery, Soho Square, 1821, p.19.
67. *Evidence Relating to the Art of Engraving …*, Report to the Select Committee of the House of Commons, 15 July 1836, p.45.
68. For instance, W.R. Smith's engraving of 'Hannibal' inscribed to R. Brandard. Woolley Collection, City Museums and Art Gallery, Birmingham, P 73 81 (x).
69. To W.B. Cooke, 4 Dec. 1814, Gage 1980, p.55; Second Colour Lecture, B.Mus. Add

Ms 46151 Af, 16v; Pye, *Evidence Relating to the Art of Engraving …*, p.28.

70 Pye 1845, p.210n.

71 C.R. Leslie, *Autobiographical Recollections*, 1860, I, p.215.

72 Pye 1845, p.244n.

73 *Poetical Works of John Milton*, I, p.xxvi.

74 *Quarterly Review*, vol.3, no.222, April 1862, p.476. See also the letter to Ruskin from his father describing the state of the engravings and the other contents of Turner's house, Ruskin XIII, p.xxvi.

75 Gage 1980, p.151.

76 *Times*, 16 Oct. 1833. See Finley 1980, p.230.

77 A.E. Bray, *Life of Thomas Stothard*, 1851, p.37.

78 Thornbury 1862, II, pp.633–6.

79 *Quarterly Review*, vol.3, no.222, April 1862, pp.340–1.

80 J.T. Bunce, Introduction, *The Exhibition of Engravings by Birmingham Men*, exh. cat., RSA, Birmingham 1877, p.5.

81 *Art Journal*, 1854, p.338. see also Rawlinson I, p.xxxii.

82 For 'The Forum' (R 363) the monks' procession carries, in the sequence of proofs a) a stretcher; b) something indistinct; c) a coffin (P 75 81). A spire is added at a later stage among the rigging of the ships in 'Traitor's Gate' (R 383; P 289 75). Turner reverses the figures completely in 'Leaving Home' (R 376; P 268 75) and 'Captivity' (R 390; 321 75 D). The latter shows particularly interesting reworking.

83 Thornbury 1862, II, p.135.

84 Day II, 23 April 1873: nos.142–52; 154–8; 199–201; 393; 603; 650.

85 Thornbury 1862, I, p.408; II, p.117.

86 Thornbury 1862, I, p.406.

87 Goodall 1902, p.226.

88 Bunce 1877, p.5.

89 V&A Ms 86 FF 73 f.89.

90 Goodall 1902, p.57.

91 *Alaric Watts: Narrative of a Life*, 1884, I, p.254. The *Literary Souvenir* was first published in 1825, Ackermann's *Forget Me Not* in 1822.

92 Bunce 1877, p.6.

93 R 648; Graves papers, B.Mus. Add Mss 46, 410, 57b.

94 See entry in Redgrave 1878.

95 M.B. Huish, *The Seine and the Loire*, 1895, pp.x–xi.

96 Cadell papers, National Library of Scotland, Ms. 21041, 28r., 20 March 1832.

97 Gage 1980, p.87.

98 Bryan 1886, I, p.342.

99 Ruskin III, pp.412–4.

100 *Art Journal*, 1874, p.124.

101 Dyson 1984, p.216, n.2, misreads a letter in supposing they were partners.

102 Turner's letter to the print publisher, Arch, of ?1824, Gage 1980, p.94, asks him to tell Miller how much he admires his work; *cf.* Rawlinson I, p.54 and Ruskin V, p.157n.

103 Gage 1980, p.185.

104 See the Turneresque 'Falls of Corriemulzie' in

the Victoria and Albert Museum (E.59.1922).

105 Ruskin VII, p.149n.

106 Vol.30, 1 Nov. 1830, p.454.

107 To James Skene, April 1819, *Letters of Sir Walter Scott*, ed. H.J.C. Grierson, 1932–7, VII, p.381.

108 National Library of Scotland, Ms. 3917, f.142.

109 Grierson XI, p.486.

110 Moore V, p.1811.

111 *Letters of Charles Dickens*, ed. M. House *et al.*, Pilgrim Edition, Oxford 1965–93, I, p.81n.

112 Moore V, p.1833.

113 Moore V, p.1870; *Letters of Charles Dickens*, I, p.170n.

114 Moore V, pp.1901, 2253.

115 Clayden 1889, I, pp.84–6.

116 *A Catalogue of the Oil Paintings &c … at Farnley Hall, Otley, Yorkshire, A.D. 1850*, National Art Library, Victoria and Albert Museum.

117 Gage 1980, p.47.

118 Turner has also pictured Fitz James again in this series as huntsman with a bugle in 'Glen Artney'.

119 Ruskin XIII, p.xlix.

120 Engraver identified by Turner's letter to W.B. Cooke, Gage 1980, pp.76–7.

121 *Turner Studies*, vol.11, no.1, Summer 1991, p.57.

11 Rogers, Byron and the Annuals

1 C. Powell, 'Turner's Vignettes and the Making of Rogers' *Italy*', *Turner Studies*, vol.3, no.1, 1983, pp.2–13.

2 Goodall 1902, pp.4–5.

3 *Athenaeum*, no.147, 21 Aug. 1830, p.526.

4 Canto V, verse lxxxix, Byron, *Life and Works*, XVI, p.92.

5 Clayden 1889, I, p.147.

6 A.E. Bray, *Life of Thomas Stothard*, 1851, p.104.

7 Ruskin XIII, p.514; W 1156, now at Vassar College Art Library, Poughkeepsie, USA.

8 'J.M.W. Turner's Illustrations to the Poets', unpublished Ph.D. thesis, UCLA 1966, e.g. p.65.

9 Ruskin XIII, p.445.

10 Titles given are those engraved on the proofs in the portfolios published at the time of the first edition.

11 *Landscape Annual*, 1830, p.77; Ruskin XIII, p.203.

12 I can find no authority for Ruskin's sentimental assertion (Ruskin XXX, p.353) that this is the funeral of a poor child.

13 Rogers's *Italy*, p.227.

14 Clayden 1889, II, p.3.

15 Bembridge, Isle of Wight, Mss. 54 I c. See Gage 1980, p.278.

16 Scott, *Miscellaneous Prose*, XI, p.126.

17 Identified as Flaxman by Cecilia Powell from the quarto edition of *Italy*, 1838; C. Powell, 'Turner's Vignettes and the Making of Rogers's *Italy*', *Turner Studies*, vol.3, no.1, Summer 1984, p.12, n.33.

18 See n.15.

19 Rogers's *Italy*, p.211.

20 Ruskin XXII, p.128.

21 As is suggested by the date of 1826 on Turner's watercolour of 'Aosta' (TB CCLXXX 145), written on the cross, before it was altered in the engraving to 1814.

22 Ruskin XIII, p.380.

23 Goodall 1902, p.5.

24 Clayden 1889, II, p.88.

25 *Athenaeum*, no.320. 14 Dec. 1833, p.841.

26 Rogers's *Poems*, p.6.

27 Ruskin XIII, p.380; Ruskin XXI, p.214.

28 Rogers to his sister Sarah. Clayden 1889, I, p.117.

29 S. Roberts, *Rogers and his Circle*, 1910, p.22.

30 Note to 'English Bards', *Life and Works*, VII, p.271.

31 W. Maginn (ed.), *The Maclise Gallery*, 1873, p.16.

32 But see the Note with an earlier Ms. reading, 'a bridge, a square', Roger's *Poems*, p.112.

33 Rogers's *Poems*, p.58.

34 Rogers's *Poems*, pp.65–8, 70.

35 See also Ruskin's fine didactic analysis, Ruskin VII, p.220, and on the emblematic plough, Ruskin XV, p.206.

36 The castle is possibly Embsay, repeated from 'The Boy of Egremond'. Turner's earlier sketch (TB CCLXXX 90) shows the figures more close. He subsequently worked in the symbolic motifs from the earlier vignettes.

37 See Goodall 1902, p.60.

38 Byron, *Life and Works*, II, p.276.

39 Clayden 1889, I, p.66; p.50.

40 *Athenaeum*, no.320, 14 Dec. 1833, p.841.

41 Rogers's *Poems*, p.228.

42 *Sir David Wilkie of Scotland*, exh. cat., N. Carolina, 1987, p.236.

43 'Life of Samuel Rogers', Rogers's *Poems*, edition of 1860, pp.xl–xli.

44 Ruskin XIX, p.151.

45 W. Irving, *History of the Life and Voyages of Christopher Columbus*, 1828, I, p.185. The engraving of Palos faces p.305, in W. Irving (ed.), *Voyages and Discoveries of the Companions of Columbus*, 1831.

46 Rawlinson I, p.246.

47 Rogers's *Poems*, p.232.

48 Ruskin V, p.137; Ruskin IV, p.299.

49 Rogers's *Poems*, p.285.

50 Rogers's *Poems*, p.251.

51 Goodall 1902, p.53, claims wrongly that Stothard supplied the long line of figures for his father's engraving of this vignette. The earlier version of this image is TB CCLXXX 99 (Finberg, 'A Vision'), which shows the crucifix, masts and palms.

52 Rogers's *Poems*, p.263.

53 Unpublished M.A. report, Courtauld Institute, University of London 1978, p.28; Gage 1989, p.204.

54 Rogers's *Poems*, p.242.

55 John Murray archive. Letter to George Crabbe (Jr), 25 Feb. 1833.

56 Prospectus to Crabbe's *Works*, 1833.

57 TB CCXXXIII f.55, 1828 (without the boats).

58 T. Taylor (ed.), *Life of B.R. Haydon*, 2nd ed. 1853, I, p.397.

59 Ruskin VII, p.191.

60 John Murray archive.

61 In the extra-illustrated copy of Thornbury in the British Library there is a letter from C.R. Cockerell, 27 Aug. 1833, sending a portfolio to Finden at Murray's request for *Illustrations of Sacred History*, VIII, p.135r.

62 W.M. Leake, *Outline of the Greek Revolution*, 1826, p.27.

63 Canto IV, verses xxvi–li; Canto III, verses xlvi–li, *Life and Works*, VIII, pp.203–13, 152–4.

64 *Arnold's Magazine of the Fine Arts*, vol.1, no.4, Aug. 1833, p.316.

65 Moore to Murray, 7 Oct. 1831, John Murray archive.

66 Moore had written on 23 Sept. suggesting an image of Byron in the Campo Santo.

67 Two undated letters, John Murray archive.

68 *Life and Works*, VI, pp.324, 259.

69 Canto II, verse lxxxvi. *Life and Works*, VIII, p.105.

70 Brown 1992, p.107.

71 W. Wilkins, *Atheniensia, or Remarks on the Topography and Buildings of Athens* (pub. Murray), 1816, p.49.

72 J. Stuart, *Antiquities of Athens* 1795, III, p.134, pl.15.

73 See the descriptions in 'The Corsair' and 'The Curse of Minerva', and also J.C. Hobhouse, *A Journey through Albania &c.*, 1809, p.307, which describes his sojourn of ten weeks with Byron in Athens and their daily contemplation of the monuments, calling the Temple of Theseus 'the most perfect edifice in the world'.

74 *Life and Works*, VI, p.219.

75 See also letter to Moore, *Life and Works*, V, p.150: 'Pope is a Greek temple, with a Gothic cathedral on one hand, and a Turkish mosque and all sorts of fantastic pagodas and conventicles about him. You may call Shakespeare and Milton pyramids, if you please, but I prefer the Temple of Theseus or the Parthenon to a mountain of burnt brickwork'.

76 J.C. Hobhouse, *Historical Illustrations of the Fourth Canto of Childe Harold*, 1818, pp.300 *et seq.*

77 2 Dec. 1832, p.154.

78 'Beppo', verse xi; 'Marino Faliero', Canto IV, verse i: *Life and Works*, XI, p.109; XIII, pp.151–3. See also vol.XI, p.182 on Venice, and on the approach of the Carnival, to Moore, vol.XI, p.314.

79 *Life and Works*, VIII, p.193.

80 Four times in *Childe Harold*, once in 'Beppo'; see also *Life and Works*, II, p.12.

81 John Murray archive.

82 E. Shanes, 'Tracking Down those Missing Turners', *Sunday Times Magazine*, 4 April 1982, p.35.

83 Canto IV, verse xxiv; *Life and Works*, XVI, p.277.

84 *Life and Works*, XVI, p.60.

85 *Life and Works*, XVI, p.325.

86 For 'the School of Homer', see *Life and Works*, VI, pp.73–4, 306. For 'the castellated Rhine', see *Don Juan*, Canto x, verses lxi–ii, *Life and Works*, XVI, p.325.

87 *Life and Works*, XIII, p.446.

88 *Mr Murray's Letter Book*, 1833, p.125. John Murray archive.

89 See also a letter from Edward Finden to Murray, 18 Nov. 1834, referring obliquely to an abandoned project.

90 W. Frost and H. Reeve, *A Complete Catalogue of the Paintings, Water-Colour Drawings and Prints in the Collection of the late Hugh Andrew Johnstone Munro, Esq. of Novar*, 1865, p.124, nos.121-2.

91 The *Art Journal*, 1876, p.106, was presumably responsible for the mistaken theory that this series was part of the *Picturesque Views in England and Wales* project of 1827–32. An obituary of James Baylis Allen (rather than the J.C. Allen who engraved them) mentions some of this series by name as part of the *England and Wales*. As Rawlinson (I, p.170) pointed out, they are 'totally unlike' that series in style, being on grey paper in bodycolour. Admittedly the size of the five 'landscape' views as engraved corresponds to the size of the plates for the *England and Wales* rather than for the smaller Byron *Landscape Illustrations*.

92 Finberg 1961, p.341.

93 *Athenaeum*, no.170, 29 Jan. 1831, p.76.

94 L. Ritchie, *Wanderings by the Loire*, 1833, p.106.

95 *Alaric Watts: A Narrative of his Life*, 1884, II, pp.312–3.

96 Ritchie 1833, pp.31, 158.

97 Scott's *Miscellaneous Prose*, IX, pp.210, 284.

98 Ruskin II, p.265.

99 *The Keepsake*, 1836, p.296.

100 Ibid., p.168.

101 *The Keepsake*, 1837, p.54. The three marine vignettes were reprinted in a publication which was called *The Book of the Sea: A Nautical Repository*; it has every appearance of a pirated book, without date or publisher. For this volume Heath presumably had also released the plate of 'The Light Towers of the Hève', which was used as the title-vignette.

III Scott, Milton, Campbell and Moore

1 The Cadell papers at the National Library of Scotland have been renumbered since Finley's book. For the list of subjects drawn up for Turner by Scott and Cadell, see Ms. 21023 f.106.

2 Cadell to Scott, Ms. 21002 f.264r.

3 Ms. 21013 f.101; ibid. f.129.

4 Ms. Acc. 5131, 15 July 1831.

5 Ms. 21041 f.25v., 15 March 1832; ibid., f.129, 24 March 1832.

6 Diary of 1836, Ms. 21026 f.1.

7 Cadell to Scott, Ms. 21002 f.264 r.

8 *Poetical Works*, VIII, p.20.

9 Ms. 3917 f.272v.

10 Ruskin V, p.333.

11 Finberg 1961, pp.76, 83–4.

12 *Athenaeum*, no.325, 18 Jan. 1834, p.44.

13 M. Huish, 'List of the Engraved Works', in *Notes by Mr. Ruskin on his Collection of Drawings by the Late J.M.W.Turner*, 13th. ed. 1878, p.172.

14 See n.12.

15 Thornbury I, pp.189–90.

16 *Poetical Works*, VII, p.40.

17 Finley 1980, pp.164–9.

18 *The Letters of Sir Walter Scott*, ed. H.J.C. Grierson, 1932–7, XI, p.486; *Poetical Works*, VII, p.137.

19 Fisher's *Landscape and Historical Illustrations*, ed. G.N. Wright, 1836–8, II, p.15.

20 *Poetical Works*, VII, p.80.

21 30 March 1831, Ms. 15980 f.55r. See also W. Partington (ed.), *The Private Letter-Books of Sir Walter Scott*, 1930, p.246.

22 Ms. 21002 f.264r.

23 *Poetical Works*, IV, p.117n. Rhymer's Glen was suggested to C.R. Leslie by Scott as a background to his portrait of him, but was not used (C.R. Leslie, *Autobiographical Recollections*, 1860, I, pp.89–90). Landseer used it for a portrait of Scott in 1833, which is now in New York.

24 Thomas Warton, quoted by Scott, *Poetical Works*, I, p.93.

25 Messrs. Moon, Boys and Graves' *Descriptive Catalogue*, no.69, quotes the first three stanzas of the ballad about the treacherous dinner invitation. See also Heath's *Picturesque Annual*, 1835, 'Scott and Scotland', p.50.

26 *Poetical Works*, I, p.178.

27 Thornbury I, p.190.

28 *Poetical Works*, III, p.346.

29 Ibid., XI, p.34.

30 Finley 1980, p.258.

31 That it is sunset is most likely, from the letter to James Lenox describing Turner's own experience in the cave. Gage 1980, p.209.

32 Gage 1969, p.112. This image was nearly lost

to the world. The first choice for 'Lord of the Isles' was Macleod's Maidens, near Dunvegan, at Skye, 'a steep pile of rocks rising from the sea in forms something resembling the human figure'. Lockhart, *Life of Scott*, 2nd ed., IV, p.306.

33 See *Miscellaneous Prose*, I, p.372.

34 Ibid., VI, pp.338 *et seq.*; Shakespeare's tomb, for Scott's essays on the drama, is placed opposite the frontispiece of Jerusalem, which illustrates the essays on chivalry.

35 Ibid., II, p.114.

36 W.F. Miller, *A Catalogue of Engravings by William Miller, H.R.S.A., 1818–71*, 1886, p.xxvi. He was paid 25 guineas for each plate.

37 The watercolour shows in place of the brazier a base in construction for an obelisk in memory of Scott. See J.R. Goldyne, *J.M.W. Turner: Works on Paper from American Collections*, exh. cat., Berkeley University Art Museum 1975, p.138.

38 Finley 1980, pp.242–2.

39 *Miscellaneous Prose*, XI, p.214–5; XIII, p.297.

40 Ibid., XV, p.388.

41 *Life and Works*, X, p.6.

42 Finley 1980, p.190.

43 Rawlinson I, p.lxxiii. Rawlinson had not seen the printed correction slip to Vol.VIII of *Miscellaneous Prose* which assigned the engraving of this plate to Horsburgh and not to Miller, who is actually named on it. The *Marlaise to Nantes* sketchbook, TB CCLVII 65a shows Turner's sketches of the details of the architecture.

44 *Miscellaneous Prose*, IX, p.398.

45 Ibid., X, p.225.

46 Ibid., V, p.221.

47 Ibid., XI, p.323; XVI, p.320.

48 Ibid., XI, p.311.

49 Ibid., XIII, p.117.

50 C. Powell, *Turner's Rivers of Europe: The Rhine, Meuse and Mosel*, exh. cat., Tate Gallery 1991, p.116.

51 *Miscellaneous Prose*, XV, p.204.

52 Turner's friend Eastlake was in one of these boats at the time, and Turner refers to Eastlake's painting of the subject, Gage 1980, p.62. See also a further reference in a letter by Turner, Henry Sotheran Ltd, booksellers' catalogue, *Piccadilly Notes*, no.27, 1977, p.19.

53 15 Aug. 1832, Ms. 21011 f.19r.

54 Finley 1980, pp.214–5.

55 Hamerton 1895, p.271.

56 *Poetical Works*, I, p.xxvi. Although it is not mentioned on the title-page, which reads 'with imaginative illustrations by J.M.W. Turner, Esq., R.A.', two vignettes of single figures in this edition are by Richard Westall, one of Satan and one of Euphrosyne.

57 Turner quotes in the Fourth Perspective Lecture at the Royal Academy, 1811, lines from 'L'Allegro' and the description of evening in *Paradise Lost*, IV, lines 598–600, which he used as epigraph to 'Harlech Castle', RA 1799 (B&J 9). See J. Ziff, *Studies in Romanticism*, Boston, III, 1964, pp.598–600.

58 See lines 44–8.

59 TB CCLXXX 87; Gage 1987, p.222.

60 Genesis, chap.I, v.18.

61 Goodall 1902, p.61.

62 For Turner's lecture mentioning Poussin's methods of allegorical allusion, see J. Ziff, 'Turner and Poussin', *Burlington Magazine*, no.105, July 1963, p.315.

63 Rawlinson I, p.314.

64 *Comus*, lines 883–8.

65 *Paradise Regained*, IV, lines 561–2.

66 'Lycidas', lines 50–1.

67 Thornbury II, Appendix, p.363, was responsible for the mistaken title of this for a separate Bunyan engraving, 'Faith of Perrin'; the reviewer in the *Quarterly*, no.222, April 1862, p.459, complaining of inaccuracies and ignorance of literature on the part of Thornbury, points out that 'Taith y Pererin' is the Welsh for 'Pilgrim's Progress', and that a Welsh edition of Bunyan came out with this same vignette-title, bearing the titles in Welsh and English. The National Library of Wales has a copy published by 'Peter Jackson, late Fisher, Son & Co.', n.d. (information from Richard H. Lewis). Fisher died in 1837. The watercolour remains untraced.

68 Beattie 1849, III, p.82.

69 Redding 1860, I, p.74.

70 Ibid., p.181.

71 Ibid., II, p.360. See also *Art Union*, Aug. 1839, p.123.

72 Beattie 1849, III, pp.194, 238.

73 Goodall 1902, p.226.

74 Redding 1860, II, p.318.

75 Redding 1860, I, p.298; Byron, *Life and Works*, V, p.70.

76 W. Hazlitt, *The Spirit of the Age*, Paris, 1825, p.136.

77 *Annual Register*, 1795, p.70.

78 See Campbell's *Poems*, p.273 (note to p.13, line 14). G.H. Bushnell, *Kosciuszko*, St Andrews 1943, p.12. The details of the events in Warsaw may be read in the *Annual Register*, 1795, pp.70–3.

79 Information from Cecilia Powell.

80 Redding 1860, I, p.56.

81 July 1827, Moore III, p.1041.

82 Moore I, p.257. In May 1819 Moore writes of a visit to Fawkes's exhibition of his watercolours, 'chiefly Turner's and very beautiful' (I, p.172). In Rome he admired Poussin's landscapes, but found 'nothing elevated or poetical in them, like those of Claude or Turner' (I, p.248).

83 Moore V, p.1811.

84 Moore V, pp.1866, 2076.

85 Rawlinson II, p.324.

86 R 638. The Marlay Collection at the Fitzwilliam Museum, Cambridge has a 'First finished proof taken expressly for B.G. Windus Esq.re with C.B. Broadley's Compts.'; on the back is the handwritten statement, 'The Poems never published'.

Charles Bayles Broadley was a Fellow in Law at Trinity College, Cambridge, and had 'a friendship of several years standing' with the Revd William Kingsley, then Tutor of Sidney Sussex College, who was in turn a friend of Turner and of Ruskin. See *Testimonials in Favour of the Rev. Dr. Broadley, of Trinity College*, privately published, Cambridge 1850, p.72; Ruskin XIII, p.335. R. Bell, preface to *Art and Song*, p.xi, says that these were the last plates supervised by Turner.

87 Canto IV, verse clxxiii, *Life and Works*, VIII, p.263.

Colour Plates

1 Henry Le Keux after J.M.W.
Turner **A Villa (Villa
Madama – Moonlight)** 1830
(App.B, no.14; not exhibited)

2 **St Maurice** *c*.1826–7
(cat.no.1)

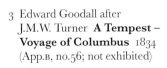

3 Edward Goodall after
J.M.W. Turner **A Tempest –
Voyage of Columbus** 1834
(App.ʙ, no.56; not exhibited)

4 **A Hurricane in the
Desert (The Simoom)**
*c.*1831–2 (cat.no.17)

5 Edward Goodall after
J.M.W. Turner **The Alps
(The Alps at Daybreak)** 1834
(App.B, no.48; not exhibited)

6 **The Alps (The
Alps at Daybreak)**
*c.*1831–2 (cat.no.20)

7 Robert Brandard after
J.M.W. Turner **Mustering
of the Warrior Angels**
1835 (cat.no.32)

8 **Mustering of the
Warrior Angels**
c.1834 (cat.no.31)

9 Edward Goodall after
J.M.W. Turner **The Fall
of the Rebel Angels** 1835
(App.ʙ, no.114; not exhibited)

10 **The Fall of the
Rebel Angels**
*c.*1834 (cat.no.33)

11 The 'Presentation'
Smailholm Tower and
Sandyknowe Farm 1832
(cat.no.42)

12 Study for 'Kosciusko'
*c.*1835–6 (cat.no.47)

13 Edward Goodall after
J.M.W. Turner **Kosciusko**
1837 (cat.no.49iii)

14 **Kosciusko** *c.*1835
(w 1273; not exhibited)
*National Galleries of
Scotland, Edinburgh*

15 **Dawn of Christianity –**
Flight into Egypt RA 1841
(cat.no.57)

16 John Ruskin
Glacier des Bois
*c.*1843 (cat.no.56)

Catalogue

Unless otherwise stated, all works are by J.M.W. Turner. Measurements are given in millimetres followed by inches, height before width. All engravings are on steel.

Works illustrated in colour are indicated with an asterisk.

Rogers's *Italy*, 1830

For an account of this series, see pp.35–9.

1 St Maurice *c.*1826–7*
Pencil and watercolour
165 × 220 (6½ × 8¹¹⁄₁₆)
TB CCLXXX 147
D27664
W 1154

Rogers describes the narrow pass and Alpine torrent. There is a preliminary study, TB CCLXXX I.

2 Hannibal Passing the Alps *c.*1827
Pencil and watercolour
140 × 205 (5½ × 8¹⁄₁₆)
TB CCLXXX 149
D27666
W 1160

Rogers's verses describe the tumult, din and the barbaric pomp of Hannibal's army, and also the shadowy and sublime mountains. The 'towered elephant' with upturned trunk is said to be about to tumble headlong into the chasm. There is a preliminary study, TB CCLXXX 6. Turner was much interested in Hannibal's crossing of the Alps, making a sketch of the subject as early as 1798 (TB XL f.67).

3 Lake of Como *c.*1827
Pencil and watercolour
160 × 202 (6⁵⁄₁₆ × 8)
TB CCLXXX 157
D27674
W 1161

Rogers describes the morning light and the noble amphitheatre of hills around the lake; he says that the harbour town to the right across the lake with its tower is like a scene from Gaspar Poussin, while the marble steps and the palace to the left are a setting for a scene from Veronese.

4 A Villa (Villa Madama – Moonlight) *c.*1827
Pencil, pen and black and brown ink, and watercolour
241 × 297 (9½ × 11¾)
TB CCLXXX 159
D27676
W 1165

The papal villa near Rome, partly designed by Raphael, was 'perhaps the most beautiful villa of its day', according to Vasari's *Lives of the Artists*. By Rogers's day it was mostly demolished; in the poem he devoutly hails the rising moon among the ruins, from an arched vestibule. Turner shows the same arcaded structure that he pictures here in the 'Claudian Harbour Scene' of 1828 (B&J 313). The engraving is titled simply 'A Villa' in the portfolio of engravings published by Cadell and Moxon in 1830.

5   Campagna of Rome *c.*1827
Pencil and watercolour, with some
gouache
70 × 185 (2³/₄ × 7¹/₄)
TB CCLXXX 161
D 27678
W 1168

Rogers contrasts the pastoral and warlike
setting of the antique Roman world, such as
his imagined sight of Aeneas and refulgent
Roman shields, with the present desolation
and the empty tombs like limbs of dismem-
bered giants. The scene was sketched in the
Vatican Fragments sketchbook of 1819–20
(TB CLXXX f.75a, mistaken by Finberg for
Lake Nemi) showing the distant aqueduct, a
monument and the line of hills. Cecilia Powell has identified the ruined tomb from
Turner's sketches in the *Smaller Roman Classical Studies* sketchbook, 1819 (TB CXC ff.1,
44, 47, 48). See C. Powell, *Turner in the South*
1987, p.135.

6   Study for 'Temples of Paestum'
*c.*1826–7
Pencil and watercolour
131 × 258 (5¹/₈ × 10¹/₈)
TB CCLXXX 92
D27609

For discussion of this and the two following
entries, see p.38. This distant view of the
temples was sketched by Turner in the
Naples, Paestum and Rome sketchbook of
1819–20 (TB CLXXXVI ff.19 verso, 29).
Turner used an approximation of this view
for the temples on the plain by the sea in the
far distance of 'Story of Apollo and
Daphne', RA 1837 (B&J 369).

7   Temples of Paestum *c.*1827
Pencil and watercolour, with some
gouache
240 × 305 (9⁷/₁₆ × 12)
TB CCLXXX 148
D 27665
W 1173

Cecilia Powell discusses the inaccuracy of
the proportions and of the number of
columns in this reconstruction of the temples by Turner, and points to his careful
studies of the ruins in the *Naples, Paestum and
Rome* sketchbook (TB CLXXXVI ff.19 verso,
19b, 29–31a, 42a–43a); C. Powell, *Turner in
the South*, p.204, n.71.

JOHN PYE (1782–1874) AFTER
J.M.W. TURNER

8   Temples of Paestum 1829
Line engraving, third published state
Image 60 × 86 (6⁵/₁₆ × 3³/₈);
sheet size 380 × 278 (14¹⁵/₁₆ × 10⁷/₈);
platemark 253 × 144 (9⁷/₈ × 5⁵/₈)
T04665
R 369
[Illustrated App.B, no.22]

**9   A Villa. Moon-Light (A Villa on
the Night of a Festa di Ballo)** *c.*1827
Pen and traces of pencil, watercolour
95 × 115 (3³/₄ × 4¹/₂)
TB CCLXXX 165
D 27682
W 1175

For Rogers's description of this villa with its
windows blazing for a scene of revelry, see
p.37. The first title above is that given in the
portfolio of engravings of 1830; the latter
title seems to be Rawlinson's invention, as
the phrase 'festa di ballo' does not appear in
the text.

Rogers's *Poems*, 1834

10   A Garden *c.*1831–2
Watercolour and gouache
121 × 133 (4³/₄ × 5³/₈)
TB CCLXXX 162
D 27679
W 1177

For ever as we run,
We cast a longer shadow in the sun.
   'Human Life', Rogers's *Poems*, p.187

For discussion of Turner's sources among
formal Italian gardens, and of the symbolism of this vignette, see pp.40–1.

WILLIAM MILLER (1796–1882) AFTER
J.M.W. TURNER

11 A Garden 1832
Line engraving, touched by
J.M.W. Turner
Image 84 × 84 (3³/₁₆ × 3³/₁₆);
sheet size 216 × 150 (8¹/₂ × 5⁵/₁₆);
cut within plate-mark
*The College Art Collections, University
College London (No.2362)*
R 373

Turner has written in the margin, 'Burnish
away the sharp lines of the water and fill in
with close work all the distance and soften
away the whole of the sky excepting the *sun*
and [?up] [...] cloud – the water much
lighter and only a little sharper at the top
thru' the cloud on the right hand in short all
the centre wants filling in in drypoint, keeping it free from hardness yet [?preserving] a
mass of light and brightness to the jet of
water where I have marked to help you and
to take away the too positive lines'. For
Turner's 'touching' of proofs, see pp.25–7.
Miller's account book records the payment
of 25 guineas for this plate in February 1832,
and adds, 'nearly finished' (W.F. Miller, *A
Catalogue of Engravings by William Miller,
H.R.S.A., 1818–71*, 1886, p.xxii).

12 Greenwich Hospital *c*.1831–2
Pencil and watercolour
105 × 152 (4¹/₄ × 5⁵/₁₆)
TB CCLXXX 176
D27693
W 1181

Noblest structures imaged in the wave!
A nation's grateful tribute to the brave.
Rogers, 'The Pleasures of Memory',
Poems, p.33

Arnold's Magazine of the Fine Arts, vol.3, no.3,
Jan. 1834, p.275, in praising this image, said
of the pensioners, 'Every one must remember the *bring-em-nears* as they call their tele-
scopes, by the loan of which they realise a
few pence during the summer months'.

**13 Falls of Lodore (Study for
'Keswick Lake')** *c*.1831–2
Pencil and watercolour
135 × 145 (5⁶/₁₆ × 5⁶/₈)
TB CCLXXX 91
D27608

The forester in 'The Pleasures of Memory',
in the 'rude romantic clime' of Cumbria,
which Rogers says Salvator Rosa would
have relished, is described thus:

the rapt youth, recoiling from the
roar,
Gazes on the tumbling tide of dread
Lodore;
And thro' the rifted cliffs, that scaled
the sky,
Derwent's clear river charmed the
dazzled eye.
Poems, p.36

14 St Herbert's Chapel *c*.1831–2
Pencil and watercolour
105 × 120 (4¹/₈ × 4¹¹/₁₆)
TB CCLXXX 180
D27697
W 1183

Turner has placed a version of Eton College
Chapel on the island on Derwentwater in
response to Rogers's mention of the ruins;
he shows Rogers's imagined solitary fisherman who formerly would have heard the
chanted hymn and seen the tapered rite
(*Poems*, p.40).

15 An Old Manor-House *c*.1831–2
Pencil and watercolour
105 × 95 (4¹/₈ × 3³/₄)
TB CCLXXX 201
D27718
W 1184

This is the old house in 'Human Life' that
stands while children succeed their parents
through the cycle of weddings and funerals.
Rogers names it as Llewellyn-hall, but the
building here is more likely an invention of
Turner's. Ruskin claimed that the house
among trees in the *Smaller Fonthill* sketchbook of 1799–1802 (TB XLVIII f.6) marked

'red' (perhaps for its brick or terracotta) was the original, but I am not convinced. There is a preliminary sketch (TB CCLXXX 15) of a spire and a house of elaborate Tudor brickwork, resembling East Barsham Manor (information from John Newman). John Britton's series *Architectural Antiquities*, to which Turner contributed a plate in 1814, had carried views of East Barsham Manor in 1809. This was a publication in which both Rogers and Turner were the dedicatees of plates. The earlier design was presumably rejected by Rogers as too grandiose. The house in 'Summer Eve – The Rainbow' (App.B, no.121), the first vignette to Campbell's *Poetical Works*, has several strong similarities, and may be intended by Turner as an allusion to this vignette.

WILLIAM MILLER AFTER
J.M.W TURNER

16 An Old Manor-House 1832
Line engraving, touched by
J.M.W. Turner
Image 95 × 86 (3¾ × 3⅜);
sheet size 212 × 151 (8⁵⁄₁₆ × 6¹⁄₁₆);
cut within platemark
*The College Art Collections, University
College London (No.2366)*
R 380

Inscribed by Turner, at top right, 'Burnished into rays', and below, 'This pediment too dark and nearest the 3 to look rich of ornament the marking of this Wing all too strong more like the right Wing the centre [?to] kept light'. Miller recorded this engraving as 'nearly finished' in February 1832, and was paid 25 guineas for it (W.F. Miller, *A Catalogue of Engravings by William Miller, H.R.S.A., 1818–71*, 1886 p.xxii).

**17 A Hurricane in the Desert
(The Simoom)** *c.*1831–2*
Pencil and watercolour, with some pen
and black ink
127 × 127 (5 × 5)
TB CCLXXX 195
D 27712
W 1189

Rogers describes the wind as causing a hollow wave of burning sand. See also Byron's note to *The Giaour*: 'the blast of the desert, fatal to every living thing, and often alluded to in eastern poetry'. Byron quotes James 'Abyssinian' Bruce on the suffocation and the 'purple haze' caused, as shown by Turner (*Life and Works*, IX, p.159).

18 St Pierre's Cottage *c.*1831–2
Pencil and watercolour
235 × 303 (9¼ × 11⅞)
TB CCLXXX 183
D 27700
W 1192

Turner shows Jacqueline and her pet deer in front of her father's cottage, with a backdrop of the Piedmontese Alps as described by Rogers, 'with blush of sunset on their snows' (*Poems*, p.146).

19 Captivity *c.*1831–2
Pencil and watercolour, with some
gouache, pen and black ink
128 × 130 (5¹⁄₁₆ × 5⅛)
TB CCLXXX 187
D 27704
W 1194

This illustrates an eight-line poem by Rogers. At the proof stage Turner changed the position of the imprisoned woman at the window (see p.25). An earlier study places the woman in an interior, a cell with straw on the floor (TB CCLXXX 10).

20 The Alps (The Alps at Daybreak)
*c.*1831–2*
Watercolour
115 × 139 (4⁹⁄₁₆ × 5½)
TB CCLXXX 184
D 27701
W 1199

Wilton calls attention to the 'vortex of light' and the effect of the paper at the edges of the image, giving the impression of 'limitless and dazzling snow' (A. Wilton, *Turner Watercolours from the British Museum*, exh. cat., International Exhibition Foundation, Cleveland, Detroit and Philadelphia 1977, p.70).

21 Columbus Setting Sail *c.*1831–2
Pencil and watercolour, with some pen
and black ink
100 × 147 (3¹⁵/₁₆ × 5³/₄)
TB CCLXXX 189
D 27706
W 1203

For a commentary on the designs for 'The
Voyage of Columbus', see pp.41–4.

23 Land Discovered by Columbus
*c.*1831–2
Pencil and watercolour
198 × 297 (7³/₄ × 11¹¹/₁₆)
TB CCLXXX 190
D 27707
W 1205

**26 Study for 'A Tempest – Voyage of
Columbus'** *c.*1831–2
Pencil and watercolour
127 × 125 (5 × 4⁵/₁₆)
TB CCLXXX 100
D 27617

**24 Study for 'The Landing of
Columbus'** *c.*1831–2
Pencil and watercolour
108 × 143 (4¹/₄ × 5⁵/₈)
TB CCLXX 194
D 27711

**22 A Vision. Voyage of Columbus. C.II
(The Vision of Columbus)** *c.*1831–2
Pencil and watercolour, with
scratching-out
108 × 133 (7¹/₁₆ × 5¹/₄)
TB CCLXXX 197
D 27714
W 1204

Compare the two studies for this work, TB
CCLXXX 203 and 204.

27 A Tempest – Voyage of Columbus
*c.*1831–2*
Pencil and watercolour
125 × 110 (4⁷/₈ × 4⁵/₁₆)
TB CCLXXX 202
D 27719
W 1207

See the studies for this vignette in pencil in
the *Berwick* sketchbook of 1831 (TB CCLXV
ff.29 verso, 30).

25 The Landing of Columbus *c.*1831–2
Pencil and watercolour
80 × 130 (7¹/₁₆ × 5¹/₈)
TB CCLXXX 191
D 27708
W 1206

The Rivers of France, 1833–5

This series of title-vignettes to *Turner's Annual Tours* is described on pp.50–1.

28 Nantes *c.*1826–30
Watercolour and gouache; pen with black and brown ink, on blue paper, faded to grey
186 × 134 (7⁵/₁₆ × 5¹/₄)
Visitors of the Ashmolean Museum, Oxford
W 930

There is a slight sketch for this subject in the *Morlaise to Nantes* sketchbook of 1826–30 (TB CCXLVII f.61 verso), including the elaborate carved poop at the right. Miller was paid 30 guineas in August 1832 for the engraving he made (W.F. Miller, *A Catalogue of Engravings by William Miller, H.R.S.A., 1818–71*, 1886, p.xxii). This watercolour was given by John Ruskin to the University of Oxford in 1861.

29 Light Towers of the Hève *c.*1832
Watercolour and gouache, with some pen and brown ink, on blue paper, faded to grey
189 × 134 (7⁷/₁₆ × 5¹/₄)
TB CCLIX 136
D24701
W 951

A scale is inscribed at foot, presumably by the engraver, John Cousen. There are sketches in the *Seine and Paris* sketchbook of 1830 (TB CCLIV ff.87 verso and 88). Colour studies for this vignette are in the Bequest (TB CCLIX 1, 2, 80). There are also an alternative design (W 1001) and three possible studies (W 1002–4); see C. Hartley, *Turner Watercolours in the Whitworth Art Gallery*, Manchester 1984, p.54.

30 Château Gaillard, from the South *c.*1832
Watercolour and gouache with some pen and black ink, on blue paper
193 × 140 (7⁹/₁₆ × 5¹/₂)
TB CCLIX 127
D24692
W 971

Inscribed 'Ferry and Petit Andyle' (*sic*). The staffage of a line of fishermen with nets is quite common in Turner's designs, e.g. the 'Kilgarren Castle' of 1798 (W 243).

Milton's *Poetical Works*, 1835

This series is discussed on pp.60–2, where the Miltonic texts are restored to the images.

31 Mustering of the Warrior Angels
*c.*1834*
Watercolour and pencil, with pen and ink
118 × 105 (4⁵/₈ × 4¹/₈)
Preston Hall Museum, Stockton Borough Council
W 1264

An illustration to *Paradise Lost*, Book VI.

ROBERT BRANDARD (1805–1862) AFTER J.M.W. TURNER

32 Mustering of the Warrior Angels
1835*
Line engraving, engraver's proof
Image 95 × 83 (3³/₄ × 3¹/₄); trimmed outside platemark 216 × 154 (8¹/₂ × 6)
T06285
[Colour plate 7; also illustrated App.B, no.113]
R 598

A note in Turner's hand on a proof in the Mummery Collection at the Victoria and Albert Museum says, 'These proofs are about the thing, but I should like to have the plate for about five minutes before you begin' (EL 123).

33 The Fall of the Rebel Angels
*c.*1834*
Pencil and watercolour, with pen and
red ink
123 × 94 (4¹³/₁₆ × 3¹¹/₁₆)
W 1265
Private Collection

An illustration to *Paradise Lost*, Book I.

**34 Sketch for 'The Temptation on the
Mountain'** *c.*1834
Pencil and watercolour
152 × 133 (6 × 5¹/₄)
TB CCLXXX 97
D 27614

An illustration to *Paradise Regained*, Book III.
No quotation was given in the Index of Illustrations in Macrone's edition, but see
lines 265 *et seq.*

JOHN COUSEN (1804–1880) AFTER
J.M.W. TURNER

35 The Temptation on the Mountain
1835
Line engraving, first published state
Image 102 × 83 (4 × 3¹/₄);
sheet size 216 × 153 (8¹/₂ × 6¹/₁₆);
platemark 434 × 297 (17¹/₁₆ × 11¹¹/₁₆)
T 06632
R 601
[Illustrated App.B, no.116]

36 The Temptation on the Pinnacle
*c.*1834
Pencil, watercolour and gouache
193 × 140 (7⁵/₈ × 5¹/₂)
T 06500
W 1268

An illustration to *Paradise Regained*, Book VI.

EDWARD GOODALL (1795–1870) AFTER
J.M.W. TURNER

**37 Ludlow Castle. Rising of the
Water-Nymphs** 1835
Line engraving, first published state
Image 110 × 82 (4⁵/₁₆ × 7³/₁₆);
sheet size 205 × 144 (8³/₁₆ × 5⁵/₈);
platemark 435 × 300 (17¹/₈ × 11¹³/₁₆)
T 06633
R 604
[Illustrated App.B, no.119]

An illustration to *Comus*.

Scott's *Poetical Works*, 1834 and *Miscellaneous Prose*, 1834–6

The vignettes for Scott are discussed on
pp.53–9.

**38 Three Poets in Three Different
Kingdoms Born** 1822
Watercolour
198 × 140 (7³/₄ × 5¹/₂)
Private Collection

This is the frontispiece for six designs for
illustrations of specific lines from Scott,
Byron and Moore, made for Walter Fawkes
of Farnley Hall in 1822. There were four illustrations for Scott, and one each for Byron
and Moore (W 1052–7). This shows Loch
Katrine in the background. For discussion
of the title and the scene with figures from
The Lady of the Lake, see p.32.

39 Edinburgh from Leith Harbour

c.1825
Pencil on grey wash
206 × 157 (8¹⁄₈ × 6)
TB CLXVIII B
D 13749
W 1063

The title-vignette for Vol.II of Scott's *Provincial Antiquities*, 1826. For discussion of Turner's emblem, see p.33.

40 Lochmaben Castle *c*.1832

Watercolour
200 × 148 (7⁷⁄₈ × 5⁷⁄₈)
Private Collection
W 1075

The title-page to *Poetical Works*, Vol.III, 'Minstrelsy of the Scottish Border'. Lochmaben Castle was a royal castle and seat of Robert the Bruce. Outside the cartouche Turner has drawn an illustration of 'Clerk Saunders', pp.175–83, showing Margaret at his grave and the murderous brother with a dirk. On Lochmaben Castle, see *Poetical Works*, Vol.I, p.422.

41 Bemerside Tower *c*.1832
Watercolour and pencil
146 × 114 (5³⁄₄ × 4¹⁄₂)
Pen Ithon Estate Ltd
W 1079

The title-vignette to Vol.V of *Poetical Works*, an edition by Scott of the 'Sir Tristrem' of the thirteenth-century Thomas the Rhymer. Sketches showing the Spanish chestnut, Sir Walter Scott's coach and the details of the sundial are in the *Abbotsford* sketchbook of 1831 (TB CCLXVII ff.82 verso, 83). For discussion of Turner's visit to Bemerside with Scott and the publisher Cadell, and their reception by Miss Mary Haig (all four are shown in the vignette, including Turner sketching under the chestnut) and of Turner's symbolism here, see p.42.

42 The 'Presentation' Smailholm Tower and Sandyknowe Farm

1832*
Watercolour
191 × 140 (7¹⁄₂ × 5¹⁄₂)
Private Collection

Turner's sketches made in the company of Scott are in the *Abbotsford* sketchbook of 1831 (TB CCLXVII ff.84 verso, 85, 85 verso, 86). Turner made this vignette as a souvenir of the excursion, which was Scott's last visit to the farmhouse in which he had been brought up, next to the tower; it shows Scott, Cadell and Turner in the coach. He sent it to the ailing Scott at Naples in March 1832. Scott wrote on 6 March to Mrs Scott of Harden, his kinswoman who owned the farm and castle, 'I have got an *esquisse* of Old Smailholme Tower from the pencil of Mr Turner' (*Letters of Sir Walter Scott*, ed. H.J.C. Grierson, 1932–7, XII, p.44). Scott recalls his early days there and 'the old castle standing in a wild patch of crags and morass to which he made an annual pilgrimage' (ibid., IX, p.370).

JOHN HORSBURGH (1791–1869) AFTER
J.M.W. TURNER

43 Mayburgh 1833
Line engraving, first published state
Image 87 × 92 (3³⁄₄ × 3⁵⁄₈);
sheet size 435 × 297 (17¹⁄₈ × 11⁵⁄₈);
platemark 208 × 150 (8¹⁄₈ × 5⁷⁄₈)
T04959
R 514
[Illustrated App.B, no.86]

This site, with its single standing stone, twenty feet high, and its circular bank of loose stones, was sketched by Turner on his journey north, in the *Minstrelsy of the Scottish Border* sketchbook (TB CCLXVI ff.26 verso, 27, 28, 29). His sketches from different points of the compass, marked W, N and E, show the stone, and he has paced out and marked his sketch from the foreground to the stone, '50 paces'. This was the title-vignette to Vol.IX of the *Poetical Works*, 'The Bridal of Triermain'.

EDWARD GOODALL AFTER
J.M.W. TURNER

44 Fingal's Cave, Staffa 1834
Line engraving, first published state
Image 122 × 83 (4¹³⁄₁₆ × 3¹⁄₄);
sheet size 436 × 300 (17¹³⁄₁₆ × 3¹⁄₄);
platemark 210 × 150 (8¹⁄₄ × 5⁷⁄₈)
T04958
R 512
[Illustrated App.B, no.85]

Title-vignette to Vol.X of *Poetical Works*, 'The Lord of the Isles'. See the *Staffa* sketchbook of 1831 (TB CCLXXIII ff.28–9v.), and the entries on Staffa in A. Lyles, *Turner: The Fifth Decade*, exh. cat., Tate Gallery 1992, pp.45–7.

WILLIAM MILLER AFTER J.M.W.
TURNER

45 Rhymer's Glen, Abbotsford 1835
Line engraving, first published state
Image 122 × 82 (4¹³/₁₆ × 3³/₁₆);
sheet size 435 × 300 (17⅛ × 11¹³/₁₆);
platemark 208 × 150 (8⅛ × 5⅞)
T04749
R 542
[Illustrated App.B, no.103]

Title-vignette to Vol.xxi of *Miscellaneous
Prose*, 'Periodical Criticism'. Turner's
sketches are in the *Edinburgh* sketchbook
(TB CCLXVII ff.49, 50 verso). This scene
was originally intended for the *Poetical Works*.
This glen on Scott's estate was his favourite
seat; the empty bench with the writer's open
book and his stick allude to the death of
Scott, on 21 September 1832. Miller records
completing the plate and the payment of
25 guineas in June 1835 (W.F. Miller, *A Catalogue of Engravings by William Miller, H.R.S.A.,
1818–71*, 1886, p.xxiii).

Campbell's *Poetical Works*, 1837

For a commentary on these vignettes, see
pp.62–5.

EDWARD GOODALL AFTER
J.M.W. TURNER

46 Camp Hill, Hastings c.1836
Line engraving, engraver's proof
touched by J.M.W. Turner
Image 80 × 73 (3⅛ × 2⅞);
sheet size 436 × 301 (17¹³/₁₆ × 11¹³/₁₆);
platemark 294 × 153 (11⁹/₁₆ × 6)
T04781
R 629
[Illustrated App.B, no.137]

Inscribed by Turner, 'More pointed rays,
starlike'; 'Little figures | army marching
up'; 'Ground Shadows too many | Shields
the strongest'.

47 Study for 'Kosciusko' c.1835–6*
Watercolour
162 × 201 (6⅜ × 7¹⁵/₁₆)
TB CCLXXX 49
D27566

See discussion of this and other studies for
'Kosciusko' on p.22.

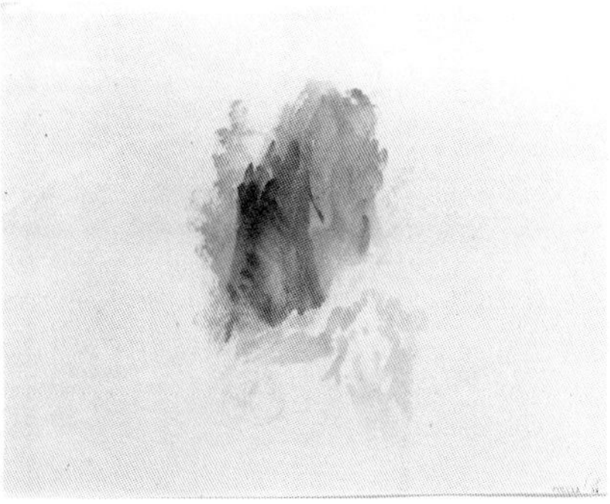

48 Study for 'O'Connor's Child'
c.1835–6
Watercolour
129 × 90 (5¹/₁₆ × 3⁹/₁₆)
TB CCLXXX 58
D27575

See discussion of this study on p.22.

49 Eight Pages from Campbell's
Poetical Works
London 1837
Line engravings by Edward Goodall
and Robert Wallis (1794–1878) after
J.M.W. Turner from the first edition,
with letter-press
Sheet size 198 × 134 (7¾ × 5³/₁₆)
i) Page 1, 'Summer Eve – The
Rainbow' (Goodall), image 84 × 84
(3³/₁₆ × 3³/₁₆) (R 613)
[Illustrated App.B, no.121]
ii) Page 3, 'The Andes Coast' (Goodall),
image 78 × 73 (3¹/₁₆ × 2⅞) (R 614)
[Illustrated App.B, no.122]
iii) Page 14,'Kosciusko'* (Goodall),
image 85 × 83 (3⅜ × 3¼) (R 615)
[Colour plate 13; also illustrated
App.B, no.123]
iv) Page 66, 'O'Connor's Child'
(Goodall), image 92 × 72 (3⅝ × 2¹³/₁₆)
(R 618)
[Illustrated App.B, no.126]
v) Page 77, 'Lochiel's Warning'
(Goodall), image 75 × 69 (3 × 2¾)
(R 619)
[Illustrated App.B, no.127]
vi) Page 87, 'Hohenlinden' (Wallis),
image 103 × 73 (4 × 2⅞) (R 621)
[Illustrated App.B, no.129]
vii) Page 104, 'The Last Man'
(Goodall), image 83 × 66 (3¼ × 2⅝)
(R 624)
[Illustrated App.B, no.132]
viii) Page 237, 'The Death-Boat of
Heligoland' (Goodall), image 74 × 68
(2⅞ × 2⅝) (R 630)
[Illustrated App.B, no.138]
Dr Jan Piggott

Turner seems to have followed many important features and details in the design for
'The Last Man' from that of his friend
George Jones RA, who illustrated the same
poem, engraved by Wallis and published
with Campbell's text, in *The Amulet* for 1828.

Moore's *The Epicurean*, 1839

Only one of the watercolours made for the engraved images appears to have survived. Moore says in his introduction to *The Epicurean* that it was Macrone's suggestion to have Turner make the designs. The following designs were commissioned by Macrone for an elaborately illustrated edition of *Alciphron* by Moore, which was an earlier version in poetry of *The Epicurean*. This edition was never published. *Alciphron* was, however, published both together with *The Epicurean* and separately, in the same year as *The Epicurean*; in the separate edition it appeared with three of the four engravings that accompanied *The Epicurean*. See pp.65–7 for a discussion of the commission and the images.

50 Memphis (The Kingdoms of the Earth) *c*.1837
Pencil and watercolour
118 × 79 (4⅝ × 3⅛)
TB CCLXXX 134
D27651

This corresponds to Moore's description of the city at the great festival of the Moon (*The Epicurean*, p.30; *Alciphron*, pp.12–13).

51 Spirits of the Sunset *c*.1837
Pencil and watercolour
102 × 75 (4 × 2¹⁵⁄₁₆)
TB CCLXXX 133
D27650

Moore's heroine Alethe dies from a poisoned coral chaplet. This appears to be a sketch for the figures, most likely representing Christian martyrs, used for the minute frieze of figures in the sky glimpsed through the upper window at the rear of the temple in 'The Chaplet' (no.71). However, see the description of 'the spirits of young and old', *The Epicurean*, p.60.

52 Alciphron and the Spectre *c*.1837
Pencil and watercolour
95 × 95 (3¾ × 3¾)
TB CCLXXX 130
D27647

The spectre advances, taper in hand, and invites the Epicurean to visit Egypt, where he will be enlightened (*The Epicurean*, pp.10–11; *Alciphron*, pp.6–7).

53 Alciphron's Swoon *c*.1837
Pencil and watercolour
100 × 75 (3¹⁵⁄₁₆ × 2¹⁵⁄₁₆)
TB CCLXXX 128
D27645

On his arrival in Egypt, Alciphron swoons (*The Epicurean*, p.45).

An Unidentified Publication on Deep-Sea Fishing

54 Cod on the Beach *c*.1835
Pencil, watercolour and gouache
202 × 153 (8 × 6)
TB CCLXXX 4
D27521

See Gage 1987, p.231. There are three other vignettes probably connected with this project, similar in theme, palette and general treatment (TB CCCLXXX 3; TB CLXIII 342–3). They were grouped by Ruskin with a note, 'Parcel containing 4 finished vignettes of fish for Mr Bicknell' (i.e. Elhanan Bicknell, Turner's patron who owned a whaling fleet). By the prominence of types of fish in the foreground they suggest chapter-headings on mackerel, lobster and plaice.

JOHN RUSKIN (1819–1900)

Vignettes for
Friendship's Offering, 1843–4

As is well known, Ruskin in *Praeterita* says that the gift to him at the age of thirteen of a copy of the illustrated edition of Rogers's *Italy* was responsible for 'the entire direction of my life's energies' (Ruskin XXXV, p.29). These two vignettes were 'worked up in exaggerated imitation of Turner's more extravagant compositions', in what W.G. Collingwood called his period of 'morbid Turnerism' (*Ruskin*, 1893, II, p.xli). They were published in an Annual which had once, in 1830, contained an engraving after Turner, 'Vesuvius in Eruption' (R 339).

JOHN RUSKIN

55 Coast of Genoa *c.*1842–3
Watercolour
190 × 156 (7½ × 6¼)
Cook and Wedderburn, no.773
Ruskin Galleries, Bembridge School, Isle of Wight (Bem. 1293)

This shows the Château de Cornolet near Mentone, with Cap St-Martin and Monaco. It was engraved by Turner's engraver, J.C. Armytage, for *Friendship's Offering*, 1843, to illustrate 'The Battle of Montenotte', a poem by Ruskin. (See no.59).

JOHN RUSKIN

56 Glacier des Bois *c.*1843*
Watercolour
204 × 132 (8 × 5¼)
Inscribed 'Le Glacier Des Bois'; signed with initials
Cook and Wedderburn, no.433
Education Trust Ltd, Brantwood, Coniston, Cumbria (Brant. 893)

This was engraved by J.C. Armytage for *Friendship's Offering* in 1844, to accompany Ruskin's undergraduate poem, 'A Walk in Chamouni', with its description of the source of the Arveron.

Miscellaneous

57 Dawn of Christianity – Flight into Egypt RA 1841*
Oil on canvas
Circular, diameter 785 (31 × 31)
Ulster Museum, Belfast
B&J 394

There is a series of rough monochrome studies for this painting in the Tate Gallery (N05508), in grey paint on a spoiled canvas.

It was first exhibited at the Royal Academy in 1841, where its title was accompanied in the catalogue by the epigraph '"That Star has risen", Rev. T. Gisborne's Walks in a Forest'. This quotation comes from line 39 of 'Walk the First. Spring' (T. Gisborne, *Walks in a Forest*, 7th ed. 1808, p.5). The Revd Thomas Gisborne's subject is vernal renewal, the 'lesson in the teeming soil, the freshening meadow and the bursting wood'. Christ, he says,

> to bewilder'd man
> Bade Spring, with annual admonition,
> hold
> Her emblematical taper.
> (lines 32–4)

There is no reference in the text to the Flight into Egypt, but Turner's crimson dawn of Christianity is suggested there:

> Till the dawn crimson'd, and the
> impatient East,
> Shouting for joy, the Day-star's advent
> hail'd.
> (lines 37–8)

Gisborne mentions Satan's defeat; Turner introduces a duality into the picture by symbolically figuring darkness, death and evil in the picture by representing Satan as the serpent, in a shape and position that mark it as a quotation from Poussin's 'Deluge' (see p.61). Here the serpent directly opposes the Christ-child. The painting shows the influence of Turner's illustrations for Milton and for Moore's *The Epicurean*, in particular the placing of the snake in the same position as in the vignette 'The Temptation on the Mountain' (nos.34–5). 'Walk the First' ends with the poet hailing 'the dawn of evangelic Day'.

58 *The Keepsake*
London 1836
Open at 'The Destruction of both Houses of Parliament by Fire, Oct. 16, 1834' 1835
Line engraving by James Tibbetts Willmore (1800–1863) after J.M.W. Turner
Image 115 × 89 (4½ × 3½)
Dr Jan Piggott

See p.51, and K. Solander, *Dreadful Fire, the Burning of the Houses of Parliament*, Cleveland Museum of Art, Ohio 1984.

59 *Friendship's Offering*
London 1842
Open at 'Glacier des Bois'
Line engraving by J.C. Armytage
(1820–1892) after John Ruskin
Image 118 × 103 (4⅝ × 4)
Dr Jan Piggott

EDWARD GOODALL AFTER
J.M.W. TURNER

60 Title-vignette to Bunyan's
Pilgrim's Progress, 1836
Line engraving
Image 159 × 102 (6¼ × 4)
Proof before title, with Turner Sale
stamp
Dr Jan Piggott

61 Rogers's *Poems*
London 1827
Open at pp.206–7, showing marginal
sketches in pencil by J.M.W. Turner
187 × 255 (7⅜ × 10 1/16)
TB CCCLXVI 206, 207
D36330

This shows Turner's rough sketch for 'The
Alps (The Alps at Daybreak)'.

62 Rogers's *Poems*
London 1834
Open at p.192: 'The Alps (The Alps at
Daybreak)'
Line engraving by Edward Goodall
after J.M.W. Turner
198 × 260 (7¾ × 10¼)
Tate Gallery Library

63 Letters of J.M.W. Turner and
Samuel Rogers
Tate Gallery Archive
TGA 7219.11 (Turner to Rogers);
TGA 7219.12 (Rogers to Turner)

To Rogers from Turner (dated by Gage
1980, p.189 as [?25 Nov 1842]):

'47 Queen Anne Street West
Friday night

Dear Sir
I will with great pleasure be with you on
Sunday night.
Yours truly
J.M.W. Turner

S. Rogers Esq.re
St James's Place'

To Turner from Rogers (dated by Gage
1980, p.171 as [?1838], but 30 December
also fell on a Sunday in 1827 and 1832):

'Pray dine with me tomorrow, if you can,
at 6 o'clock.
Yours very truly
S. Rogers

St James's Place
Sunday 30th december'

64 Scott's Miscellaneous Prose
Edinburgh 1834–6
Ten volumes, open at frontispieces and
title-vignettes, line engravings by
William Miller, John Horsburgh and
Edward Goodall after J.M.W. Turner,
illustrating the *Life of Napoleon*, and
Paul's Letters to his Kinsfolk
Vol.v: 'Brussels. Distant View' (Miller),
image 82 × 140 (3¼ × 5½) (R 519);
'Hougoumont' (Miller), image 100 × 88
(3 15/16 × 3 7/16) (R 520)
Vol.VIII: 'Hôtel de Ville, Paris'
(Horsburgh), image 107 × 86
(4¼ × 3⅜) (R 525) (mistakenly
attributed on plate to Miller; Cadell's
cancel slip reads: 'The name of
WILLIAM MILLER is adhibited to the
Vignette to this Volume, in place of
J. HORSBURGH').
Vol.IX: 'Brienne' (Miller), image
82 × 145 (3¼ × 5⅝) (R 527);
'Napoleon's Logement, Quai Conti'
(Horsburgh), image 119 × 70
(4⅝ × 2¾) (R 526)
Vol.x: 'Piacenza' (Miller), image
82 × 144 (3¼ × 5⅝) (R 529);
'Venice', (Miller), image
103 × 85 (4 × 3⅜) (R 528)
Vol.XI: 'Verona' (Miller), image
82 × 145 (3¼ × 5¾);'Vincennes'
(Miller), image 78 × 82 (3 1/16 × 3¼)
(R 531)
Vol.XII: 'St Cloud' (Miller), image
82 × 131 (3⅛ × 5⅛) (R 532); 'Mayence'
(Miller), image 77 × 85 (3 1/16 × 3⅜)
(R 533)
Vol.XIII: 'Milan' (Horsburgh), image
82 × 140 (3¼ × 5½) (R 534); 'The
Simplon' (Miller), image 113 × 79
(4½ × 3⅛) (R 535)
Vol.XIV: 'Paris from Père Lachaise'
(Miller), image 78 × 118 (3⅛ × 4⅝)
(R 536); 'Malmaison' (Miller), image
115 × 83 (4½ × 3¼) (R 537)

Vol.XV: 'Fontainbleau' (Miller), image
97 × 76 (3⅞ × 3) (R 538)
Vol.XVI: 'Field of Waterloo, from the
Picton Tree' (Miller), image 82 × 144
(3¼ × 5⅝) (R 539); 'The Bellerophon,
Plymouth Sound' (Goodall), image
107 × 86 (4¼ × 3⅜) (R 540)
Dr Jan Piggott

For a discussion of the Napoleon series, see
pp.56–9.

Paris and Environs sketchbook

65 Vincennes 1832
Pencil
175 × 127 (6⅞ × 5)
TB CCLVII f.47
D24257

This shows the sketch for the upper part of
'Vincennes'. The small figure of Savary,
Napoleon's Chief of Police, is already shown
on the battlement, from which he witnessed
the execution of the Bourbon Duc d'Enghien. See pp.58–9.

JOHN HORSBURGH AFTER
J.M.W. TURNER

66 Napoleon's Logement, Quai Conti
*c.*1834
Line-engraved steel plate
210 × 150 (8¼ × 5 5/16)
St Bride Printing Library, London
R 526

Engraved for title-vignette of Scott's *Miscellaneous Prose*, Vol.IX, 1835.

WILLIAM MILLER AFTER
J.M.W. TURNER

67 Sandy Knowe, or Smailholm 1838
Line-engraved steel plate
208 × 143 (8 3/16 × 5⅝)
St Bride Printing Library, London
R 566

Engraved for the title-vignette of Vol.IV of
the second edition of Lockhart's *Life of Scott*
(2nd ed. 1839). Miller was paid 25 guineas in
December 1838 (W.F. Miller, *A Catalogue of
Engravings by William Miller, H.R.S.A, 1818–71*,
1886, p.xxiii).

JOHN HORSBURGH AFTER
J.M.W. TURNER

68 Ashestiel 1833
Line-engraved steel plate for title-vignette to Scott's *Poetical Works*, Vol.VII
191 × 126 (7½ × 4¹⁵⁄₁₆)
St Bride Printing Library, London
R 506

JOHN HORSBURGH AFTER
J.M.W. TURNER

69 Mayburgh 1833
Line-engraved steel plate for title-vignette to Scott's *Poetical Works*, Vol.XI
196 × 129 (7¹¹⁄₁₆ × 5¹⁄₁₆)
St Bride Printing Library, London
R 514

70 Byron's *Life and Works*
London 1832–3
Five volumes, open at frontispieces and title-vignettes, line engravings by Edward Finden (1791–1857) after J.M.W. Turner
Vol.VII: 'The Gate of Theseus. Athens', image 104 × 77 (4¹⁄₈ × 3) (R 416); 'The Plain of Troy', image 75 × 85 (2¾ × 3³⁄₈) (R 417)
Vol.VIII: 'Bacharach. On the Rhine', image 90 × 84 (3⁹⁄₁₆ × 3⁵⁄₁₆) (R 418); 'The Castle of St Angelo', image 68 × 86 (2¹¹⁄₁₆ × 3⁷⁄₁₆) (R 419)
Vol.XIV: 'Parnassus. And Castalian Spring', image 95 × 80 (3¾ × 3¹⁄₈) (R 424); 'The Field of Waterloo. From Hougoumont', image 53 × 95 (2¹⁄₈ × 3¾) (R 425)
Vol.XV: 'Scio. Fontana dé Melek Mehmet, Pasha', 85 × 80 (3³⁄₈ × 3³⁄₁₆) (R 426); 'Genoa', 60 × 100 (2⁵⁄₁₆ × 3⁷⁄₈) (R 427)
Vol.XVII: 'School of Homer. Scio', 81 × 87 (3³⁄₁₆ × 3¹⁄₈) (R 430); 'The Castellated Rhine', 73 × 97 (2⁷⁄₈ × 3⁷⁄₈) (R 431)
Dr Jan Piggott

71 Moore's *The Epicurean*
London 1839
Three copies, open at line engravings by Edward Goodall after J.M.W. Turner
i) Open at frontispiece: 'The Garden', image 99 × 86 (3⁷⁄₈ × 3³⁄₈) (R 634)
ii) Open at p.148: 'The Nile', image 105 × 87 (4¹⁄₈ × 3½) (R 636)
iii) Open at p.206: 'The Chaplet', image 107 × 82 (4¼ × 3¼) (R 637)
Dr Jan Piggott

72 Moore's *Alciphron, a Poem*
London 1839
Open at frontispiece: 'The Ring'
Line engraving by Edward Goodall after J.M.W. Turner
Image 105 × 84 (4¹⁄₈ × 3¼)
Dr Jan Piggott

Appendix A

TB CCLXXX: 'Studies for Vignettes – Chiefly Rogers'

Key

B   for Byron's *Life and Works*, 1832–4
TC for Campbell's *Poetical Works*, 1837
JM for Milton's *Poetical Works*, 1835
TM for Moore's *The Epicurean*, and *Alciphron*, 1839
R(I) for Rogers's *Italy*, 1830
R(P) for Rogers's *Poems*, 1834

The finished watercolours for the engravings in the two Rogers volumes are given in capitals. They carry the titles given by Rogers or Moxon which appear below the engraving in the two portfolios and in the quarto editions of 1838; other traditional titles follow in brackets.

1. Study for 'St Maurice' (TB CCLXXX 147). R(I)
2. Study of Piazza S. Marco, Venice. Campanile, Duomo, yellow canopy (?puppet booth). R(I)
3. Lobsters on the Beach. Finished design, unengraved
4. Cod on the Beach. Finished design, unengraved (cat.54)
5. Study for staffage of 'Hohenlinden' (W 1279; R 621). Horse, cannon, gore. TC
6. Study for 'Hannibal Passing the Alps' (TB CCLXXX 149). Mounted elephant, sworded figure, standards. R(I)
7. Ship, *cf.* 'The Andes Coast' (W 1272; R 614). TC
8. Study for 'Hannibal Passing the Alps' (TB CCLXXX 149). Mountain cleft; Alpine pass; outlandish military figures in pencil. R(I)
9. Study of a castle on a lake with mountainous sides. R(I)/R(P)
10. Study for 'Captivity' (TB CCLXXX 187). R(P)
11. Study for 'The Andes Coast' (W 1272; R 614) without ship. TC
12. Study for 'The Landing of Columbus' (TB CCLXXX 191). Boats with crosses, figures. R(P)
13. Study for 'Bay of Naples' (TB CCLXXX 143). R(I)
14. Leaning Towers of Bologna (Torre Asinelli and Torre Garisenda). Watermark 'T Edmonds 1825'. R(I)
15. Rejected study for 'An Old Manor-House' (TB CCLXXX 201). East Barsham Manor and ?Grantham spire. R(P)

16. Study for 'An Old Oak' (TB CCLXXX 174). Villagers, tent. R(P)
17. Study for 'A Garden' (TB CCLXXX 162). Three-columned temple; outline of old man to l.; palette and style of no.16. R(P)
18. ?Palos. Study for 'Columbus Setting Sail' (TB CCLXXX 189). Church on rock and town. R(P)
19. ?Palos. Study for 'Columbus Setting Sail' (TB CCLXXX 189). Tower and hill; masts to r. R(P)
20. Colour study for 'Corinth, from the Acropolis' (W 1224; R 420). Minaret, temple, columns. B
21. Two drawings: (i) inscr. 'Rats'. Raft and turreted building. ?Ratisbon (Regensburg) on the Danube; (ii) Bridge with many bays. Watermark '&S 1843'
22. Florence: Palazzo Vecchio and Loggia dei Lanzi. Basin of the Great Fountain with figures of Neptune and tritons, and water. *Cf. Rome and Florence* sketchbook (TB CXCI f.37). R(P)
23. Hill-town and ?Via Mala by moonlight. Watermark 'J. Whatman, 1839'
24. Inscr. 'Hadrian's Villa', but more likely Vesuvius and Bay of Naples. Verso, a villa. R(I)
25. (i) Capriccio: waterfall crossed by bridge in hill town. (ii) Continental city on a river; bridge of 8 or 10 bays. By palette a pair with no.23. Watermark 'J Whatman 1839'

Nos.26–38 are in a 'roll sketchbook' with covers of marbled paper, containing images mostly to do with the life of Napoleon; none is a vignette. Watermark on nos.32 and 38 'J. WHATMAN TURKEY MILL, 1825'.

26. River, fortifications on hill, bridge
27. Ehrenbreitstein. Inscr. 'The March of N – from Cob[lenz]'.
28. Storm over light-house; ?Dutch port from the sea, with wharf
29. Inscribed 'Adieu Fontainbleau'; (*cf.* W 1115; R 538)
30. ?Waterloo. Sentry. Inscr. 'The Rival's the Divine Hand of N' and 'N'
31. ?Pyre and sail-boat. Inscribed 'Form [...] the [...] in Dido'
32. View of Rhine downstream to Coblenz (left) and Ehrenbreitstein (right), with twin spires of St Castor's church, Coblenz, the

bridge of boats and a timber raft. Inscr., referring to [?'the second raft'], with 'N' and 'The Curse of Z' below.
33. Inscr. 'Sauve Qui Peut'. Column of red figures, some on horseback. See Scott's *Life of Napoleon, Miscellaneous Prose*, Vol.XV, p.157, and Vol.XVI, p.19
34. Alps with town. Illegible place names
35. Mounted figures on wet sand. Inscr. '[...] wet sand. N'. See Scott's *Life of Napoleon, Miscellaneous Prose*, Vol.X, p.349
36. View from hillside; bridge of boats with troops, looking north onto Ehrenbreitstein. Inscr. 'March of Napoleon on Coblenz'
37. Inscribed 'N and the Lady'. See *Life of Napoleon*, Scott's *Miscellaneous Prose*, Vol.XV, p.250
38. Sea-shore with goats and ?figures.
39. Sky, trees, figures. TC
40. Beach, storm, figures. TC
41. Boat in storm. Study for ?'Lord Ullin's Daughter' (W 1280; R 622). TC
42. Beach, headland, solitary figure. TC
43. Preparatory study: figures below trees. TC
44. Preparatory study: ?military figures. TC
45. Study for 'Kosciusko' (W 1273; R 615). TC
46. Boat in storm. TC
47. Trees and crowded figures. TC
48. Preparatory study: figure below tower. TC
49. Study for 'Kosciusko' (W 1273; R 615) (cat.47)
50. Preparatory study: figures. TC
51. Preparatory study: storm at sea. TC
52. Preparatory study: ?waterfall, 'Gertrude of Wyoming' (W 1284; R 626). TC
53. Preparatory study: figures. TC
54. Preparatory study: ?sky. TC
55. Ship for 'The Andes Coast' (W 1272; R 614). TC
56. Study for 'Kosciusko' (W 1273; R 615). Military figures; soldiers on towered bridge; isolated hero. TC
57. Female figure by hilly shore. TC
58. Study for 'O'Connor's Child' (W 1276; R 618). TC (cat.48)
59. Study for 'O'Connor's Child' (W 1276; R 618): sea, castle, kneeling female figure. TC
60. Figure in a garden. TC
61. Preparatory study: storm. TC
62. Figures at fence with dog; illustration to 'The Pleasures of Hope', Pt.I, lines 295–314, describing a homeless wretch

looking longingly at a cottage and its garden; derives closely from illustration by Edward Francis Burney (1760–1848) to Longman's 'new edition' of the poem, 1816, facing p.25. TC

63. Preparatory study: island in a storm. TC
64. Study for 'Lord Ullin's Daughter' (W 1280; R 622). TC
65. Stormy sky over a valley with river. Study for ?'Hohenlinden' (W 1279; R 621); compare no.61. TC
66. Figures on crest of cliff: study for ?'Lord Ullin's Daughter' (W 1280; R 622). (TB number printed wrong way up). TC
67. Preparatory study: ?conflagration. TC
68. Preparatory study: study for ?'The Last Man' (W 1282; R 624). TC
69. Preparatory study. TC
70. Study for ?waterfall, 'Gertrude of Wyoming' (W 1284; R 626). TC
71. Preparatory study: boat in waves. Study for ?'Lord Ullin's Daughter' (W 1280; R 622). TC
72. Preparatory study. TC
73. Storm and outline of ?La Haye Sainte. Study for ?'The Field of Waterloo' (W 1116; R 539), for Scott's *Life of Napoleon*.
74. Preparatory study: two seated figures. TC
75. Preparatory study: storm for ?'The Death-Boat of Heligoland' (W 1288; R 630). TC
76. Preparatory study: pencilled figures. TC
77. Pharos, in palette of TM designs. Watermark 'SE & Co 1837'.
78. Not a vignette. Watermark with nos.79, 83 and 85, together making one sheet, is 1841. Wilton (*Turner Watercolours*, 1987, p.112) suggests that this is a study for Satan rousing his legions, for Macrone's Milton, but the watermark is too late. In that the other figures are not on a burning lake but form an ellipse on the right, perhaps an early study for 'The Angel Standing in the Sun', RA 1846 (B&J 425)
79. Not a vignette. Preparatory study: ?light towers. Watermark 'J. Whatman 1841'
80. Figures in sky or on a wave: ?'Death-Boat of Heligoland' (W 1288; R 630) TC or ?'Ludlow Castle. Rising of the Water-Nymphs' (W 1270; R 604). JM
81. ?St Michael's Mount and sketch of Angel. Inscr. 'Vol 1' and 'In these fell regions by Wyvera caught' and other illeg. lines. Not for Macrone's Milton, as watermark is 'Whatman 1842'
82. Sky for 'The Nile' (W 1300; R 636). Watermark 'S E & Co 1837'. TM
83. Not a vignette. River or coastal subject. ?Light towers. Watermark 'J. Whatman 1841'. *Cf.* no.24
84. Sunset over a city. With nos.96 and 98, views of continental cities with a bridge from above, using similar palette and pencil work. See nos.21, 23 and 25 for similar palette and loose pencilling

85. Not a vignette. River subject. Watermark 'J Whatman 1841'
86. Sea and sun ?'O'Connor's Child' (W 1276; R 618). TC
87. Study for 'Galileo's Villa' (TB CCLXXX 163). Diagram of system of spheres; globe and telescope; house and vines. R(I)
88. Study for 'Tivoli' (TB CCLXXX 166). R(I)
89. Study for ?'Gertrude of Wyoming – The Valley' (W 1283; R 625). TC. [Formerly identified, by Finberg, as the first study for 'Tornaro' (TB CCLXXX 172)].
90. Study for 'Evening' ('Datur Hora Quieti') (TB CCLXXX 199). R(P)
91. Falls of Lodore, study for 'Keswick Lake' (TB CCLXXX 181). R(P) (cat.13)
92. Study for 'Temples of Paestum' (TB CCLXXX 148). R(I) (cat.6)
93. Study for 'Traitor's Gate, Tower of London' (TB CCLXXX 177). R(P)
94. Study for 'Greenwich Hospital' (TB CCLXXX 176). R(P)
95. The Ponte Vecchio, Florence. Unfinished design. R (I)
96. See no.84
97. Study for 'Temptation on the Mountain' (W 1267; R 601). JM (cat.34)
98. See no.84 (same pinkish paper). Watermark 'J. Whatman. Turkey Mill. 1832'
99. Study for 'The Landing of Columbus' (TB CCLXXX 191). R(P)
100. Study for 'A Tempest – Voyage of Columbus' (TB CCLXXX 202). R(P) (cat. no.26)
101. Town on a rock. Detail to l. of 'Amalfi' (TB CCLXXX 167). R(I)
102. Leaning tower, *cf.* no.14. R(I)
103. Study for 'The Forum' (TB CCLXXX 158). R(I)
104. Funeral procession for 'The Forum' (TB CCLXXX 158). R(I)
105. Study for ?'The Chapel of William Tell' (TB CCLXXX 155). R(I)
106. Lake with mountains and village. ?Geneva. R(I)
107. Market and piazza. R(I)
108. Study for 'Venice (The Rialto – Moonlight)' (TB CCLXXX 196). R(P)
109. Duplicated by Finberg as no.135
110. Inscr. by Turner '4 Vig for the East Coast'. Church on a quay. Blue paper
111. Holy Island. Blue paper
112. Sea fortifications, or ruined castle. ?Lowestoffe. Line of fishermen with nets, horse and cart, boats. Blue paper
113. Study for 'The Nile' (W 1300; R 636): sunset, meanders, distant architecture, boats with figures. TM
114. Study for 'The Ring' (W 1299; R 635): falling mid-air figure over river; outlines of ghouls and falling balustrade. *The Epicurean*, p.58. TM
115. Nymphs of the Nile. Bathing scene. See *Alciphron*, p.14. TM

116. Rock of Pharos and Harbour of Eunostus at Alexandria. *The Epicurean*, p.16. TM
117. Study for 'The Chaplet' (W 1301; R 637) Orcus, figures and flames, Egyptian idols. TM
118. Study for 'The Expulsion from Paradise' (W 1266; R 600). JM
119. The Spirits of the Orb. Lethean cup; dancing figures. *The Epicurean*, pp.76–7. TM
120. The Veiled Priestess of the Moon. *The Epicurean*, p.79. TM
121. Study for ?'Lord Ullin's Daughter' (W 1280; R 622). Figures on crest in pursuit; boat. TC; however, style of TM
122. Temple at ?Necropolis with rainbow. ?TM
123. Study for 'The Ring' (W 1299; R 635). TM
124. Study for descent of Alciphron into the well, *cf.* no.129. TM
125. Study for 'The Chaplet' (W 1301; R 637). ?Forum with High Priest of Memphis, tribunal and flames for martyrs. *The Epicurean*, pp.199–200, 205–6. TM
126. The Grotto of the Anchoret. *The Epicurean*, pp.164–7. TM
127. Study for 'The Chaplet' (W 1301; R 637). Figures, Anubis and martyrs. TM
128. Alciphron's Swoon. Finished design, un-engraved; *The Epicurean*, p.45. TM (cat.53)
129. Descent into the Well. *The Epicurean*, pp.50–1: 'massy iron gates' &c. TM
130. Alciphron and the Spectre. Finished design, unengraved. *The Epicurean*, pp.10–11. TM (cat.52)
131. Embarcation for the Festival of the Moon. Pyramids, boats. TM
132. Embarcation for the Festival of the Moon. Palms, boats, pencilled figures. *Cf.* no.115. TM
133. Spirits of the Sunset. TM (cat.51)
134. Memphis (The Kingdoms of the Earth). Many figures. TM (cat. no.50)
135. Inscribed 'Raff Villa' ?Madama. *Cf.* no.24 verso. R(I)
136. Pine trees. R(I)
137. Study for 'The Andes Coast' (W 1272; R 614). Compare no.11. TC
138. Study for 'The Chaplet' (W 1301; R 637). TM
139. Not a vignette. ?Medea. On back of envelope, with red rim of seal as sun. Franked 5 July 1824
140. ?Upper Rhine view. Raft in foreground (W 1285; R 627). TC
141. ?Pont Neuf, Paris. *cf. Rivers of France*
142. Claudian scene, with massed architecture in pencil. Church with campanile to left. ?Villa Madama. Compare *St Peter's* sketchbook (TB CLXXXVIII ff.13v., 14). Inscr. 'Br[...]'. R(I)
143. BAY OF NAPLES (W 1172; R 368). R(I) A preparatory study for this watercolour is TB CCLXXX 13.
144. PERUGIA (W 1170; R 366). R(I)
145. AOSTA (W 1158; R 354). R(I)
146. MARENGO (W 1157; R 353). R(I)

147. ST MAURICE (W 1154; R 350; cat.1). R(I)
A preparatory study for this watercolour is
TB CCLXXX 1.

148. TEMPLES OF PAESTUM (W 1173; R 369;
cat.7). R(I)
A preparatory study for this watercolour is
TB CCLXXX 92.

149. HANNIBAL PASSING THE ALPS (W 1160;
R 356; cat.2). R(I)
Preparatory studies for this watercolour
are TB CCLXXX 6, 8 and 151.

150. LAKE OF COMO, II (A FAREWELL)
(W 1176; R 372). R(I)

151. Study for 'Hannibal Passing the Alps'
(TB CCLXXX 149). R(I)

152. THE LAKE OF GENEVA (W 1152; R 348).
R(I)

153. THE HOSPICE. GREAT ST BERNARD
WITH THE LAKE (I) (W 1155; R 351). R(I)

154. MARTIGNY (W 1159; R 355). R(I)

155. THE CHAPEL OF WILLIAM TELL
(W 1153; R 349). R(I)
A preparatory study for this watercolour is
TB CCLXXX 105.

156. FLORENCE (W 1163; R 359). R(I)

157. LAKE OF COMO (I) (W 1161; R 357; cat.3).
R(I)

158. THE FORUM (W 1167; R 363). R(I)
Preparatory studies for this watercolour
are TB CCLXXX 103 and 104.

159. A VILLA (VILLA MADAMA –
MOONLIGHT) (W 1165; R 361; cat.4). R(I)

160. ROME (CASTLE OF ST ANGELO) (W 1166;
R 362). R(I)

161. CAMPAGNA OF ROME (W 1168;
R 364; cat.5). R(I)

162. A GARDEN (W 1177; R 373; cat.10). R(I)
A preparatory study for this watercolour is
TB CCLXXX 17.

163. GALILEO'S VILLA (W 1164; R 360). R(I)
A preparatory study for this watercolour is
TB CCLXXX 87.

164. BANDITTI (W 1171; R 367). R(I)

165. A VILLA. MOON-LIGHT (A VILLA ON
THE NIGHT OF A FESTA DI BALLO)
(W 1175; R 371; cat.9). R(I)

166. TIVOLI (W 1169; R 365). R(I)
A preparatory study for this watercolour is
TB CCLXXX 88.

167. AMALFI (W 1174; R 370). R(I)
A preparatory study for this watercolour is
TB CCLXXX 101.

168. A VILLAGE. EVENING (W 1178; R 374).
R(P)

169. LEAVING HOME (W 1180; R 376). R(P)

170. ST ANNE'S HILL, I. (W 1188; R 384). R(P)

171. ST ANNE'S HILL, II. (W 1201; R 397). R(P)

172. TORNARO (W 1185; R 381). R(P)

173. THE GIPSY (W 1179; R 375). R(P)

174. AN OLD OAK (W 1195; R 391). R(P)
A preparatory study for this watercolour is
TB CCLXXX 16.

175. SHIP-BUILDING (AN OLD OAK DEAD)
(W 1196; R 392). R(P)

176. GREENWICH HOSPITAL (W 1181; R 377;
cat.12). R(P)
A preparatory study for this watercolour is
TB CCLXXX 94.

177. TRAITOR'S GATE, TOWER OF LONDON
(W 1187; R 383). R(P)
A preparatory study for this watercolour is
TB CCLXXX 93.

178. THE BOY OF EGREMOND (W 1197; R 393).
R(P)

179. BOLTON ABBEY (W 1198; R 394). R(P)

180. ST HERBERT'S CHAPEL (W 1183; R 379;
cat.14). R(P)

181. KESWICK LAKE (W 1182; R 378). R(P)
A preparatory study for this watercolour is
TB CCLXXX 91.

182. LOCH LOMOND (W 1200; R 396). R(P)

183. ST PIERRE'S COTTAGE (W 1192; R 388;
cat.18). R(P)

184. THE ALPS (THE ALPS AT DAYBREAK)
(W 1199; R 395; cat.20). R(P)

185. VALOMBRÈ (W 1191; R 387). R(P)

186. ST JULIENNE'S CHAPEL (W 1193; R 389).
R(P)

187. CAPTIVITY (W 1194; R 390; cat.19). R(P)
A preparatory study for this watercolour is
TB CCLXXX 10.

188. COLUMBUS AND HIS SON (W 1202; R 398).
R(P)

189. COLUMBUS SETTING SAIL (W 1203;
R 399; cat.21). R(P)
Preparatory studies for this subject are
TB CCLXXX 18 and 19.

190. LAND DISCOVERED BY COLUMBUS
(W 1205; R 401; cat.23). R(P)

191. THE LANDING OF COLUMBUS (W 1206;
R 402; cat.25). R(P)
Preparatory studies for this watercolour
are TB CCLXXX 12, 99, 194.

192. CORTES AND PIZARRO (W 1208; R 404).
R(P)

193. VENICE (W 1162; R 358). R(I)

194. Study for 'The Landing of Columbus'
(TB CCLXXX 191). R(P) (cat.24)

195. A HURRICANE IN THE DESERT (THE
SIMOOM) (W 1189; R 385; cat.17). R(P)

196. VENICE (THE RIALTO – MOONLIGHT)
(W 1190; R 386). R(P)
A preparatory study for this watercolour is
TB CCLXXX 108.

197. A VISION. VOYAGE OF COLUMBUS. C.II
(THE VISION OF COLUMBUS) (W 1204;
R 400; cat.22). R(P)
Preparatory studies for this watercolour
are TB CCLXXX 203 and 204.

198. 'Going to School', finished design,
unengraved. R(P) (fig.18 on p.40)

199. EVENING (DATUR HORA QUIETI)
(W 1209; R 405). R(P)
A preparatory study for this watercolour is
TB CCLXXX 90.

200. A VILLAGE-FAIR (W 1186; R 382). R(P)

201. AN OLD MANOR-HOUSE (W 1184; R 380;
cat.15). R(P)

A rejected design for this subject is
TB CCLXXX 15.

202. A TEMPEST – VOYAGE OF COLUMBUS
(W 1207; R 403; cat.27). R(P)
A preparatory study for this watercolour is
TB CCLXXX 100.

203. Study for 'A Vision. Voyage of Columbus.
C II (The Vision of Columbus)'
(TB CCLXXX 197). R(P)

204. Study for 'A Vision. Voyage of Columbus.
C II (The Vision of Columbus)'
(TB CCLXXX 197). R(P)

205. Bonneville, St Michael

206. Distant blue mountains, with bridge in
foreground

207. Chamonix

208. Alpine lake. Inscr. 'Lucerne', not in
Turner's hand Cf. 'Lake Leman' (W 1313)

209. Study for the boat in 'The Andes Coast'
(W 1272; R 614). TC. [Formerly known as
'The Black Boat'].

Appendix B

Turner's Collected Literary Vignettes

The vignettes are illustrated as half-size reproductions on pp.101–17.
The references to the 'w' and 'tb' catalogues are to the watercolours on which the engravings are based.

Rogers's *Italy*, 1830

1. Lake of Geneva (R 348; T04632) E. Goodall
   (W 1152; TB CCLXXX 152)
2. The Chapel of William Tell (R 349; T04633)
   R. Wallis
   (W 1153; TB CCLXXX 155)
3. St Maurice (R 350; T04634) R. Wallis
   (W 1154; TB CCLXXX 147; cat.1)
4. The Hospice. Great St Bernard with the
   Lake (I) (R 351; T04636) W.R. Smith
   (W 1155; TB CCLXXX 153)
5. The Hospice. Great St Bernard (II)
   (R 352; T04638) W.R. Smith
   (W 1156; Vassar College Art Gallery,
   Poughkeepsie, USA)
6. Marengo (R 353; T04639) E. Goodall
   (W 1157; TB CCLXXX 146)
7. Aosta (R 354; T04641) H. Le Keux
   (W 1158; TB CCLXXX 145)
8. Martigny (R 355; T04643) W. Cooke
   (W 1159; TB CCLXXX 154)
9. Hannibal Passing the Alps (R 356; T04644)
   W.R. Smith
   (W 1160; TB CCLXXX 149; cat.2)
10. Lake of Como (I) (R 357; T04645) E. Goodall
    (W 1161; TB CCLXXX 157; cat.3)
11. Venice (R 358; T04646) E. Goodall
    (W 1162; TB CCLXXX 193)
12. Florence (R 359; T04648) E. Goodall
    (W 1163; TB CCLXXX 156)
13. Galileo's Villa (R 360; T04650) E. Goodall
    (W 1164; TB CCLXXX 163)
14. A Villa (Villa Madama – Moonlight) (R 361;
    T04651) H. Le Keux
    (W 1165; TB CCLXXX 159; cat.4)
15. Rome (Castle of St Angelo) (R 362; T04652)
    R. Wallis
    (W 1166; TB CCLXXX 160)
16. The Forum (R 363; T04654) E. Goodall
    (W 1167; TB CCLXXX 158)
17. Campagna of Rome (R 364; T04656)
    E. Goodall
    (W 1168; TB CCLXXX 161; cat.5)
18. Tivoli (R 365; T04658) J. Pye
    (W 1169; TB CCLXXX 166)

19. Perugia (R 366; T04659) E. Goodall
    (W 1170; TB CCLXXX 144)
20. Banditti (R 367; T04661) R. Wallis
    (W 1171; TB CCLXXX 164)
21. Bay of Naples (R 368; T04663) E. Goodall
    (W 1172; TB CCLXXX 143)
22. Temples of Paestum (R 369; T04665; cat.8)
    J. Pye
    (W 1173; TB CCLXXX 148; cat.7)
23. Amalfi (R 370; T04667) R. Wallis
    (W 1174; TB CCLXXX 167)
24. A Villa. Moonlight (A Villa on the Night of
    a Festa di Ballo) (R 371; T04668) E. Goodall
    (W 1175; TB CCLXXX 165; cat. 9)
25. Lake of Como. II (A Farewell) (R 372;
    T04670) R. Wallis
    (W 1176; TB CCLXXX 150)

Rogers's *Poems*, 1834

26. A Garden (R 373; T04671; cat.11) W. Miller
    (W 1177; TB CCLXXX 162; cat.10)
27. A Village – Evening (R 374; T05114)
    E. Goodall (W 1178; TB CCLXXX 168)
28. The Gipsy (R 375) E. Goodall
    (W 1179; TB CCLXXX 173)
29. Leaving Home (R 376; T04672) E. Goodall
    (W 1180; TB CCLXXX 169)
30. Greenwich Hospital (R 377; T04673)
    E. Goodall
    (W 1181; TB CCLXXX 176; cat.12)
31. Keswick Lake (R 378) E. Goodall
    (W 1182; TB CCLXXX 181)
32. St Herbert's Chapel (R 379; T04674)
    H. Le Keux
    (W 1183; TB CCLXXX 180; cat.14)
33. An Old Manor-House (R 380; T06163;
    cat.16) W. Miller
    (W 1184; TB CCLXXX 201; cat.15)
34. Tornaro (R 381; T06164) R. Wallis
    (W 1185; TB CCLXXX 172)
35. A Village-Fair (R 382; T06165) E. Goodall
    (W 1186; TB CCLXXX 200)
36. Traitor's Gate, Tower of London (R 383;
    T06166) E. Goodall
    (W 1187; TB CCLXXX 177)
37. St Anne's Hill, I (R 384; T06167) E. Goodall
    (W 1188; TB CCLXXX 170)
38. A Hurricane in the Desert (The Simoom)
    (R 385) E. Goodall
    (W 1189; TB CCLXXX 195; cat.17)

39. Venice (The Rialto – Moonlight) (R 386;
    T06645) W. Miller
    (W 1190; TB CCLXXX 196)
40. Valombrè (R 387) E. Goodall
    (W 1191; TB CCLXXX 185)
41. St Pierre's Cottage (R 388) E. Goodall
    (W 1192; TB CCLXXX 183; cat.18)
42. St Julienne's Chapel (R 389; T04676)
    E. Goodall
    (W 1193; TB CCLXXX 186)
43. Captivity (R 390) E. Goodall
    (W 1194; TB CCLXXX 187; cat.19)
44. An Old Oak (R 391; T05117) E. Goodall
    (W 1195; TB CCLXXX 174)
45. Ship-building (An Old Oak Dead) (R 392;
    T05118) E. Goodall
    (W 1196; TB CCLXXX 175)
46. The Boy of Egremond (R 393; T05120)
    E. Goodall
    (W 1197; TB CCLXXX 178)
47. Bolton Abbey (R 394; T05121) R. Wallis
    (W 1198; TB CCLXXX 179)
48. The Alps (The Alps at Daybreak) (R 395;
    T05122; cat.62) E. Goodall
    (W 1199; TB CCLXXX 184; cat.20)
49. Loch Lomond (R 396; T06188) W. Miller
    (W 1200; TB CCLXXX 182)
50. St Anne's Hill, II (R 397; T06169) E. Goodall
    (W 1201; TB CCLXXX 171)
51. Columbus and his Son (R 398; T06170)
    E. Goodall
    (W 1202; TB CCLXXX 188)
52. Columbus Setting Sail (R 399; T06171)
    E. Goodall
    (W 1203; TB CCLXXX 189; cat.21)
53. A Vision. Voyage of Columbus. c.II (The
    Vision of Columbus) (R 400; T06172)
    E. Goodall
    (W 1204; TB CCLXXX 197; cat.22)
54. Land Discovered by Columbus (R 401;
    T06173) E. Goodall
    (W 1205; TB CCLXXX 190; cat.23)
55. The Landing of Columbus (R 402; T06174)
    E. Goodall
    (W 1206; TB CCLXXX 191; cat.25)
56. A Tempest – Voyage of Columbus (R 403;
    T04677) E. Goodall
    (W 1207; TB CCLXXX 202; cat.27)
57. Cortes and Pizarro (R 404; T05131)
    E. Goodall
    (W 1208; TB CCLXXX 192)
58. Evening (Datur Hora Quieti) (R 405; T05132)
    E. Goodall
    (W 1209; TB CCLXXX 199)

Byron's *Life and Works*, 1832–4

59. Santa Maria della Spina, Pisa (R 415;
    T06182) E. Finden
    (W 1219; Visitors of the Ashmolean
    Museum, Oxford)
60. The Gate of Theseus, Athens (R 416; see
    cat.70) E. Finden
    (W 1220; untraced)
61. The Plain of Troy (R 417; T06647) E. Finden
    (W 1221; private collection)
62. Bacharach on the Rhine (R 418; T06648; see
    cat.70) E. Finden
    (W 1222; Vassar College Art Gallery,
    Poughkeepsie, USA)
63. The Castle of St Angelo (R 419; T06183; see
    cat.70) E. Finden
    (W 1223; Tate Gallery)
64. Corinth from the Acropolis (R 420; T06649)
    E. Finden
    (W 1224; Syndics of the Fitzwilliam
    Museum, Cambridge)
65. The Bridge of Sighs, Venice, (R 421; T06650)
    E. Finden
    (W 1225; untraced)
66. The Bernese Alps (R 422; T06184) E. Finden
    (W 1226; Vassar College Art Gallery,
    Poughkeepsie, USA)
67. The Walls of Rome (Tomb of Caius Sestius)
    (R 423; T06651) E. Finden
    (W 1227; Tate Gallery)
68. Parnassus and Castalian Spring (R 424;
    T06652; see cat.70) E. Finden
    (W 1228; Tate Gallery)
69. The Field of Waterloo, from Hougoumont
    (R 425; T06185; see cat.70) E. Finden
    (W 1229; private collection)
70. Scio, Fontana dé Melek Mehmet, Pasha
    (R 426; T06186; see cat.70) E. Finden
    (W 1230; private collection)
71. Genoa (R 427; T05188; see cat.70) E. Finden
    (W 1231; private collection)
72. Cologne (R 428; T06189) E. Finden
    (W 1232; private collection)
73. Santa Sophia, Constantinople (R 429)
    E. Finden
    (W 1233; private collection)
74. The School of Homer, Scio (R 430; T06190;
    see cat.70) E. Finden
    (W 1234; Visitors of the Ashmolean
    Museum, Oxford)
75. The Castellated Rhine (R 431; see cat.70)
    E. Finden
    (W 1235; Beit Collection, Blessington, Co.
    Wicklow, Ireland)

Scott's *Poetical Works*, 1833–4

76. Smailholm Tower (R 494; T05135)
    E. Goodall
    (W 1071; private collection)
77. Johnnie Armstrong's Tower (R 496; T05136)
    E. Goodall
    (W 1073 Taft Museum, Cincinnati, Ohio)
78. Lochmaben Castle (R 498; T05138)
    J.T. Willmore
    (W 1075; private collection; cat.40)
79. Hermitage Castle (R 500; T05140) R. Wallis
    (W 1077; private collection)
80. Bemerside Tower (R 502; T04951)
    J. Horsburgh
    (W 1079; private collection; cat.41)
81. Newark Castle (R 504; T05143) W.J. Cooke
    (W 1081; private collection)
82. Ashestiel (R 506; T04953; cat.68)
    J. Horsburgh
    (W 1083; Syndics of the Fitzwilliam
    Museum, Cambridge)
83. Loch Achray (R 508; T04954) W. Miller
    (W 1085; Yale Center for British Art, New
    Haven)
84. Bowes Tower (R 510; T04956) E. Webb
    (W 1087; untraced)
85. Fingal's Cave, Staffa (R 512; T04958; cat.44)
    E. Goodall
    (W 1089; private collection)
86. Mayburgh (R 514; T04959; cats.43 and 69)
    J. Horsburgh
    (W 1091; untraced)
87. Abbotsford (R 516; T04960) H. Le Keux
    (W 1093; private collection)

Scott's *Miscellaneous Prose*, 1834–6

88. Dryden's Monument (R 517; T04961)
    J. Horsburgh
    (W 1094; untraced)
89. Dumbarton Castle (R 518; T04962)
    W. Miller
    (W 1095; private collection)
90. Hougoumont (R 520; T04730; see cat.64)
    W. Miller
    (W 1097; private collection)
91. New Abbey, near Dumfries (R 521; T04965)
    W. Miller
    (W 1098; private collection)
92. Shakespeare's Monument (R 524; T04966)
    J. Horsburgh
    (W 1101; untraced)
93. Hôtel de Ville, Paris (R 525; T04733; see
    cat.64) J. Horsburgh
    (W 1102; Indianapolis Museum of Art)
94. Napoleon's Logement, Quai Conti (R 526;
    T04968; see cats.64 and 66) J. Horsburgh
    (W 1103; untraced)
95. Venice (R 528; T04970; see cat.64)
    W. Miller
    (W 1105; private collection)

96. Vincennes (R 531; T04973; see cat.64)
    W. Miller
    (W 1108; private collection)
97. Mayence (R 533; T04740; see cat.64)
    W. Miller
    (W 1110; Museum and Art Gallery,
    Blackburn, Lancashire)
98. The Simplon (R 535; T04977; see cat.64)
    W. Miller
    (W 1112; untraced)
99. Malmaison (R 537; T04979; see cat.64)
    W. Miller
    (W 1114; untraced)
100. Fontainbleau (R 538; T04980; see cat.64)
    W. Miller
    (W 1115; Indianapolis Museum of Art)
101. The Bellerophon, Plymouth Sound (R 540;
    T04982; see cat.64) E. Goodall
    (W 1117; private collection)
102. Chiefswood Cottage, near Abbotsford
    (R 541; T04983) W. Miller
    (W 1118; National Galleries of Scotland,
    Edinburgh)
103. Rhymer's Glen, Abbotsford (R 542;
    T04749; cat.45) W. Miller
    (W 1119; National Galleries of Scotland,
    Edinburgh)
104. Dunfermline (R 544; T04986) J. Horsburgh
    (W 1121; private collection)
105. Craigmillar Castle, near Edinburgh (R 546;
    T04987) W. Miller
    (W 1123; untraced)
106. Linlithgow (R 548; T04755) W. Miller
    (W 1125; Victoria and Albert Museum)
107. Killiecrankie (R 550; T04757) W. Miller
    (W 1127; untraced)
108. Fort Augustus (R 552; T04991) W. Miller
    (W 1129; private collection)
109. Calais (R 554; T04761) J. Horsburgh
    (W 1131; private collection)
110. Abbeville (R 556; T04994) J. Horsburgh
    (W 1133; private collection)

Lockhart's *Life of Scott*, 1839

111. Sandy Knowe, or Smailholm (R 566;
    cat.67) W. Miller
    (W 1140; Vassar College Art Gallery,
    Poughkeepsie, USA)
112. No. 39 Castle Street, Edinburgh, the Town
    Residence of Sir Walter Scott, for upwards
    of Twenty-five Years (R 567) W. Miller
    (W 1141; Pierpont Morgan Library, New
    York)

Milton's *Poetical Works*, 1835

113. Mustering of the Warrior Angels (R 598;
      T06285; cat.32) R. Brandard
      (W 1264; Preston Hall Art Gallery,
      Stockton-on-Tees; cat.31)

114. The Fall of the Rebel Angels (R 599;
      T06286) E. Goodall
      (W 1265; private collection; cat.33)

115. The Expulsion from Paradise (R 600;
      T06631) E. Goodall
      (W 1266; private collection)

116. The Temptation on the Mountain (R 601;
      T06632; cat.35) J. Cousen
      (W 1267; private collection)

117. The Temptation on the Pinnacle (R 602;
      T06287) F. Bacon
      (W 1268; Tate Gallery; cat.36)

118. The Death of Lycidas – Vision of the
      Guarded Mount [St Michael's Mount]
      (R 603; T06288) E. Goodall
      (W 1269; Taft Museum, Cincinnati, Ohio)

119. Ludlow Castle. Rising of the Water-
      Nymphs (R 604; T06633; cat.37) E. Goodall
      (W 1270; untraced)

Bunyan's *The Pilgrim's Progress*, 1836

120. Title-vignette (R 605; T06626; cat.60)
      E. Goodall
      (W 1302; untraced)

Campbell's *Poetical Works*, 1837

The watercolours for the Campbell series are all
now in the National Galleries of Scotland,
Edinburgh. The whole series is reproduced in
colour in the catalogue of the Turner
watercolours at Edinburgh by Mungo Campbell
(1993).

121. Summer Eve – The Rainbow (R 613;
      T04764; cat.49i) E. Goodall
      (W 1271)

122. The Andes Coast (R 614; T04766; cat.49ii)
      E. Goodall
      (W 1272)

123. Kosciusko (R 615; T04767; cat.49iii)
      E. Goodall
      (W 1273)

124. Sinai's Thunder (R 616; T04768)
      E. Goodall
      (W 1274)

125. A Swiss Valley (R 617; T04769) E. Goodall
      (W 1275)

126. O'Connor's Child (R 618; T04770; cat.49iv)
      E. Goodall
      (W 1276)

127. Lochiel's Warning (R 619; T04771; cat.49v)
      E. Goodall
      (W 1277)

128. Battle of the Baltic (R 620; T04772)
      E. Goodall
      (W 1278)

129. Hohenlinden (R 621; T04773; cat.49vi)
      R. Wallis
      (W 1279)

130. Lord Ullin's Daughter (R 622; T04774)
      R. Wallis
      (W 1280)

131. The Soldier's Dream (R 623; T04775)
      E. Goodall
      (W 1281)

132. The Last Man (R 624; T04776; cat.49vii) E.
      Goodall
      (W 1282)

133. Gertrude of Wyoming – The Valley (R 625;
      T04777) E. Goodall
      (W 1283)

134. Gertrude of Wyoming – The Waterfall
      (R 626; T04778) E. Goodall
      (W 1284)

135. Rolandseck (R 627; T04779) E. Goodall
      (W 1285)

136. The Beech Tree's Petition (R 628; T04780)
      E. Goodall
      (W 1286)

137. Camp Hill, Hastings (R 629; T04781;
      cat.46) E. Goodall
      (W 1287)

138. The Death-Boat of Heligoland (R 630;
      T04783; cat.49viii) E. Goodall
      (W 1288)

139. Ehrenbreitstein (R 631; T04784) E. Goodall
      (W 1289)

140. The Dead Eagle – Oran (R 632; T04785)
      W. Miller
      (W 1290)

Moore's *The Epicurean*, 1839

141. The Garden (R 634; T06622; see cat.71)
      E. Goodall
      (W 1298; private collection)

142. The Ring (R 635; T06623; cat.72)
      E. Goodall
      (W 1299; untraced)

143. The Nile (R 636; T06624; see cat.71)
      E. Goodall
      (W 1300; untraced)

144. The Chaplet (R 637; T06625; see cat.71)
      E. Goodall
      (W 1301; untraced)

The Keepsake, 1836–7

145. The Destruction of both Houses of
      Parliament by Fire, Oct. 16, 1834 (R 332;
      T06157; cat.58) J.T. Willmore
      (W 1306; private collection)

146. A Fire at Sea (R 333; T04629) J.T. Willmore
      (W 1305; private collection)

147. The Wreck (R 334; T04630) H. Griffiths
      (W 1304; private collection)

148. The Sea! The Sea! (R 335; T05109)
      J.T. Willmore
      (W 1303; private collection)

1

2

3

4

5

6

7

8

9

10

11

12

13

14

15

16

17

18

9

20

21

2

23

24

5

26

27

28

29

30

31

32

33

34

35

36

7

38

39

0

41

42

3

44

45

46

47

48

49

50

51

52

53

54

56

57

59

60

62

63

64

65

66

67

68

69

70

71

72

74

75

77

78

80

81

82

83

84

85

86

87

88

89

90

92

93

4

95

96

7

98

99

100

101

102

103

104

105

106

107

108

09

110

111

2

113

114

15

116

117

118

119

120

121

122

123

124

125

126

127

128

129

130

131

132

133

134

135

136

137

138

139

140

141

142

143

144

45

146

147

48

Checklist of Books Illustrated by Turner's Vignettes

The following list is chronological. All books published in London unless otherwise stated. 'Landscape' refers to a rectangular engraving, longer horizontally than vertically.

Walter Scott, *The Provincial Antiquities and Picturesque Scenery of Scotland, with Descriptive Illustrations by Sir Walter Scott, Bart.*, 2 vols., 1819–26 (2 title-vignettes and 11 'landscape' views by Turner; 41 by other hands)

Samuel Rogers, *Italy, a Poem*, 1830 (25 vignettes by Turner; 19 designs by Stothard and 5 by other hands)

George Gordon, Lord Byron, *The Works, with his Letters and Journals and his Life by Thomas Moore, Esq.*, (referred to as *Life and Works*), 17 vols., 1832–3 (17 vignettes by Turner; 7 vignettes by Clarkson Stanfield; 10 designs by other hands)

Walter Scott, *The Poetical Works of Sir Walter Scott, Bart.*, 12 vols., Edinburgh 1833 (12 vignettes and 12 'landscape' illustrations by Turner)

Samuel Rogers, *Poems*, 1834 (33 vignettes by Turner; 34 designs by Stothard and 4 by other hands)

Turner's Annual Tour:
Leith Ritchie, *Wanderings by the Loire*, 1833 (title-vignette and 20 'landscape' views by Turner)
Leith Ritchie, *Wanderings by the Seine*, 1834 (title-vignette and 19 'landscape' views by Turner)
Leith Ritchie, *Wanderings by the Seine*, 1835 (title-vignette and 19 'landscape' views by Turner)
The engravings from all three were reissued in *The Rivers of France*, 1837

Walter Scott, *The Miscellaneous Prose Works of Sir Walter Scott, Bart.*, 28 vols., Edinburgh 1834–6 (23 vignettes by Turner; 17 'landscape' views by Turner and 16 designs by other hands)

John Milton, *The Poetical Works of John Milton*, ed. Sir Egerton Brydges, 6 vols., 1835, reissued in one vol., 1848 (7 vignettes by Turner; 2 vignettes by Richard Westall)

John Bunyan, *The Pilgrim's Progress*, 1836; also *Illustrations of the Pilgrim's Progress*, with text by B. Barton, n.d., and John Bunyan, *Taith y Pererin*, n.d. (title-vignette by Turner; 12 illustrations by other hands)

The Keepsake, ed. Charles Heath: 1836 (3 vignettes by Turner); 1837 (1 vignette by Turner)

Thomas Campbell, *Poetical Works*, 1837 (20 vignettes by Turner)

J.G. Lockhart, *Memories of the Life of Sir Walter Scott, Bart.*, 2nd. ed., 10 vols., Edinburgh 1839 (2 vignettes by Turner; 1 'landscape' view by Turner; 17 designs by other hands)

Thomas Moore, *The Epicurean, a Tale, and Alciphron*, 1839 (4 vignettes by Turner); *Alciphron*, 1839 (3 vignettes by Turner from *The Epicurean*, omitting R 637)

Art and Song: A Series of Original Highly Finished Steel Engravings from Masterpieces of Art of the Nineteenth Century, Accompanied by a Selection of the Choicest Poems in the English Language, ed. Robert Bell, 1867 (1 vignette by Turner; 5 'landscape' views by Turner; 26 designs by other hands)

Select Bibliography

All books published in London unless otherwise stated.

Beattie, W., *Life and Letters of Thomas Campbell*, 3 vols., 1849

Brown, D.B., *Turner and Byron*, exh. cat., Tate Gallery 1992

Bryan, M., *A Dictionary of Painters and Engravers*, 1886

Clayden, P.W., *Rogers and his Contemporaries*, 2 vols., 1889

Butlin, M., and Joll, E., *The Paintings of J.M.W. Turner*, rev. ed., 2 vols., 1984

Dyson, A., *Pictures to Print: The Nineteenth Century Engraving Trade*, 1984

Finberg, A.J., *The Life of J.M.W. Turner, RA*, 2nd ed., Oxford 1961

Finley, G., *Landscapes of Memory: Turner as Illustrator to Scott*, 1980

Gage, J., *Colour in Turner: Poetry and Truth*, 1969

Gage, J. (ed.), *Collected Correspondence of J.M.W. Turner*, Oxford 1980

Gage, J., *J.M.W. Turner: A Wonderful Range of Mind*, 1987

Goodall, F., *Reminiscences of Frederick Goodall, RA*, 1902

Hamerton, P.G., *The Life of J.M.W. Turner, RA*, 2nd ed., 1895

Herrmann, L., *Turner Prints: The Engraved Work of J.M.W. Turner*, 1990

Hunnisett, B., *Steel-Engraved Book Illustration in England*, 1980

Lyles, A. and Perkins, D., *Colour into Line*, exh. cat., Tate Gallery 1989

Moore, T., *The Journal of Thomas Moore*, ed. W.S. Dowden, 5 vols. Newark, Toronto and London 1983–8

Powell, C., *Turner in the South: Rome, Naples, Florence*, New Haven and London 1987

Pye, J., *The Patronage of British Art*, 1845

Rawlinson, W.G., *The Engraved Work of J.M.W. Turner, R.A.*, 2 vols., 1908–13

Redding, C., *Literary Reminiscences and Memories of Thomas Campbell*, 2 vols., 1860

Redgrave, S., *Dictionary of Artists of the English School*, new ed., 1878

Ruskin, J., *Works* (Library Edition), ed. E.T. Cook and A. Wedderburn, 39 vols., 1903–12

Thornbury, W.G., *The Life of J.M.W. Turner, RA*, 1862

Wilton, A., *The Life and Work of J.M.W. Turner*, 1979

Wilton, A., *Turner in his Time*, 1987

Index

Photographic Credits

Thomas Agnew and Sons Ltd; Ashmolean
Museum; James Austin; Birmingham Museum
and Art Gallery; The British Library; The
British Museum; Christie's; National Galleries
of Scotland; Stockton-on-Tees Borough Council;
Strang Print Room, University College London;
Tate Gallery Photographic Department; Frank
Taylor; Tyne and Wear Museums; Ulster
Museum; John Webb

Lenders

Friends of the Tate Gallery

Since their formation in 1958, the Friends of the Tate Gallery have helped to buy major works of art for the Tate Gallery Collection, from Stubbs to Hockney.

Members at £25 are entitled to free admission to Tate Gallery exhibitions with a guest, invitations to previews of Tate Gallery exhibitions, exclusive Friends Gallery Evenings, special events, *tate - the art magazine* mailed three times a year, free admission to exhibitions at Tate Gallery Liverpool and Tate Gallery St Ives, and use of the Friends Room at the Tate Gallery.

Three categories of higher level memberships, Associate Fellow at £100, Deputy Fellow at £250, and Fellow at £500, entitle members to a range of extra benefits including invitations to exclusive special events.

The Friends of the Tate Gallery are supported by Tate & Lyle PLC.

Further details on the Friends may be obtained from:

Friends of the Tate Gallery
Tate Gallery
Millbank
London SW1P 4RG
Tel: 071-887 8752

Patrons of the Tate Gallery

The Patrons of British Art support British painting and sculpture from the Elizabethan period through to the early twentieth century in the Tate Gallery's collection. They encourage knowledge and awareness of British art by providing an opportunity to study Britain's cultural heritage.

The Patrons of New Art support contemporary art in the Tate Gallery's collection. They promote a lively and informed interest in contemporary art and are associated with the Turner Prize, one of the most prestigious awards for the visual arts.

Annual membership of the Patrons ranges from £350 to £750, and funds the purchase of works of art for the Tate Gallery collection.

Benefits for both groups include invitations to Tate Gallery receptions, an opportunity to sit on the Patrons' acquisitions committees, special events including visits to private and corporate collections and complimentary catalogues of Tate Gallery exhibitions.

Further details on the Patrons may be obtained from:

The Development Office
Tate Gallery
Millbank
London SW1P 4RG
Tel: 071-887 8744

Sponsorship

Tate Gallery, London – Sponsorships since 1990

AFAA, Association Française d'Action Artistique, Ministère des Affaires Etrangères, The Cultural Service of the French Embassy, London
1993, *Paris Post War: Art and Existentialism* exhibition
Agfa Graphic Systems Group
1991, *Turner: The Fifth Decade* exhibition and catalogue
Barclays Bank PLC
1991, *Constable* exhibition
Beck's
1992, *Otto Dix* exhibition
The British Land Company PLC
1990, *Joseph Wright of Derby* exhibition
1993, *Ben Nicholson* exhibition
The British Petroleum Company plc
1990–3, *New Displays*
British Steel plc
1990, *William Coldstream* exhibition
Carroll, Dempsey & Thirkell
1990, *Anish Kapoor* exhibition
Channel 4 Television
1991–3, The Turner Prize
Clifton Nurseries
1990–2, Sponsorship in kind
Daimler-Benz AG
1991, *Max Ernst* exhibition
Debenham Tewson & Chinnocks
1990, Turner *Painting and Poetry* exhibition
Digital Equipment Co Ltd
1991, *From Turner's Studio* touring exhibition
1993, Library and Archive Computerisation
Alfred Dunhill Limited
1993, *Burne-Jones: Watercolours and Drawings* exhibition
The German Government
1992, *Otto Dix* exhibition
The Independent
1992, *Otto Dix* exhibition
1993, *Paris Post War: Art and Existentialism* exhibition
KPMG Management Consulting
1991, *Anthony Caro: Sculpture towards Architecture* exhibition
Lloyd's of London
1991, Friends Room
Nuclear Electric plc
1993, *Turner: The Final Years* exhibition
Olympia & York
1990, Frameworkers Conference
Pearson plc
1992–5, Elizabethan Curator Post
Reed International P.L.C.
1990, *On Classic Ground* exhibition
SRU Ltd
1992, *Richard Hamilton* exhibition
Sun Life Assurance Society plc
1993, *Robert Vernon's Gift* exhibition

Tate Gallery, London –
Corporate Members

Tate & Lyle PLC
  1991–3, Friends relaunch marketing
  programme
THORN EMI
  1993, *Turner's Painting Techniques* exhibition
TSB Group plc
  1992, *Turner and Byron* exhibition
  1992–5, *William Blake* series of displays
Volkswagen
  1990–4, The Turner Scholarships

Tate Gallery Liverpool – Sponsorships since 1990

AIB Bank
  1991, *Strongholds* exhibition
American Airlines
  1993, *David Hockney* exhibition
Barclays Bank PLC
  1990, *New Light on Sculpture* display
BASF
  1990, *Lifelines* exhibition
Beck's
  1990, *Art from Köln* exhibition
  1993, *Robert Gober* exhibition
British Alcan Aluminium plc
  1991, *Dynamism* display
  1991, *Giacometti* display
British Telecom plc
  1990, Outreach Programme
Concord Lighting
  1990, Sponsorship in kind
Cultural Relations Committee,
  Department of Foreign Affairs, Ireland
  1991, *Strongholds* exhibition
English Estates
  1991, Mobile Arts Project
Granada Television plc
  1990, *New North* exhibition
Korean Air
  1992, Sponsorship in kind
The Littlewoods Organisation plc
  1992–5, *New Realities* display
Merseyside Development Corporation
  1990, Outreach programme
  1992, *Myth-Making* display
  1992, *Stanley Spencer* display
Mobil Oil Company Ltd
  1990, *New North* exhibition
Momart plc
  1990–3, Artist's Fellowship at Tate Gallery
  Liverpool
NSK Bearings Europe Ltd
  1991, *A Cabinet of Signs* exhibition
Ryanair
  1991, Sponsorship in kind
Samsung Electronics
  1992, *Working with Nature* exhibition
Volkswagen
  1991, Sponsorship in kind

Partners

ADT Group PLC
The British Petroleum Company plc
Glaxo Holdings p.l.c.
Manpower PLC
THORN EMI
Unilever

Associates

Brunswick Public Relations
BUPA
Channel 4 Television
Drivers Jonas
D.T.Z. Debenham Thorpe
Global Asset Management
Herbert Smith
Lazard Brothers & Co Ltd
Linklaters & Paines
Refco Overseas Ltd
S.G. Warburg Group